Graffiti Heart

Eliza Jonas

Contents

Designations & Pack Dynamics   vii

Prologue   1
1. Danika – fifteen years later   13
2. Emmett   19
3. Danika   26
4. Jonah   33
5. Colin   40
6. Danika   46
7. Danika   53
8. Jonah   59
9. Danika   67
10. Emmett   74
11. Danika   83
12. Emmett   90
13. Danika   97
14. Colin   104
15. Danika   111
16. Colin   119
17. Danika   125
18. Jonah   133
19. Danika   140
20. Emmett   148
21. Danika   155
22. Danika   163
23. Jonah   169
24. Colin   176
25. Danika   183
26. Danika   190
27. Jonah   196
28. Danika   203
29. Emmett   210
30. Danika   217

31. Jonah 224

32. Danika 230

33. Emmett 237

34. Jonah 243

35. Colin 250

36. Danika 256

37. Danika 262

38. Danika 269

A Note From Eliza 277

Also by Eliza Jonas 279

About the Author 281

For the women who have dimmed themselves for any reason. Let's shine bright like we're meant to.

Designations & Pack Dynamics

Alpha – Providers and caregivers. Overall dominant designation, can "bark" to command, but it's considered taboo to do that. Historically financial providers to their pack, but in recent years more alphas have stayed home to raise kids. This fulfills the caregiver drive in them.

Beta – Completes the pack, bonds can't snap into place without one. They act as a balance to the alpha and omega hormones and pheromones, but only when in a pack. In a single mate, they can't balance things. Don't produce their own extreme pheromones but do have unique scents

Omega – Center and heart of the pack, goes into heats three times per year. CAN get pregnant outside of one but less than 1% chance. Require physical touch regularly to avoid overactive pheromones which can lead to other health issues.

Touch Sickness – Omegas can get Touch Sickness if not touched or cuddled enough. It causes them to pull away from people they don't know and can have physical signs of sickness such as fatigue and numbness in the skin. Treatable with regular snuggles.

Touch Loss – The ultimate disease from Touch Sickness. Not transmissible. Prevents the Omega from finding their Match via touch. Also causes them to crave comfort more than others, leading to increased nesting and cuddling if they are bonded or matched with someone. Touch outside of a match or bond is draining for them.

Packs – Cannot complete pack bond without each designation. Designations can mate bond each other, but things will always be "off" until a pack is formed with at least one of each designation. Nature's way of keeping balance between the designations.

Mate Bond – Mate bonds are between two or more people, must be consensual. Will not take if one party is unwilling. Does not have to be a match, can be chosen. Mate bonds will give you insight to a person's emotions. (Mate bonds between two people are unstable unless they are in a pack bond with all 3 designations.)

Pack bond – Pack bonds are between three or more people, as long as there is one of each designation. Will not take if one is missing, will not take if one is unwilling. Pack members are naturally drawn together (Pack Pull) with or without the match bond.

Pack Pull – the feeling that pack members get when they find others meant to be in their pack. It draws you to those people like a magnet but there's no forced bonding.

Matches – Matches are uncommon. There are two indicators to show that a match is present. One is scent, meaning the scent of the other person is extremely appealing and you're drawn to it. The other is touch, at the first touch there will be a physical sensation that has been described as tingling, a small zap, and/or a rush of energy. Matches solidify with a mated match bond, but do not replace a pack bond. Matches do not *have* to solidify the bond, but most do.

Mated Match Bond – When two or more matched bond together. It's stronger than a typical mate bond, also allows for awareness of other person's location and mental communication in small distances.

Prologue

Danika

My room is officially a sty of clothing and shoes. I don't even have that many of either, but I've managed to spew them on every possible surface of my room, and I *still* can't find my damn crop top. There's a party over in the back field tonight, and I'll be damned if I look anything less than edible with Benny being there. It's been a month since I presented, and everybody in our tiny town knows, so I'm big news.

There's only one other omega in town, and she's got herself a pack. I'm gonna be just like her and pack up. We have plenty of alphas, and I could easily tolerate a beta male. Collecting a beta female for my pack would even be okay. I don't swing that way, but she could find a second beta or her own alpha; I wouldn't restrict her. I'm not *that* petty.

"There you are!" I exclaim, snatching the white sparkling top.

It shimmies perfectly onto my body, showing the inch or two of skin that drives the boys wild. We may be a small town ... well, village really, but that's never stopped me from embracing how good I look. Don't get me wrong, I can throw down when I need to, but I never resist the opportunity to look *good*.

Eliza Jonas

My room isn't much, but my dresser is at a good height to double as a vanity, so I plop myself down and fix my makeup before pulling my hair into a high ponytail. My mouth stretches into a grin in my old, cheap mirror, and I leave my room. Unfortunately, my older brother is standing across from my door, his arms crossed and face full of judgement.

"What?" I ask, popping my hip out.

"You ain't goin' tonight. Stay home. It's all the older students. Don't be there," he tells me in his almost-southern lazy drawl.

I glare in response. "You don't get to control me! Who knows? Maybe I'll find my match tonight!"

"If you had one in this small town, you'da met him. I'm warnin' you, stay home, Dani. I'm tryin' to protect you."

He stomps off after that, and I sneer behind his back before closing my door behind me. Talk about being an alpha-hole. My brother is insufferable. He has no idea what I deal with as an omega. He should pay more attention ... I don't need him to protect me. I stalk after him and lightly bounce down the steps, trying to avoid making too much noise. Unfortunately, it didn't help anything.

"*Danika!*" my father roars.

"Fuckin' great," I mutter, dragging my ass over to his easy chair where, sure enough, he's sittin' with an open beer and cars flying by on the TV.

"What?" I ask when I'm within his sight.

"You ain't goin' to no party tonight. Especially not dressed like that. You look like a call girl. I don't care if you're an omega, you ain't old enough yet."

He turns back to the TV as though that's the end of the conversation. I suppose for him it is, but I'm not leaving until I've had my say.

"This is fashion, Daddy, not some floozy outfit. Being an omega means I gotta make sure I'm seen! I won't cause problems, honest. Just let me go for a bit?" I ask.

My brother rolls his eyes from the other side of the room. Instead of answering me, though, my father decides to talk to him.

"Tuck! Make sure if she tries to leave, you lock her up in her room. Got it?"

Tucker sighs loudly. "Pop, I'll be out at the party."

Our father growls softly. "Fine. I'll lock you up myself, Danika. Don't test me, girl!"

Snarling in frustration, I turn and stomp up the stairs. Gotta put on a show or they'll know what's up. I'm gettin' out of this house tonight if it's the last thing I do. I keep my bedroom door open a crack, and listen for the sound of Tucker leaving. Sure enough, about five minutes later he calls out a goodbye and my parents both shout their reply. *Okay, he's gone.* I can stay out of sight if I make sure I'm plastered to the far wall of the stairs while I descend.

At the top of the stairs, I hear a new beer can being opened and my mother clearing her throat. My parents are an alpha beta pair ... bonded, but the longer they go without an omega, the shakier things get. They fight too much and don't smile enough. It'll be okay, though, when I'm eighteen I'm leavin' this place for good. Knowing they are both in the same room, I quietly make my way down the stairs, avoiding any creaking spots. I've done this enough that you'd think they know better, but they never seem to learn.

At the base of the stairs, I take a quick look down the hallway and grab my Chucks before silently opening the back door and stepping outside. Breathing a small sigh of relief, I quickly get my shoes on, and bolt from the house. The door I just went through is right next to the kitchen, and it would be too easy for my mother to see me if she goes back in there.

When I'm four houses away, I slow down. Our town is about five blocks and a few scattered stores around beside that. Like I said, basically a village. It does have its charm though. We're surrounded by forest and nestled close to a mountain. It's pretty, and I find myself staring more than I care to admit, wishing I had somethin' to draw with. I used to draw all the time, but I ran out of supplies last year and my parents won't buy more. I guess they'd rather have beer.

The party is out in the grove, a spot that's tradition to be used as a

3

place for parties. Every adult has been here, so there's no secret, just the rite of passage. I make my way through town and saunter into the trees. I'm making a fuckin' entrance tonight.

Benny better appreciate this. I know he's my brother's best friend, but I also know he likes to look at me.

As I approach the bonfire, I can see the party's been underway for a little bit now, even before Tucker left the house. My eyes snag on Benny, who has his hand resting awfully high on that beta girl's thigh. Well, that won't do. I walk over there and stop in front of him, letting my pony swing so it drapes down my shoulder. My finger finds a few strands of my hair and starts to twist it a bit.

"Hey, Benny," I greet him with a smile.

"Ho-ly shit, Dan, you look great tonight," he says, raking his eyes over me.

There's a twinge of irritation that he's using that nickname, but I push past it. He gave it to me when I got mad as a child because it's a boy name, and I'm clearly not a boy. However, he can call me that if it means I get his attention tonight. I'm hoping he'll stake his claim, and we can be together. Besides, I smell way better than that beta. She smells like expired flower perfume.

Benny takes his hand off the beta and gestures for me to sit on the other side of him. Over the years, furniture has been carved into some tree logs, so there are several benches around the area. Thankfully, this one only fits about three people.

I cross my legs toward him and turn my body. "How ya doin'?" I ask.

"A lot better now," he says. "You finally convince your old man to let you leave for a party?"

"As if I need his permission. I sneak out all the time, you know that," I scoff.

He grins, but it doesn't make my stomach flutter like usual. It feels a little aggressive, almost like he's baring his teeth. He presented as an alpha a couple years ago, but he's never been aggressive except for his first rut. Town rumors ran for days after it. Thankfully, I haven't had my first heat yet. It takes omegas a bit longer to go into heat than it does for an alpha to go into rut.

Benny places his hand on my knee, and I can feel the heat of it straight through my jeans, warming the skin underneath. His smoked cheese scent is usually delicious to smell, but tonight it's a little sour.

"You're right, you make your own way. Sometimes you gotta rebel a bit, y'know?"

Smiling, I scoot a little closer to him but freeze when I hear someone growling behind me. *Shit, that didn't take long.*

"You were supposed to stay home," Tucker says, his voice deeper than usual.

When I turn to look at him, I see some smudged lipstick on his throat, his clothes look a little disheveled, and there's a faint lingering fruity scent coming off him. Seems like he was having some fun. My eyebrows raise in response to his aggression.

"You know you're supposed to take care of your girl, right? I don't need your assistance, but whoever was sucking on your neck needs new lipstick. That's a terrible color," I comment.

Benny laughs and moves his hand so he can wrap an arm around me. "Good point, Dan. He should be over there, *taking care of her.*"

Tucker growls and points his finger at me. "Don't go gettin' ideas, this ain't over."

"Tell you what," Benny says as Tucker walks away, "that deserves a drink. You want one?"

"Sure, I'd love one."

That sharp smile is back, and I ignore my uneasy stomach. Tucker's really getting to me tonight, and I need to just focus on me, not him. Or his stupid nagging voice in my head. It'll be fine. I know Benny is a good guy. Proof of it arrives with him handing me a Solo cup, full of some kind of punch that smells like pure alcohol.

"Is there any actual punch in here?" I laugh after smelling it.

Benny shrugs. "Maybe a drop or two. Who needs it anyway? It just waters down the good stuff."

Benny and I flirt and chat the night away, and soon enough the punch doesn't faze me anymore. It's actually really good stuff, which I tell Benny. Maybe he and I can make it sometime. I find his eyes just staring at me, and pretty soon nothing makes any sense. I lose all track of time, but I know Benny's got me.

There are some *loud* fuckin' birds this morning. Why the hell do they have to sound so chipper? I try to roll over and snuggle back down in my bed, but something pokes me as I do.

"The fuck?" I mutter.

Opening my eyes is a hazard and it takes me a couple tries. Everything is so damn bright this morning. Maybe that juice *was* a little too much. When I finally get my eyes open and adjusted to the light, I realize with horror why I'm being poked in the side.

I'm laying out on the woods, and a stick is the source of my irritation. The source of my horror, though? That's the fact that I'm in the woods, mostly naked and shivering. My mind tries to think back to last night, but everything is just barely out of reach in my head. I remember Benny being there for me, even when I threw up. That was really nice of him. What the hell happened after though?

Pushing myself up from the ground, I notice my pant legs are only attached to one ankle now, and I can feel leaves trying to nestle where they don't belong. There's a faint whining noise in the air and I can't figure out where it's coming from. It's obnoxious whatever is making it. Shakily, I put my clothes back where they belong. There's something in the back of my head screaming that I should be more upset right now, but I can't figure out why.

I just feel kind of numb. At first it was horrifying, then my brain decided no more emotions for me. Finally, I get my clothes covering me again, and start my walk home. The sun is up, but not high yet, so early morning. Maybe I can make it home without being seen. That damn whining noise is still going, and I take a minute to rub my ears. Maybe I hit my head or something.

When I get to my house, I find luck is *not* on my side, and my entire family is awake. There's only four of us so it's not a large firing squad, but they all look ready to pull a trigger. The three of them stare from their spots in the kitchen as I toe off my shoes and turn to go up the stairs. It's silent except for that damn whining noise until my dad snaps out of it.

"Where the *fuck* have you been all night? Cut it out with the damn whining sound, nobody here gives a shit and it's obnoxious!"

Part of my mind is impressed that his face has gotten so red.

His words take a second to permeate. *Oh, I'm the source of the noise.* I'm whining, a high-pitched, keening sound that hasn't stopped. It takes me a moment of focusing but I finally cut it off and the following silence is almost deafening. The whine is threatening to come back up.

"Your daddy asked you a question, miss. You'd best tell him where you've been," my mother chimes in.

"I ... uh, I don't know," I finish lamely.

Tucker scoffs, "You were at the damn bonfire last night, that's where you were!"

My father glares at me. "You snuck out? You go whorin' yourself out to all the older boys? You think that now you're an omega you've got some special pass? If you think we're gonna put up with this shit, you are *sorely* mistaken!"

All I can do is stare as some pieces start falling into place in my head. The alcohol, feeling so out of control, Benny being attached to me all night, waking in the woods almost naked. That initial wave of horror from the woods washes over me again, and I sit on the stairs as it hits me.

"I was raped," I say to nobody in particular.

"Excuse me?" Tucker says, actually looking like he cares.

My eyes fly up to look at their faces. Tucker looks angry, but my parents seem annoyed.

"I woke up in the woods with my clothes not right. Why would I do that on my own? Someone raped me," I tell them again, my throat tightening as I say the words.

Tears start to escape my eyes, and my father scoffs at me, almost sneering. "You think you're gonna go out in public like that and not get a reaction? You were askin' for whatever you got. Get yourself cleaned up, you're grounded for the next year."

Part of me wants to check his scent and see what he's really feeling. Maybe he's just scared, not mad. Sometimes people say things they don't mean if they're just scared. My nose, however, can't quite pick anything up right now. That part of my brain isn't working.

Numbly, I stand again and turn to walk up the stairs, the tears falling faster now. I don't want to cry until I'm in the shower, at least then they'll get washed away with everything else. I hear footsteps behind me and turn when my hand is on the doorknob to the bathroom.

"Who?" Tucker asks, anger lacing his tone.

"What?"

"Who was it? I'll beat the shit out of them."

Relief hits me, and it's a struggle to keep my knees from buckling. Someone in this house cares.

It takes a moment to clear my throat of the tightness. "Benny."

His face changes ever so slightly from anger to disgust. If I didn't know better, I wouldn't think he'd been concerned at all. I know he was, though, he had his Big Brother game face on. Now? Now he's looking at me like I'm a bug on his shoe.

"Fuck you. Benny would never. I wanted to believe you, but naming Benny? No, whatever happened with him was asked for. You've been panting after him for years, and there's no way he'd do that to you. Mom and Dad were right, you dress like that and you get what you ask for."

Any hope I had for an ally is shattered. Not in this house, no allies here. I nod my understanding and go into the bathroom, telling myself I'm not crazy and I didn't ask for it. That doesn't help the tears that come under the hot spray of water though.

For the next few days, whispers follow me around town. We don't have school right now, but that doesn't stop people from spittin' toward me or insulting me under their breath. It comes from all sides, and when someone lets it slip that I blame Benny? All bets are off at that point. I can't step foot outside of my house without someone callin' me a liar and a whore. So, I stopped going outside.

I'm spending another evening in my bed, wishing I never presented as an omega. It's what got me into trouble. I thought I was hot shit, but I guess I'm just a hot mess. My room is actually clean, since I had a ton of nervous energy the first day I stayed in the whole day, but I haven't had motivation to do anything else. So, I stay in bed, playin' dumb apps on my phone.

When I presented as an omega this year, I almost downloaded some social apps, but never got around to it. Now, I'm thankful. I'm sure there's nothing but nasty words waiting for me there. After losing at this virtual card game for the fifth time, I turn it off and actually leave my bed. I need some fresh air. Perhaps if I go sit on the back porch people won't see me as easily. Maybe I could make it five minutes out there.

It's a nice evening, and for a moment, I'm grateful for the fresh air. It's not quite twilight but the sun is pretty damn low in that sky. Closing my eyes, I savor the feel of the wind as it gently breezes past me. It's then that I get my first whiff of a scent. Smoked cheese. My eyes fly open, and I move to run back into the house, but Benny's already too close. He can easily grab me if I try to run.

"I hear you've been tellin' everybody I touched you when you didn't want it," he says, like we're discussing the weather.

"That's 'cause you did. I never wanted to go that far that soon, you know I've said that for years. I wanted to wait for a full pack. Then you decided to just take without askin'." I try to sound angry in my retort, but I'm pretty sure it's just filled with sorrow. I try to hide the fear.

"I didn't hear you complain. Seems like you're sore that I didn't bring you home. You know what though?"

My body starts to tremble as the full weight of understanding hits me. Benny didn't just *do* something bad, Benny *is* bad.

He leans in closer. "I don't bring whores home to my house."

A whine starts to build up again, and only a small squeak hits the air before I push it back down. I will *not* whine for him.

Benny chuckles in a low tone. "See you around. Can't wait to use that sweet cunt again. Remember, you ask for it every time."

Scrambling up off the porch, I race into the house, barely making it to the toilet before my stomach purges itself of its contents. I sob into the toilet between waves of nausea and hate myself. I hate this town, I hate the bigots who live here, I hate Benny, I hate myself, and I *hate* my omega. When I pull myself up, I splash some cold water on my face to wipe away my sick and try to get out of my head. In the mirror I can see myself, but she doesn't look the same. The girl in the mirror has my dark hair, my deep blue eyes, and full lips, but I don't recognize her. She looks like she's lost something. Like she's on the edge of a knife and doesn't know which way she will fall.

As I stare, I realize which way I'm going to fall. I'm going to choose it, and nobody can take that away from me. I pack a bag as full as I can get it, and snag a second one to put a few additional items in —my electronics, a couple of knick knacks, and a pinecone I painted as a kid. Without a word, I turn and leave my house. Honestly, it's never been a home anyway, why would I want to stay? Striding out to the shed, I find Daddy's blowtorch and snag it too.

The sun is almost setting now, twilight is just about in full effect, which is helpful for me to stay unseen. When I get to the house I'm aiming for, I'm pleased to hear the TV up loud enough to hear outside. Excellent, that means Mr. Durst is sound asleep and Mrs. Durst has the TV on. She needs hearing aids but that's not something you get in a small village. Creeping around to the garage, I find the bike he restored years ago but refuses to sell. The keys are still in it, and I find a two-gallon bucket of gas to dump in it. Based on the sounds, there was some already in, so that will get me even farther. I stuff my extra bag into the saddle bag of the motorcycle, and even though I know it won't fit, I try to shove in my duffle.

Giving up, I toss the blowtorch in the second saddle bag, tighten the strap on my duffle so it sits tightly across my back, and snag the single helmet he has. There are a few cobwebs in it, but I wipe those out and shoo away the spiders. Pushing hard, I get the bike moving and then walk it to the edge of the woods, right near the clearing. There's a few trees to wade through, but it won't take me long and I can run back to the bike quickly.

I grab the blow torch from the saddle bag and walk over to where I woke up, wanting to erase it from existence before I erase myself from this town. Once it's fired up, I hold the flame to the ground and watch as the leaves and underbrush burn up, erasing anything my body may have touched when it lay here. Fuck this place.

I lock the blow torch in the on position and chuck it into the woods before jogging back to the bike. Smoke is starting to drift up into the sky as I fire up the bike, slam the helmet on, and speed through town. A few people watch me speed off, not knowing who is on the bike, looking perplexed. There's a hill you have to drive over as you leave the village, and once I hit the top of it, I stop and turn my bike around, looking to see what the result is of my fun with fire.

Smoke is billowing now, and I can see flames licking through the trees, spreading faster than I would have guessed. My gaze stays locked on the town and the growing fire as everyone panics and tries to stop the inevitable burn. It's dark out now, the flames a stark bright spot in the inky darkness of the rural village. When the grey ash starts falling into my hair, I shake it out and put the helmet back on.

I'm done here.

Chapter 1

Danika – fifteen years later

My studio is blissfully quiet as I apply another splash of paint to the canvas. I'm sure a lot of other artists play some kind of music, but if you ask me, it's just a distraction. The silence lets my art speak for itself, and leaves my mind clear to let the creativity flow. My only companion is the sound of my brush along the canvas and other layers of paint.

When I started exploring art, I was surprised to find that the calm I'd been seeking was actually in the silence as I watched my image come to life. I'd spent so long avoiding the quiet, afraid of what memories and thoughts it would bring. When I painted for the first time, I finally understood the value of silence. It doesn't bring back old memories, the reason why I refuse to ever be in a vulnerable position again. I've clawed my way here and I'm going to stay here.

My concentration is broken by the sound of my doorbell. I pull my hand away from the canvas and sigh loudly. On a nearby stool, my phone is lit up with a video doorbell notification. Deciding my hands feel dry enough, I grab the device and smirk when I see who's waiting for me. I debate leaving well enough alone and ignoring my visitor, but I don't think I can get away from it.

"I am not accepting solicitors or religious conversion unless Girl Scout cookies are involved," I say into the device.

The response is a snort. "Woman, open the damn door. I brought cookies."

"Ooo! Cookies!" I reply before hitting the lock to let her in.

Part of me felt that the electronic lock may have been overkill, but the bigger part of me wanted to make sure I could keep people away. For some reason, the electronic lock felt safer. Don't ask me for logic, it's not my strong suit. I'm an unbonded, artistic omega. I'm allergic to logic.

My phone chimes to tell me the lock is re-engaged, and I turn back to my work in progress. I see some shading that I'm not super happy with. Faintly, I register the sound of footsteps and the presence of someone new in my studio. She's quiet for a few moments, letting me get the last brushstrokes out before I sit back with satisfaction.

My hand whips out to the side. "Cookie."

"They're in the kitchen, you heathen," she admonishes me as she places one in my hand.

I turn, grinning. "Yeah but you always bring me one anyway."

My best friend laughs and rolls her eyes. She waits patiently as I scarf the cookie down and clean my brushes. I get to hear all the details of the horrible outfits people were wearing at the office today. She sounds so distressed that I snicker as I finish up the cleaning process.

"Well, I guess your eyes will never be the same, which is just going to send your fashion sense into the drain. Pity, I'll never be able to walk around with you again."

Sophie laughs, delighted by my snark. "That would require you to leave your house for something *other* than an exhibition opening."

"I leave the house! To get my mail." I giggle.

She's not wrong, though. I've retreated into myself over the last fifteen years, and she's only known me for seven of them. I've never really shown her who I used to be, even though she knows my entire story. The thing is, Sophie doesn't care. She takes me as I am, encourages me, then supports me in my decisions. If she were a guy, I'd totally bone her.

"We really need to get you out more. I bet it would do you a world of good to go to a coffee shop or something and just sit there in public," Sophie insists.

I chew my bottom lip a bit. "I hear you. Maybe after my next exhibition we can plan something."

"Really?"

"No promises," I warn her.

She nods. "Okay, so it's a done deal."

Laughter escapes me as I roll my eyes at her. We've reached the kitchen now, and I grab another cookie to cram into my mouth. She plops down on a stool in the kitchen, making herself comfortable. My place isn't a typical place to live, but it's been mine for ten years now. This small cottage was originally a rental until the owner offered to sell it to me. I'm not sure what they used the cottage for when they owned it, but it's perfect for what I need.

The kitchen is just big enough for me to cook for myself, and maybe one other person. My living room can fit three or four people with one couch and a chair, and I have my bedroom and bathroom. There's no nest space, and I'm very okay with that. What I fell in love with is the wide-open back room. There's plenty of room for several canvases, even my large ones, and the light is sublime. It's almost a challenge for me to find bad light in there.

The result of my oddly spaced dwelling means I don't seek or receive many visitors. After I found myself in the city at sixteen, I quickly decided that socializing didn't hold the appeal it once did to me. My cottage isn't in the middle of the woods, it's part of a smaller neighborhood, but it's quiet and there's decent space between each house. My truck fits nicely in the cheap carport I found, so it stays dry in the elements. Mostly.

"Speaking of exhibitions, are you ready for your next one?" Sophie asks.

I sigh and take another bite of cookie.

"I'm close. I have one piece I'm finishing up, then I think I'm good. It's a big one this time, so I had to find a new venue," I tell her.

"The venue you use now is huge, what do you mean you had to find a new one?"

"Yeah, but the problem is that they don't do solo exhibitions. So, with having to share, I wouldn't get enough spots to hang all my pieces. The new place is physically smaller, but it will be *just* my art showing."

"It's a solo? Why didn't you tell me? That's so exciting!" Sophie is grinning, and I'm pretty sure her bounce on the stool is partially involuntary.

"I thought I told you." I frown in confusion.

Sophie holds up a hand. "The past is past, let's not dwell. Do you need help with anything before the exhibition?"

I fight the urge to laugh. Sophie can be so mercurial, but she also doesn't hold on to grudges. In the span of thirty seconds, she was thrilled, then hurt, then forgiving, then moving on. I don't know how she processes emotions so quickly, but I admire it. My mouth tips into a smile and I shake my head at her.

"No, I just need to finish up my current painting, then get them ready for transport," I tell her.

She grins. "Excellent! Make sure you send me the address and all that. I don't want to go to the wrong spot."

I pretend to think about it for a moment. "Well, I might be able to send that over to you. If you're lucky."

Sophie laughs, and we spend the next couple of hours talking about whatever comes to mind. She has a fantastic love life and hearing all her stories settles my resolve to be on my own. However, the stories are also hilarious, and I beg to hear each one of them. Eventually, dinner time rolls around, and she packs up to leave. I make sure she has the exhibition information and give her a hug. She squeezes me quickly, knowing that I crave the touch, but that it also drains me.

As I stand at the window, I see her climb into her car, then ease her way out of my driveway and back to the road. My heart feels warm and light after her visit, like it always does. She's an omega, same as me, but she revels in it. Nothing makes Sophie quite as happy as when she can doll up and try to entice some alphas and betas her way. She looks soft and cute, but she's extremely well versed in self-defense, and I've heard more than one story where a guy underestimated her and paid the price.

The long-buried part of me wishes I could be a badass like she is, but it always fades quickly when I remember that I'm safer this way. Sometimes I miss the girl I used to be. Confident and happy with myself and enjoying the attention I got. An omega should enjoy the attention they get; they're meant to be loved on and cherished. Unfortunately, the world doesn't see it the same way. I've learned hiding is a better choice.

I check my last painting one more time, ensuring that it's fully covered and wrapped just how I like it to be. Before I start to load my truck up, I can't resist pulling my phone out one more time to check my email. I've probably looked at it so many times that if it were paper, it would have torn several times. The times have not changed, nor has the address, but my nerves feel better after checking for the thousandth time. Stupid anxiety. The assistant who will be there tonight is a man, which is setting me off a bit.

"You can do this. You're an adult, you have a taser gun, you can run fast," I tell myself as I haul the first painting out of my house.

It's a cool evening, and the scent of lilac washes over me. The perfect scent of spring. I reach the back of my truck and lean my painting against one pole of the carport, safely on the cement pad. I don't need dirt getting in the cracks. I open the window of the camper shell on my truck bed, then the bottom hatch.

My truck is not fancy. It's about ten years old, has a little rust, and the camper shell clashes horribly with the truck bed, but it protects my livelihood. My paintings are safe in any weather back there, and it eases my nerves. I'm finally loaded up, so I grab my bag and hop in the cab. Since it's just me, there's no back seats and my bag sits on the passenger seat. I put the truck in drive and ease onto the road with my precious cargo. Time to go set things up.

Chapter 2

Emmett

My feet bop around the gallery, music on the overhead speakers giving me dance energy. My favorite nights are set up nights. I get to turn on all the lights and play whatever music I want for a couple hours. Normally, there's other people here, or the giant front windows light our space enough that I don't need lights on. Having the lights on means I can stop under some of them and pretend I'm under a spotlight as I swirl my hips around.

After grabbing another new bulb from my box, I head over to one of the display spaces I haven't prepped yet. Each of the bright lights we would normally use to highlight the paintings are being replaced with a UV light. We also modified our normal switches to link to a button by the space. Guests can push the button to see the UV light on the painting.

It's definitely different, but that's one of the things we love about having a gallery. We can do whatever we want and we love different. Jonah offered to be here with me since we have a new artist, but I assured him he would just throw off my groove. So he and Colin are at home keeping each other company. My dick hardens at that idea, and I have to take some deep breaths to get it to calm down. I'll have fun with them another night. Part of me wishes that we were bonded, but with three of us instead of two, we all worried about the dynamic being off without an omega. So as much as it's a bummer to not feel their pleasure, I know I'll get to experience it later.

"Gertie! What do you think? Is it looking good?" I ask.

The room remains silent around me.

"You could help out a *little* you know."

No response. Sighing, I walk over to where I left her in one of the seated areas. I pick her up and stare into her lifeless black eyes. Her fur is somehow still ridiculously soft, and I can't help but melt at her little ears. Damn hamster.

"Fine, be adorable. I don't need you to respond anyway!" I fake pout.

I bring her little taxidermized body close to my chest and drop her in the little pocket of my polo shirt. The slight weight of her body is familiar and calms any nerves building as I wait for the new artist. There are always a few nerves when someone new shows here, but I make a point of taking a few deep breaths. I don't want my scent flooding the place, especially if I'm stressed.

Jonah is incredibly over-protective of our little pack, so when I hear an alert sound in the back, I jog over to the security cameras. There's an older truck approaching the building, and my excitement increases a notch. Anyone getting close to our building on the back side is here to deliver art or supplies. That or someone coming to take us all hostage and hold us for ransom, but apparently that's not likely. Colin keeps telling me my imagination is too active.

He's probably right.

Invested in the outcome, I watch the older truck reverse in toward the back doors. It's in good shape, but clearly a few years older and has a camper shell on it that doesn't match. Matching is overrated, anyway. When the truck finally stops, a woman steps out from the cab and my jaw drops. She is gorgeous. Gorgeous isn't even a good enough word to use for her. Dazzling. Glorious. Beautiful. Still not good enough. I'll keep thinking.

Her clothes are baggy, almost like she's trying to blend in with her surroundings. They're not falling off her body baggy, but they're clearly too big for her, and she continuously fidgets. Her hands pull the sleeves down any time they start to rise, and while most people would look right past her, I can see past the exterior. Her hair is bound in a truly messy bun, black as night and messier than the thoughts in my head. I can see her deep blue eyes briefly when she looks into the video camera to push the button.

The ringing of the video doorbell snaps me out of it, and I frown down at Gertie.

"Why didn't you snap me out of it earlier? I could have met here at the door!" I scold her.

Shaking my head in exasperation, I head toward the back door. Gertie is lucky she's cute, it's hard to stay mad at her. I skip my way to the door and fling it open dramatically. My arms are spread wide and I'm grinning as I face the artist.

"Welcome!" I say loudly.

Apparently, I am too loud and move too quickly for her because the next thing I hear is a scream, and the most pain I've ever experienced flows through my body. My muscles lock up, and I can feel the strain they're under from whatever is happening. There's a low-pitched noise of pain filling my ears, as if someone is growling through a wail of torture. Belatedly, I register that my knees have slammed down into the pavement. I'm pretty sure I'm dying.

A voice enters the chaos, and I think I fall in love.

"Oh shit, oh shit, oh god, shit, fuck. Here, come this way, shit. I knew I shouldn't have kept it in my hand. Fuck."

Smaller hands wrap around my biceps and hold me upright while on my knees. The pain abruptly stops, but the lingering ache floods my system along with the lovely feeling of nostalgia. *Did I have a seizure? What the hell was that?* I manage to flutter my eyes open, and I find myself staring into the deep blue eyes of the woman I saw on our security camera.

"Just breathe through it, you're gonna be fine. Fuck. I'm *so* sorry!

There you go, you got this," she coaches me through the myriad of sensations from the taser.

I take another deep breath and sit up on my own, holding up my body weight so she knows she can let go. Once she figures out that she doesn't have to hold on to me anymore, she wrings her fingers as we sit and look at each other.

The world slows as I take in her scent, minty and sweet. A breath of fresh air that swirls through the air and through my senses. I've never smelled something so tempting and so comforting in the same moment. If I wasn't obsessed before, I sure as fuck am now. I want to bury my nose in her neck and take a deep inhale. Thankfully, she speaks before I can do something stupid.

"Are you okay?" she asks in a small voice.

"I think I came a little," I reply oh so smoothly.

Her eyes widen before she grins at me, a small giggle escaping her.

"Is that good?"

I hum as I think of a response. "I've had worse experiences with cumming awkwardly, so I think we'll call this one a good experience."

She laughs. "I'm glad."

We stand up, and I brush the knees of my pants before suddenly moving my hand to my shirt pocket. What if Gertie got damaged or fell out? Panic starts to rise until I feel her familiar shape and fur. I glance down to validate what my hand feels and I breathe easier. My hand shoots out between the woman and I once my Gertie check is complete.

"Name's Emmett. I'm here to help you get set up. Assuming you're the artist and not someone trying to rob me," I introduce myself.

She grins at me, but doesn't take my hand. Belatedly, I realize I didn't ask if she's okay with touching, and I quickly yank my hand back with a mumbled apology.

"It's fine." She smiles warmly at me. "I'm Danika, and I am your artist. Although, I could just be tricking you into thinking that. Maybe I'll rob you when you're not looking."

Chuckling, I reply, "Noted. The best pens to steal are on the information desk. I'll look the other way."

"I'll keep that in mind." She giggles.

We walk through the gallery, and I show her the different spaces where her art will hang. I indicate the UV lights we installed at her request, and she seems impressed with what we came up with. I can see some insecurity on her face, though.

"What's wrong?" I ask her.

"What do you mean?"

"You look a little upset. Is there something we can fix?"

She sighs. "No, it's honestly just nerves. I've never done a solo show before, and I'm really hoping it will go well."

I nudge her gently with my elbow, our layers of clothing serving as a barrier against our skin. No fear of unwanted touch here. "I'm sure it'll be great."

My reward for reassuring her is a small smile. She gestures for me to assist her with her artwork. I listen closely as she tells me where to hold the art, and we put all of the paintings in the main room. I'm super excited to see her work, but I try to keep my energy at bay. I don't want to freak her out.

"Are you excited to see the art, Gertie?" I whisper to my hamster.

Danika looks over at me from her spot across the room.

"Did you say something?"

My head whips up, and I look at her with widened eyes. My eyes look back and forth in the room, hoping that Jonah will magically appear and say something. Unfortunately, there's no magic to be had here. Shuffling my feet, I take a deep breath. May as well own up to it now.

"Um, yes?" I tell her.

"Oh, sorry. I couldn't hear it from here. Can you repeat it? I'll move closer."

She turns from her spot and starts to walk over to me. There's something about her that does me in. She's not trying to be sexy as she walks, but she effortlessly is. Even in baggy clothes and a messy bun. I don't want Gertie to think I'm drooling, so I make sure my mouth is closed and subtly wipe my mouth.

"Uh, well, I was just saying that it's exciting to see your art," I tell her.

She arches a brow at me. "I haven't unveiled anything yet. You haven't seen the art."

"I'm excited to see it when you unveil it," I insist.

She smiles at me, like she knows I'm bluffing a bit. Thankfully, she doesn't call me on my bullshit. I'm not quite ready to discuss Gertie, even though I'm not ashamed of her. It's just a lot to explain, and I don't know if she'll be able to handle it all. I hope she is, but I don't want to get my hopes up. Before I know it, she's got her pieces in the rooms and wall spots that she wants and she's ready to unwrap them to hang them.

I move to stand near her, ready to help if she asks, and anxious to see her work. My eyes watch her patiently as she puts her hands on her hips and takes a deep breath. Unconsciously, I breathe along with her. When she notices, her mouth quirks up in a smile and her eyes meet mine.

"Feel ready?" I ask

"Yeah, it just always feels nerve-wracking when I show someone the art for the first time. Once you see it, it's officially public, so it's easier after."

"Take your time, there's no rush."

After one more deep breathe, she leans close to the piece and grabs the canvas covering. Slowly, the picture is revealed, although I notice a slight shake to her hands as she pulls it off the painting. My heart stops for a moment as I take in the image. It's beautiful, but there's an underlying darkness that I can sense. There's a woman in the image, sitting on a log and surrounded by trees. Her face is serene as she gazes through the nature surrounding her.

"Want to see the switch?" she asks quietly.

I nod, not trusting my voice at the moment. When she pushes the button, I almost lower to my knees. The scene changes from a calm and serene picture to horror and anger. The woman is no longer only sitting peacefully; she now has a spirit version of herself screaming as she tears at her hair. Tears stream down her face in the image, facing the trees that are now covered in flames. Smoke swirls between the woman and the trees, blocking her from getting to them while they burn.

Belatedly, I realize my cheeks are wet with tears. My heart feels like it's constricting as I see the dichotomy of the woman's image. Pain lances through me at the horror of the fire and the anguish showing on the woman's spirit. Silence passes between Danika and me, an understanding of sorts connects us. Understanding without words the gravity of the piece. This exhibit is going to be one of the most emotional things I've ever seen.

Chapter 3

Danika

"You have checked your appearance no less than ten times. You look *great*. Can we go now?" Sophie asks.

I huff out a frustrated breath.

"Fine. Yes. We can go. I want to make sure we're there at least an hour early. Emmett said that's an okay time to arrive."

"Ah yes, the man of your dreams! Mr. Tall, Dark, and Delicious with a scent of home," Sophie waxes.

"We're not talking about this." I roll my eyes as I walk to my purse, double checking its contents.

Taser? Check. Keys? Check. ID? Check. I've got the necessities, and this time I'll be keeping the taser put away unless there's actual danger. I still feel bad for tasing Emmett, although he was a good sport about it. It wasn't a hardship helping him sit up, either. He was covered enough that I wasn't at risk for skin contact, but his scent about knocked me over. It was a sense of home, cozy, and safety all rolled into one.

Unfortunately for me, the concepts of home, cozy, and safety do not go together. Therefore, I will not be pursuing this. Stupid trauma.

"Fine, I'll drop it, but I'm keeping an eye on both of you tonight," Sophie promises.

Well, promises may be generous. I keep my face turned from her as I roll my eyes, slide my feet into a pair of kitten heels, and smooth my hands down my dress. I found a black maxi dress a couple years back in a secondhand store, and it's been my go-to for every exhibit I display. The V-neck is elegant without too much cleavage, and the short sleeves cover my shoulders.

"I heard that eye roll," she teases.

"You know me too well." I giggle in response.

Finally, I turn, facing her head-on, expecting her to appear amused. Instead, she's staring at me with an affectionate smile, something held in her hands. My eyes drop down to the box and look back up at her, confusion furrowing my brow.

"You know I love you, but I'm not going to marry you if you kneel right now," I tell her.

Sophie barks out a laugh, head thrown back for a moment.

"Babe, you can't afford me. *I* can't afford me most days. Um, I wanted to get you something special for tonight. I know you have one extra special to you painting tonight, even if I haven't seen it yet, and I know it took a lot for you to get to this point. You are amazing, brave, and beautiful."

Pressure builds behind my eyes, and I blink furiously to try and avoid crying. When I finally glance down, I see the now-open box and duck my head, pointing my grin at the floor. Looking back at Sophie, I feel tears start to fall down my face a bit, which causes her to panic.

"Shit, I know it's not really fancy, but is it that bad?"

Giggling, I reach out to the box and gently lift the handmade necklace out of it. My best friend made me a necklace woven like a friendship bracelet, with small medallions hanging from it. Each medallion has an encouraging or uplifting word on it. I run my fingers across them, muttering some of the words as I go.

"Brave, resilient, gorgeous, amazing ..." I grin directly at Sophie now.

She smiles as if my wonder at her gift is the best thing she has ever seen.

"I know you don't love bling like I do, so I tried to make something you wouldn't mind having around even if you don't wear it," she says softly.

I pull her into a brief, fierce hug and turn my back to her, passing the necklace behind me. She easily takes the hint and fastens it on. Thankfully, she wove an actual necklace fastener to it instead of having to tie it on. She spins me around and surveys the necklace.

"It's perfect."

Smiling, I nod my head to agree, then pull us toward our cars. Sophie refuses to ride in my truck, citing the lack of class, and I refuse to go to an exhibition without it. So, we're driving separately, a fact that I have ribbed her about several times. When we arrive, she smoothly parks next to me and holds out her hand as I exit my truck. I clasp her hand in mine, and we walk toward the back door. Emmett told me I could enter from the front or back tonight, and I decided the back would be better. Then I don't have to worry about running into anybody if I leave early. It's awkward walking out with a patron, especially if they don't like your art.

Emmett opens the door before I have a chance to knock, but has tapered his exuberance this time. He grins at us, and I can't help but smile back. Sophie nudges me in the ribs, mouthing 'Cute!' at me. My eyes roll good naturedly and we finish crossing the distance to the door.

"No taser tonight?" Emmett teases.

"I left it in my *other* bag," I say haughtily.

My smile grows as he chuckles and steps outside to wave us in before him.

"Do you want me to take your purses or anything?" he asks.

We both decline, and he nods. "Not a problem. We have not officially opened yet, so I'll introduce you to Jonah. He's the boss around here."

"Sounds good," I reply, following him through the back halls just like yesterday.

As we walk behind him, I can't help but ogle his ass. It fills out the black dress pants he's managed to squeeze into. I don't mean that in a bad way, he's just allllll muscle and my eyes are very grateful for that fact. Sophie nudges me and looks between my eyes and his ass a few times.

"Oh shut it!" I hiss at her.

This bitch just silently cackles at me. It's why I love her. Thankfully, her opportunity to tease me about my refusal to admit attraction hits its end when we step into the brightly lit room. There are a few walls interspersed throughout to break up the views, but otherwise it's open and I almost tear up a little seeing only *my* work being displayed. There's no set theme to my paintings other than they reveal something that you wouldn't expect to see.

Sophie gasps, and I know she's seen the one painting I refuse to sell. My big, personal reveal. She scuttles over to it, checking each detail once she's closer. Her mouth is slightly open, and her eyes are wide. Sophie knows enough of my story that she's well aware of what will show when that black light goes on. She just doesn't know what it will look like. She bites her lip and looks over at me as I approach. She asks without words, and I respond in kind by pushing the button that turns on the UV light.

Her hand flies up to cover her mouth as her eyes rove across the canvas. I can see her taking in all the details and storing them in her memory. The anguish in the woman who is standing and screaming in this new light. How all the trees are on fire in front of her, smoke billowing out toward the woman. She even catches the little detail I painted; the small flame thrower I used to start it. It's hidden toward the back of the trees, but if you know to look, it's there.

She presses the button back to the regular light, then places her hands on my face. Unafraid, I meet her eyes directly, my hands gently holding on to her forearms.

"Beautiful," she says softly.

My eyes close in a mixture of relief and overwhelm. Relief that she likes it, even if I tell myself it doesn't matter, and overwhelm from how much I love and appreciate her friendship. She's brought me back from the dark place in my mind many times. I don't know how I survived the years before her, but they've been brighter since she made her grand entrance.

Sophie's forehead touches mine gently, and then she pulls away. "Why do you have to be so clingy?"

I laugh at the joke. "I'm just pandering to you, this is a you problem."

We both laugh and take a small stroll around the gallery so she can see the paintings I've chosen to show. All of them are available for sale with the exception of the forest and the girl painting. That one I'm keeping. I've been waiting a few years to finally finish it and feel ready to show it, so tonight's the night. Eventually, it occurs to me to check in with the guy in charge.

Turning my body around, I survey the space and my eyes land on a man slightly taller than Emmett staring at me with intense chocolate eyes. Subtly, I try to take in the rest of him. Dirty blond hair styled to perfection, a perfectly fitted deep blue suit with a tie containing a myriad of colors all swirled together. Emmett is standing next to him, and I'm sure he thinks he's being casual, but I can see him holding his body stiffly, glancing between blondie and I. A quick check tells me that yes, Emmett also brought along his hamster tonight. I think he thought I didn't notice it yesterday, but I did. Just didn't want to say anything to embarrass him.

Finally deciding to do more than just stare, I move my feet to get closer to the blond man. I assume he's Jonah, but we'll see if I'm right. He decides to meet me halfway with an easy smile on his face. When we get close, I make sure both of my hands are on my purse, hoping he picks up on the fact that I don't wish to touch him. Then I get a whiff of his scent and I'm pretty sure that's the moment I really start drooling.

I didn't wear any kind of scent block on myself or to avoid smelling others. I'm torn between grateful and upset about this fact because the warmest and most tantalizing smell of coffee wafts off this man. It's the scent of calm mornings sitting in the sun. Contemplating life as I sip on the liquid gold as I sit in my studio. The beautiful sunrise I used to watch as a child while coffee brewed at home, *before* everything went to shit. I feel frozen to the spot, unsure how I want to proceed. All I know is absolutely no touching.

I can see his nostrils flare and his eyes widen as he takes my own scent in. Emmett is right behind him, smirking as if he holds the world's biggest secret. He whispers something into the new guy's ear, and I can see a minute nod in response. He stops a couple feet away from me, his arms clasped behind his back.

"You must be Danika. I'm Jonah, owner of the gallery and pack mate to this guy," he introduces himself.

Emmett blushes lightly as he gives Jonah an affectionate glance. Jonah winks in reply, as though it's an old joke they share.

"Yes, I'm Danika, and this is my emotional-support Sophie," I reply.

Sophie turns to me with a devious sparkle in her eye. Shit, should have thought that joke through before making it. She's going to milk this one for a while. I make a mental note to buy her something nice to avoid any future embarrassment. For now, Sophie places her hand gently on my shoulder.

"Do you need to sit down? You seem overwhelmed. Do you want me to hug you tight?" she asks in faux sympathy.

I hear Emmett snicker in the background and give him the stink-eye before turning to Sophie.

"No, I'm okay. Good girl, Sophie, you'll get a treat later." I pat her head.

Should I egg her on? No. Can I help it? Also no.

Jonah looks between us uncertainly. It seems like he's not quite sure how to handle this moment. Deciding to take pity on the guy, I give him a small head nod in acknowledgement.

"Thank you for hosting my art this evening. Is there anything I need to do to prepare?" I ask him.

He shakes himself out of whatever thought he's having and assures me he's got it all covered. The purchase process seems simple enough based on how he explains it, and I've got the option to do a toast or speech if I want to. I definitely appreciate how relaxed this entire process is. Now I just need to wait for the public to arrive.

Chapter 4

Jonah

The second I laid eyes on her, I knew I was a goner. Her eyes are a fascinating mix of haunted, soft, and guarded. I'm itching to find out why and help it go away, but I remind myself I only just met her and it's probably creepy to think that. Watching her sway through the room, talking with guests, though, is making it hard to remember manners. Thank God Emmett warned me about her being anti-touch. I kind of remember from our emails, but I'd totally forgotten when I saw her. Would have put a damper on things if I'd ignored that.

The room almost feels like a rave with lights randomly switching to UV then back to normal. Maybe I should find some classical music played by EDM DJs. I'm sure it exists. A mix of classy and crazy rolled into one. Smirking, I realize I just described Emmett and me. Speaking of Emmett, I can tell he's walking up behind me while my gaze is glued on Danika.

"She's perfect, isn't she?" he asks dreamily in my ear.

I smile softly. "I don't think I know her well enough to say, but she sure is amazing. Fuck, her scent ..."

Emmett groans in my ear. "Right? I thought I was hallucinating the first time I smelled her. Good thing I wasn't, I much prefer having the reality."

"Did you introduce her to Gertie?" I ask, turning my head so I can see him.

"No, I don't think she's ready for that yet." His reply is soft, almost vulnerable.

Turning fully, I grab his hand and pull him close. He comes easily, laser focused on me in the moment. My other hand reaches up to caress his cheek.

"Don't do that. I can hear your insecurity. You're wonderful, and if she doesn't see that, then she's missing out."

His answering smile eases my concern, and we both turn back to the event around us. When my eyes catch Danika's, her cheeks flush and she holds my gaze for a moment before a patron asks her a question. My teeth bite softly on my lower lip in response to the interaction. I want to see her blush all the time.

"You think she even wants to stick around to get to know us?" Emmett asks.

"Did you see her face when she caught our scents? She's at least intrigued, and that's a good start. We just can't push her. I can see she's a bit skittish. If she's putting on a face for the patrons, she's fine, but when she looks at us, it's not quite the same. Her friend gets the real her," I tell him.

Emmett hums and nods next to me. We watch some more as she smoothly talks with any patron to ask her questions. Now and again, Emmett and I get flagged to come help with a sale, and each time I get excited about adding that red dot. When I glance at Danika, she looks shocked each time, and I can't help but smile and wink at her. Her genuine shock and joy is refreshing. Usually our artists are in the business long enough that they're no longer shocked, or it's not a sale event so there are no sales.

I have a feeling her art is going to be extremely popular. If she doesn't already have someone to help manage her or act as her agent, she's going to need someone. Maybe that's where we can come in and help. If she happens to fall in love with us along the way ... well, that's just kismet, isn't it?

As the event winds down, my nerves start to make themselves known. What if she doesn't want to talk? What if she just runs for the door? I'm dying for this chance to talk with her. Quick introductions and business processes isn't enough for me. There's a deep need within me to get to know her, understand her, be a support for her. I've not felt like this before, and there's a thought that flits through my head before I dismiss it.

Maybe she's our match ...

My feet carry me over to her where she's standing with the last two guests, talking about the one painting that isn't for sale. I try to angle my approach so I don't distract her, but I clock the quick glance she gives me before looking back at the guests.

"I'm just so captured by the pain and destruction hiding beneath the beauty. Is there an inspiration for it?" The guest is a woman, likely in her mid-fifties, well put together but ostentatious. To her right is a man who appears to be her mate based on how his hand rests on her lower back.

Danika smiles shyly. "There is, but it's not a story I like to share. But I think there are more people in the world who have pain sitting under the surface of their calm."

The woman nods slowly, her eyes glued to the picture. Her mate squeezes her gently into him, and she turns, giving him a glassy-eyed smile. She sighs, resigned.

"Well, it's selfish of me, but I truly wish you were willing to part with this one. I understand your reasons, though."

The two women look into each others' eyes for a moment, and Danika offers her a nod of understanding, which is reciprocated to her.

"When is your next showing?" the patron asks.

Danika's hands go to where a long-sleeved shirt would end at her wrists before realizing there's nothing there to grasp onto. She covers the motion by weaving her fingers together, but not before I note the nervous gesture.

"I'm honestly not sure, but I do try to announce them on my business socials. I can give you a card with those listed on it if you'd like," she replies softly.

The patron lights up. "Yes, please! I think you have a bright future ahead of you, my dear, and I would love to watch as it unfolds."

A blush covers Danika's cheeks, but she fishes for the card in her purse before handing it over. The patrons depart with well wishes, and I note Emmett walking behind them, thanking them for coming before locking the door. The small click feels like the signal for everyone to let out a collective breath. Danika's friend turns to her and squeals in excitement.

"I cannot with how amazing this night went for you, babe! Are you proud? Because I am."

"I think so." Danika smiles. "I'm pretty surprised."

"Why's that?" I ask gently, inserting myself into the conversation.

Danika turns, surprised at my voice, but quickly relaxing.

"I've never sold paintings in this volume before. Maybe one or two, enough to get by, but this was such a success that it's throwing me for a loop. It feels like a mistake."

My eyebrows raise in surprise. "Really? That's surprising to me. You clearly have talent and a good following."

"Well, usually I show with other artists. And while I market some, I did more for this one." Her lips curl, and a warm feeling grows in my chest.

Emmett walks up to where we are standing and celebrates Danika with zero preamble.

"That was *amazing*, Stargazer!" he declares loudly, raising his arms above his head.

Danika's brow furrows. "Stargazer?"

"Yeah! I looked up animals who have electricity, and since you're way too extraordinary to be an eel, I picked the stargazer. It's a fish that uses electricity. Just like you used on me," he explains, almost dreamily.

"That can't be a real thing," Danika's friend chimes in.

"Oh, it's definitely real! Just ... maybe don't look up any pictures. I didn't choose the fish based on looks." Emmett rubs the back of his head.

I can see Danika's lip twitching as she wrestles with the desire to laugh or stay professional. She's so fucking cute.

"So, if you're free to swing by tomorrow, we can work with you to get the pieces packaged up and sent out. We have plenty of shipping supplies in the back, but you're welcome to bring your own as well. We'll ship from here since we have the capacity for it. That way you don't have people getting your address from the return information," I step in, saving the three of them from their potentially disastrous conversation.

Emmett means well, but he goes all in, and it can be over-whelming to someone new. Especially someone who smells as amazing as Danika does. There's no way he's going to hold back with her. I'll need Colin's help with this one. I manage to get focus back on business, then walk Danika and her friend to their cars. They both parked in the back, so I make sure our floodlights are on and I stand and watch them drive away.

A deep sigh sounds in my ear, and my body instinctively leans back into Emmett's solid body. He easily accepts my weight, and we step back fully into the building, closing the door. The second I hear the door click after closing, I spin and push Emmett back into a wall. My hand lands on his throat, firm enough so he knows not to move, but not blocking his windpipe.

"You need to be careful with her," I growl at him.

"Why?" he whines at me.

I run my nose from his collarbone, up to the top of his ear, inhaling his delicious leather scent as I do.

"Because we want to keep her. If you push too hard too fast, she might run. Do you need Colin and I to tame you so you can focus?"

Emmett shivers under my hand and our bodies are so close that I can feel how I'm affecting him. My own body is rising to the occasion, and I can't help but brush my body against his, giving both of us just the barest hint of friction. The jolt of pleasure that runs through me is delicious and I need more. Desperate to feel more of him, I press our hips together fully. My teeth nip at his ear, and a low groan rolls through him.

"Let's go home, I'd hate to deprive Colin of this sweet body." My voice is thick and heavy, desire altering the sound.

"Please, I can't wait. I need you, Jonah." Emmett's voice is on the edge, our years together telling me exactly how far I can push him.

Right now, he really does need relief. If I push him too hard to wait, he'll spiral. The last thing I want to do is make him feel unwanted, it's not something he could handle from me. As I wrap my lips around his earlobe and suck, he moans and squirms. Instead of words, I kiss my way to his lips, and he greets me happily. Our mouths caress each other, and when I flick my tongue against his lips, he opens and our tongues dance.

My hand stays on his throat, holding him exactly where I want him. When I squeeze gently and relax again, I can feel the full body shudder that runs through Emmett, his submissive side coming out to play. My spare hand lands on his hip, but slowly moves to the front of his shirt before moving up his chest. The feeling of his skin flexing in response to my touch thrills me. We've been together as an unbonded pack for five years and this never seems to get old. After getting their fill, my fingertips slide down to the button on his pants and flick it open.

"Are you going to stay still? Be a good boy for me?" I growl lowly in his ear.

Emmett nods frantically. "Yes, I'll be good, I won't move."

I nip his jaw in response and finish opening his pants before sliding them down as I kneel in front of him. Do I want relief? Absolutely. Does Emmett need it more? Also absolutely. My mouth waters as I watch his dick pop out as I reveal inch by inch of his skin. Anticipation runs through me, and I forego any kind of teasing, taking him immediately as deep as I can.

"Oh, *fuck*, Jonah!"

I can hear the slight bang of Emmett's head hitting the wall behind him when he throws his head back. My mouth still full of him, I chuckle and hollow out my cheeks before pulling back. His legs shake beneath the grip I have on his thighs, and I swirl my tongue in his slit before drawing him deep again. My cock is rock hard as I savor Emmett's, the feel of his velvety skin a treat for my senses. Unable to contain it, a moan of pleasure escapes me as I feel him getting harder, closer to his finish.

Reaching around, my fingers slide between his cheeks, spreading them open with one hand, leaving a single digit for me to tap against his hole. He jerks at the sensation, and I feel him drive deeper into my throat. Continuing the motion, I tap each time my mouth brings him in, and between the two sensations, he doesn't last long. There's a warning twitch and he explodes in my mouth. I greedily take it all down, enjoying the unique flavor of Emmett. You wouldn't think worn leather would taste good, but for some reason my alpha loves it, and who am I to question my biology?

Pulling myself to standing, I bring his pants with me, tucking him back in and fastening them. He's breathing hard, his head leaned back on the wall. When he realizes I'm standing again, he grasps the back of my head and pulls me in for a kiss. We both love the debauchery of sharing his cum between us, and I let myself get lost in him for another moment. When we finally part, I decide we've been here long enough.

"Come on, let's get home to Colin."

Chapter 5

Colin

I can feel the sweat dripping down my face as I finish my last sparring exercise. Walking forward, my opponent and I bump fists. We're both breathing heavily but grinning at each other. Otto is my favorite sparring buddy, but we only get to spar a few times per month. His schedule is pretty busy, so we don't get the chance as often as either of us would like. I'm grateful we have the chance to spar, even if it is at the ass crack of dawn.

"Did you pick up some new moves?" he asks me as we wipe down with towels.

"Nah, man, you've just been gone too long!" I grin at him.

His boisterous laugh fills the sparring area, and anyone close enough to the spot turns their heads curiously to see where the noise is coming from. Otto is a big guy, there's nothing small or quiet about him. I met him ten years ago when I was young and looking for an outlet for my frustration. We were both pretty scrawny, but Otto filled out quickly. It took me a bit longer, but I'm pleased with my muscles now.

"Let me tell you, private security is no joke, man. I work out but there's not much action," he replies.

"Really? I assumed people only hired private security for really bad situations."

Otto scoffs, "Nah, most of it is rich, paranoid people who like to say they have bodyguards. The guys and I still workout and spar, but it's not the same as real action."

I motion down my body, displaying it like it's on show with my hands. "It's hard to replace all this action, I know," I tease.

Otto laughs again, and we head to the locker rooms to clean up and go home. I decide to skip the shower and get fully cleaned at home. Waving to the staff on my way out, I climb into my car and head toward home. My alphas got home late last night, and I'm looking forward to hearing about how the exhibit went.

The house smells like bacon and eggs when I walk in, and my stomach rumbles its appreciation. Looking into the kitchen, I find Jonah cooking breakfast, happily humming as he does so. After dropping my duffel bag on the floor, I walk over and wrap my arms around Jonah's waist. My lips land a kiss on his neck, then I rest my chin on his shoulder.

"Making breakfast?" I ask.

He hums and leans back into me for a moment before standing up straight again.

"Breakfast is only for my mates who don't smell like ass," he tells me with a smirk.

"Hey, that's the smell of hard work and manliness!" I protest.

"Ehhhhh, Gertie says otherwise," Emmett calls from the other side of the kitchen. "She says you stink."

I turn toward him and place a hand on my chest in faux outrage. "Gertie! I thought we were friends. How could you be so hurtful?"

My feet carry me over to Emmett where I lean down to look Gertie in the eye with a pout on my lips.

"How can I earn your favor back, little one?" I whisper.

Emmett cocks his head to the side, listening to whatever reply he thinks Gertie is saying. I'll be honest, the first time we met I was a little weirded out by Gertie. As I got to know him more, I discovered who he is and looked past his quirks. Once I finally realized that Gertie was his way of socializing through his anxiety, it was easy to go along with it. Now my life goal is to get her to like me best.

Emmett sighs like he received rough news. "She says it will take a shower and some groveling post-shower for her to be nice again. Pretty harsh, even for her."

"It's a burden I'll happily take on." I suppress a smile.

I grab my duffel before moving past Emmett, stopping in front of Emmett to grab his face and pull him close for a kiss. Then I smack his ass before walking upstairs to get clean. My body is still on my post-workout high, so after holding Jonah close to my body and kissing Emmett, I'm feeling antsy. As I lather my body with soap, it's so fucking temping to wrap my hand around my cock, but I leave it. The lead up makes the final event so much better.

Instead, I get dressed with my cock still rock-hard and head downstairs to see if food is ready yet. When I saunter into the kitchen, Emmett takes one look at me and groans deeply. Jonah looks over at the sound, smirking when he sees me standing there.

"What?" I ask.

Emmett gestures at me wildly. "Did you *have* to wear grey sweatpants today? Really?"

My lips pull into a playful smirk, and I take my seat at the table, ignoring both of them while I fill my plate. My own deep groan escapes me as I take my first bite of salty bacon. Satisfaction fills me when grease and saltiness flood my mouth, a crispy texture between my teeth. I think bacon might be the best food ever invented. Looking at Emmett and Jonah, I see that they're both watching me with satisfied smiles on their faces.

"So, how did things go last night?" I ask.

Emmett just adopts a dreamy smile, one that I've seen him wear the last two days as he's prepared for the showing. When I asked him about it the first time, he just continued smiling and any further conversation was lost. Jonah's currently wearing a similar smile. I give both of them the stink eye, waiting for an explanation for the smiles.

"It went really well," Jonah finally says.

Then the talking stops. Frustration starts to rise within me; I don't want to have to pull answers out of them. I just want them to give me all the details.

"And ..." I prompt.

"Oh, and the artist did fantastic, she sold most of the paintings on display. Her work is incredible, I don't think I've ever seen something like it before. Looking at her art is like someone reached into your soul and pointed out your secrets. It's breathtaking," Jonah finally explains.

"Sounds like an evening Wonder would be proud of," I tell him softly, my joy at his success filling me with a warm feeling.

Jonah smiles, happiness and sorrow mixed in together. "She would be."

A smile comes to my lips at Jonah's information and the love he still holds for Wonder. My heart swells a bit as I think on this artist he mentioned, and I feel my own excitement ramp up in response to his words. Jonah's got great taste, so his shows are usually impactful, but I've not seen him this thrilled over an artist's work before. There's something more here, I can feel it.

Time to poke the beast.

"Sounds amazing! I'd love to take a look, but I bet the artist is a total bitch if she has good art."

As expected, they snap their eyes to me, indignity rising in both of them. *Bingo.* They're attracted to her, which means she's definitely special and ramps up my own curiosity.

"She's absolutely wonderful, thank you. You can keep that talk to yourself," Jonah snaps.

"Yeah! She was super nice to me after she tased me. She felt really bad!"

I lock eyes with Emmett, and the sincerity in his face makes it extremely hard to keep the smile off mine. My alpha is so damn adorable, my heart feels full any time I look at him. He looks almost distraught in his sincerity, so I stand and move to his chair, plopping myself in his lap. Despite our equal size, I manage to snuggle in close to him, giving my alpha the sense of dominance he doesn't know he needs.

Emmett prefers to be on the submissive side, but he's an alpha and still craves those dominant moments. My innate desire as a beta is to help take care of my alphas, so I'm happy to create these moments for him without making a fuss about it. If we ever find an omega and actually bond, it will be even easier to take care of him *and* Jonah. Unfortunately, we've struggled to find an omega that accepts Emmett, and while we can mate bond each other, we want the pack bond, too. So, we're still waiting.

"Tell me more about your amazing artist," I demand from Emmett's lap.

"The second I saw her on the security video, I was hooked. So, when I swung the doors open to greet her, I may have been too enthusiastic, and she tased me," Emmett explains with a smile.

Jonah's laughing next to us. "Never gets old."

"She leaned down to help me up, and she has the gentlest touch. It was like her hands belonged on my arms always. Her scent though?" Emmett groans. "Her scent was the sweetest, cleanest mint. I wanted to breathe her in for hours, basking in how fresh her smell is."

My attention turns to Jonah and I smile, waiting to hear his input also. The same dopey smile that I saw on Emmett's face is slowly forming on Jonah's face.

"She's that special, eh?"

Jonah just nods, smiling for a moment. Shaking himself out of whatever thoughts he was entertaining, he heaves a big sigh.

"Her name is Danika. She doesn't like touch, but I think it's only if it's bare skin since she helped Emmett up. She had a woman come in with her, who she described as her 'emotional support'." He chuckles.

"So she had a Gertie?" I ask.

Emmett giggles behind me.

"No, the woman was alive," Jonah quips.

We dissolve into laughter, and I can't stop laughing over the image of a woman I've never met trying to cart around a stuffed pillow shaped like a person. Or pulling a "Weekend at Bernie's" situation.

"Anyway, Danika brought her over to a painting and showed her what it looks like under a different light, and the two of them hugged. It was beautiful to watch, seeing Danika so vulnerable with her friend and strong as fuck with everyone else. It was breathtaking. I just want to sit down with her and get to know her and how her mind works, but I also know she's a bit skittish of others. I'm looking forward to seeing her today," Jonah finally finishes.

"She sounds amazing."

I drop a kiss on Emmett's temple, and we bask in the comfortable silence that descends after my response to Jonah.

"When is she moving in?" I inquire cheekily.

"How about tomorrow?" Emmett suggests.

I stand up. "Sounds good! I'll prep her room!"

My alphas laugh as I saunter away toward our empty omega space, but joke's on them because I really am going to make sure the room is cleaned out and has what an omega would need. A smile lifts my lips, and I get down to work, pulling off old bedsheets, dusting the room, vacuuming, cleaning the bathroom, and writing a list of things we'll need for our omega. There's no fooling me, she's going to be ours.

Chapter 6

Danika

My dry, gritty eyes stare up at my ceiling, noting that a few spiders are trying to move in. There are wisps of webs in a few spots that I'll need to dust out of here. I can co-exist peacefully with spiders. As long as they're not in my house. Then all bets are off. Dryness makes it hard to blink, resulting in my hands rubbing them harder than they should. I'm gonna need some eye drops today.

I tossed and turned most of the night before admitting defeat and lying in bed awake for the majority of my time in bed. Thoughts of Jonah and Emmett ran through my head, preventing sleep from fully setting in. Fear flooded my body any time I silently acknowledged my attraction to them. They are absolutely mate potential with how their scents call to me. Any time I started thinking too much about them, my body would begin to heat and I could feel slick starting to build between my thighs. Memories then popped in and cooled things to ice.

Heaving a sigh, I realize that I need to finally admit defeat. It's after eight a.m., so I need to get out of bed if I want to have any semblance of normalcy today. Thoughts continue to tangle through my head as I go through my morning routine, and I eventually give in to the fact that I need to talk with Sophie. It's easier to keep it inside and figure it out over time, but this time I'm ill-prepared to process what's happening, and I have promised Sophie that I will open up more with her. Maybe it's time to tell her about my first two years on the street when I left home.

Once I'm clean and dressed, I make my way to the kitchen for a breakfast of leftover cookies. Sophie bakes the best cookies. She can cook really well and bakes a few good desserts, but her cookies are absolutely amazing. I've told her she could make a business off them, but she laughs me away each time. A dozen make their way to my house any time I have an exhibit coming up. It's an odd ritual we've gotten into, a dozen cookies every few months, but it's what keeps my nerves steady. A pattern I can rely on no matter what else is happening. A sigh escapes me after I finish my breakfast of champions, and I grab my phone out.

"Well good morning, my little cookie monster! To what do I owe the pleasure?" Sophie greets me.

Despite my less-than-happy mood, a smile comes to my face when I hear her.

"Any chance you want to go grab a coffee? I need to wrap up stuff at the gallery, but I was hoping you would have time for coffee before that."

The line is dead silent after I finish talking.

"Sophie?" I ask.

"I'm sorry, *you* want to go *out* to grab coffee?!"

"I know, I know, harass me about it later. I need some Sophie wisdom right now."

"Oh, must be bad, eh? Okay, let's meet at the coffee shop and we can sit outside. It's a decent day," she suggests.

"Sounds good. Thanks, Sophie," I tell her.

"Always."

We disconnect and I grab my keys, not wanting to chicken out.

I've got a lightweight, long-sleeved shirt on and some flowy pants, so I'm comfortable and covered. Just the way I like it. Wearing that dress yesterday was a challenge for me. I hop in the truck and start making my way to our usual coffee joint. We don't often meet up at the shop, but when she drags me out, this is the one we always end up at. They have delicious muffins. Somehow, I beat Sophie here, so I stand near the door, waiting for her before going inside.

Sophie finally shows just as I'm considering calling her again. She looks a little harried, and my gut sinks with guilt. Did I make her rush through her morning? The last thing I want is to create chaos for her. When she reaches me, she pulls me into a brief, tight hug and then steps back quickly.

"Sorry, if you're calling me for coffee, you need a hug. Deal with it," she says, opening the door to usher me through.

A snicker escapes me as I walk into the café. Sophie knows exactly what I need even if I'm not sure sometimes. Once we have coffee in hand, we manage to find an empty booth near the back of the shop that seats two. We take a moment in comfortable silence to settle in and get our first sips of coffee. Knowing that Sophie isn't going to push me, I decide to bite the bullet.

"I really hate saying this."

Sophie smirks, knowing exactly what I'm about to say. "Go on."

"You were right," I grumble.

She just grins and waits for me to continue.

"I have a thing for Emmett," I start, pausing when I see her raised brow, "and Jonah."

She nods, satisfied.

"I couldn't sleep last night. It was like their scents wouldn't leave me alone. Their faces keep flashing in my mind, especially when my eyes closed. I'm terrified, Soph." I tell her.

Sophie frowns. "What are you scared of? What do you think will happen?"

As she asks, my stomach sinks, a cold feeling of dread creeping from the base of my skull through my body. Memories are right there, wanting to take me down and swallow me whole. The two years that I lived in the city before finding my cottage weren't great. That's probably an understatement. The memories of hands that are not mine try to creep in, but I force myself to take deep breaths for a moment, pushing the memories away.

"I'm terrified to share my body with someone. You know I left my home at sixteen and you know why. But I don't think I've ever told you about the two years basically living on the streets. It was ... not great."

I stare at my coffee cup as I speak, but I can see Sophie still in my periphery.

"There were shelters that I used for sleep, I made sure to get there an hour before closing so I always had a spot to sleep in. It was divided by designation, but didn't mean that things were safe. Most of the omegas staying there were supportive, but not all of them. If you brought anything of value there, you were likely to lose it. When the alphas snuck in, though ... let's just say my trauma may have started at home but it kept going for a few years."

My voice falters and I take a break to sip at my coffee, hoping it will soothe my throat even though it didn't falter for physical reasons. When I glance up at Sophie, she's sitting with her coffee in one hand on the table, and her other hand is covering her mouth. Her eyes glitter with a mix of sorrow and anger. The latter surprises me. Maybe it shouldn't, though. Sophie's always been a fierce friend.

"What the actual fuck?" she whispers behind her fingers.

Heat rushes through me and my cheeks feel like they're on fire. I shouldn't be embarrassed, not with Sophie, but I am. It's an irrational shame that I carry with me, and I can't ever seem to really get rid of it. When I paint in silence, I can ignore it, but it never really disappears. Not fully.

"Dani, you're one of the strongest people I've ever known. I've always thought that, but it's solidified now. You should *never* have had to go through that. Any of it. Most people wouldn't be here, but I'm so damn grateful you are."

A few tears drip down my cheeks, but I keep my gaze firmly on my coffee, unsure if I can keep myself together right now. Sophie's fingers touch mine, and I release one hand and let her hold onto my fingers. It's a small tabletop, so neither of us have to stretch to reach the other. After avoiding touch for so long, I've got Touch Loss. Normally I don't mind, I don't want people to touch me anyway, but moments like this make me a little regretful. I know that I will start to feel drained if we touch for much longer, but it's worth it. I'm able to take comfort mentally from the touch, even if my body feels drained.

Sophie clears her throat as her hand retracts. "Well, I imagine that's not the topic you want to stay on. So, let's talk it out. I can assume why you feel uncomfortable, but can you spell it out for me?"

"Yeah, I can do that." I nod and take a sip of my coffee. "What if they try to touch me?"

"Well, my first response is a counter question. Have they given you reason to think they won't keep their hands to themselves?"

"Okay, I see your point, they've been pretty respectful so far. Will they be mad if we *do* touch and I can't feel if we're matches?"

"You think they might be?" Sophie asks, completely pulling me away from my line of thinking.

"I don't know! They could be!" I snap a little.

Chuckling, she holds her hands up in surrender. "Okay, okay, we can table that. Maybe put that worry out of your mind for now?"

"Yeah, okay. What if ... what if they find out about my past and think that I'm too broken?"

"Then fuck them!" Sophie hisses.

My eyes jump to hers, wide with surprise at her vehemence. Her face is set in what I call her "don't fuck with me" mode. So I don't fuck with her and wait.

"I don't care if they are your matches ... if they think you're broken then they're fucking idiots and you deserve better. You are not broken, you hear me?"

My eyes sting with tears, and I pretend that a couple aren't escaping down my cheeks.

"Thanks, I'll keep working on remembering that," I whisper, my throat thick from the holding my tears back.

"Got any more fears I can shoot down?" she asks with a small smile.

"What happens if I can't let them all the way in? If I can't trust them?"

Her gaze remains soft as she looks at me, a touch of sorrow now present when I look in her eyes. "That one I can't help you with, babe. But I can be here to back you up no matter what choice you make. After I knock some sense into you, of course."

"Good point." I smile.

We move on to lighter topics and sip at our coffee for a little bit longer. It's nice to just exist together for a while. When both of our coffees are empty, I let a sigh escape me, a mix of contentment and slight dread. I need to get over to the gallery and collect my remaining art and wrap up business. My dread comes from all of my insecurities, not any fear of safety. Somehow that makes the dread worse. If it was solely safety, I could take measures and have a plan. This emotional stuff is way harder.

"Time to face the music," I tell Sophie.

As we grab our things and stand up, she grins at me.

"You mean, time to ogle the alphas!"

I laugh as we throw our trash away and walk out of the shop together. Being friends with Sophie has been the brightest spot in my life so far. Maybe these alphas will measure up to be a good thing, too. Sophie and I part ways, and I make my way over to the gallery. Belatedly, I realize I should have called to check that they're open. Jonah did say to come by any time, but I should have clarified. Too late now. I use the doorbell on the service door and wait patiently, my taser gun safely tucked away.

When the door opens, the first thing I am hit with is the smell of warm, roasted coffee. Reflexively, I take a large inhale through my nose, my eyes fluttering closed as I take in the scent. Although it was a brief moment, when my eyes open again I see Jonah looking at me, a smirk of satisfaction on his face.

"Come on in, I'm ready for you," he says.

My stomach flutters as I think about the fact that *I* might not be ready for *him*.

Chapter 7

Danika

O nce I'm inside of the gallery, my nerves settle a little bit more. The unknown of what will happen when I arrive is gone, and now I just need to make it through our next few interactions. I let Jonah go ahead of me, even though I've been here before. I'm not quite comfortable leading the way in a building that isn't mine yet.

"How are you feeling about last night?" he inquires.

"What do you mean?" I ask, my mind immediately trying to figure out if something happened between us and I forgot.

"With the show. It was pretty successful from my perspective."

"Oh! Um, yeah, I'm really pleased with it. It's always hard to let my work go, but I could tell people actually resonated with the pieces and that was truly great to see."

Jonah turns to look at me. "Good, I'm really glad to hear that."

We stop at the welcome desk, which is just as empty as it was during the show. It seems like mostly decoration save for the tablet that's set up with a keyboard. Smart, really, having it minimal like that; then there's no temptation for passers-by to try and break in. As I examine the walls, I note that all the paintings have been removed from their displays on the wall and are resting on the floor beneath where they had been. I'm glad he didn't try to package them up. I've got plenty of supplies for that in my truck and I like them wrapped a certain way.

Jonah turns on the tablet and goes over the numbers with me. I sold about seventy-five percent of my work, which absolutely blows my mind. On top of my fee to book the space, the gallery charges ten percent of the total profits so both the gallery and myself are benefitting from the success of last night. A warm, fuzzy feeling starts in my chest and soon I'm smiling, knowing that I really can do this on my own. I don't need to rely on shared space or online sales. There's no plan to stop my online sales, but I have hope that I can continue to show my art on my own. I won't always have to rely on a bigger name to pull in an audience and hope my stuff gets seen.

"You're pretty special, you know that?" Jonah comments.

My smile continues. "I was hoping that my work would be loved and it is. It's exciting to know that my skills are something people want to appreciate."

"Well, yes, your art is special, but so are you."

My eyes meet his, and I see sincerity radiating from his face.

"Oh, I don't know if I'm that special, but I appreciate the compliment," I deflect.

He hums noncommittally and asks if he can help to wrap up the existing pieces. Appreciating the help, I accept and go back out to my truck to get the supplies. Grabbing the closest piece, I ask him to hold it up a little for me and slide the padded cover underneath the canvas. It wraps up over the top, where I fasten it with velcro, and do similar with the sides. Working together, we get the art wrapped up quickly, chatting about whatever comes to mind as we do. Jonah's actually really soothing to be around, and I'm feeling more relaxed the longer I'm with him.

"The pièce de résistance," he comments as we come to the one painting I wouldn't sell.

I smile at his words. "I'm not sure it's anything quite so dramatic.

But it is incredibly precious to me. It was meant to be a healing piece."

"Did it work?" he asks, holding the painting gently a few inches off the floor.

I shrug as I move the wrap around the art. "In a way."

"I'm glad you painted it then. Even if it only helped a little bit."

Once I fasten the last parts of the wrap, I stand and look at him, my mind whirling with responses, unsure which one to use.

"You don't have to reply, I can see your brain working a mile a minute," Jonah says softly, full of understanding.

"You're a pretty understanding alpha, you know that?"

His brows raise a little. "I would hope most alphas are understanding, at least with omegas, but I know that's not the world as a whole. I'm glad I can be that for you."

"Okay, Mr. I have a perfect answer for everything, can you help me put these in my truck?" My mouth is tilted in a teasing smirk.

"As you wish," he says.

Aw, dammit, he's quoting *The Princess Bride* now. How am I supposed to keep my distance? Maybe it was a slip up. I direct him to grab the piece in front of us, and once we're back at my truck, I show him how I want it set on the ground as I open my truck bed.

"Can you bring out the rest and just set them like this? Then I can put them in carefully how I like them to be."

"Sure thing. I'll be right back with more art for you."

Do I pause what I'm doing and lean to check out his ass as he walks away? Yes, yes, I do. It's a damn sexy ass. Once he's out of sight, I yank my attention back to loading up my truck. With the bed open and the camper window up, I grab the canvas and set it gently on the tailgate. I push it forward enough for it to rest against the inner wall of the camper top, then hop up so I can pick it up a little as I shift it fully into the bed of the truck. When I turn to see if Jonah's back yet, I notice he's standing at the tailgate, a piece of art in his hands and jaw totally slack.

"See something you like?" I tease him as he gathers his wits again.

"Don't ask questions that you're not ready for, sweetheart," he replies in a husky voice.

My cheeks flush, and I pray that I don't slick or perfume on accident. He is a sexy man, and as much as my body might want his, I'm not sure I'm mentally there yet. Thankfully, we get back to business, and my truck is loaded up in no time. I'm pretty sure he gets a few more glimpses of my ass while I adjust my precious cargo, but I get my own glimpses as he walks inside each time. Feels like we're even.

"So, uh, thanks for letting me show at your gallery again," I say as we stand awkwardly.

Putting his hands in his pockets, Jonah nods. "Yeah, yeah, I'm really glad you did. Um, I would love to have you."

I stand and stare at him for a moment, letting what he said hang in the air. Part of me wants him to figure out what he said, but the other part of me is nervous that he's aware of what he said and doesn't regret it. If he's well aware of the creepy factor and is okay with it, then I'm out faster than a left swipe on a dating app.

Slowly, his eyes widen and a flush starts to show on his cheeks.

"Oh, shit! I mean, here at the gallery, we'd love to have you here again. Showing your art. Like you just did. Shit, I'm so sorry if I made you uncomfortable."

"Thanks for the clarification. It's okay. I think showing here again would be great. The set up is wonderful." I smile.

He grins in response. "Great! Uh, could I take you out for coffee to talk about it more? Or, we don't have to talk about it at all if you don't want to. You can pick what we talk about."

My stomach swoops with butterflies, my smile widening just a bit more. "Sure. Sounds great. You have my number?"

"Yes, I do."

"Okay then, text me later."

Without waiting for a response, I turn and climb into the driver seat of my truck and start the engine. After ensuring Jonah isn't standing in my path, I back up my truck and turn to head home again.

My brain is firing on all cylinders as I work to make sense of that entire interaction.

Okay, *obviously* he wants to go out with me, I'm not that dense, but I wasn't expecting to feel so pleased about it. It's been a long ass time since I felt butterflies for someone. Last time it didn't end well, but Jonah's coffee scent brings me comfort, almost an anticipation for a new day. I would happily take coffee and Jonah every morning, that's for sure. Then combining it with Emmett's comforting worn leather scent? It would be like the home I never really had. Cozy, warm, and loving.

Whoa there, let's slow down on the 'L' word, shall we? I think to myself.

A snort escapes me as my omega instincts war with my logical side, causing me to talk to myself. At least it's just in my head instead of out loud. For now. If those two are serious, it's going to be an interesting ride for them. Sophie has seen my crazy plenty of times and has been there for countless panic attacks, paranoia periods, and a slew of mental breakdowns. Most of which are me battling with myself regarding nesting.

My phone is ignored as I finish my drive home and get my art put away. The studio doubles as storage, and the line between chaos and order is clear. A row of completed paintings sit neatly on one side of the room, slotted carefully into an oversized paper divider. A memory of splinter-covered fingers passes through me, and I check the wood to ensure I've properly sanded and sealed it. After ten years, it's still smooth as the day I finished building it, but the next time I store canvases I'll check again. My fingers twitch each time I go near it until they feel the wood.

Everything is labeled in neat, clear letters. I practiced for hours upon hours to write neatly instead of the chaos scribble I used to have. Chaos doesn't bring anything good, so I push away anything messy or confusing unless it's in my painting space. Anything goes there, but the rest of the house is soothingly orderly. A sense of satisfaction washes through me, knowing that all the things I touched are where they are supposed to be. A kernel of irritation starts up in my head, not unlike a tiny pebble in a shoe. Unlike a pebble, it starts to grow. Something is off, and the awareness of it continues to grow and my hands wring together. My eyes catch on the labels that are empty of canvases, waiting for pieces that won't return to that spot.

"It's fine, I can update labels tomorrow. I need to eat some food and relax," I murmur.

Silence answers me. My feet shuffle back and forth, and a whine tries to escape me while I stare at what's not right in front of me. I squeeze my eyes shut, removing my ability to see what's wrong. The feeling doesn't dissipate, though. The need to fidget is now running throughout my body, creating urgency where none existed just moments ago.

"Goddammit," I growl.

My body continues to push as I begin to take down old labels, and I know this is far from over. There won't be any relaxing tonight.

Chapter 8

Jonah

It's been a few days since I got permission from Danika to message her and set up a date. Any time I try, I can't type anything; my hands shake and I can't see what I'm doing. The nerves fill me, causing butterflies to erupt in my stomach and restlessness seeps into my legs as they bounce my feet. Warmth seeps into the case on my phone as I run my fingers up and down, focusing on the smooth texture.

"It's just a text message, not a marriage proposal," I tell myself.

My body flops back against the couch I'm sitting on. This is ridiculous, I'm not a nervous guy. I've never had a situation where I feel uncertain or nervous. It's not a brag, it's a fact of my life. Danika, though? She turns me into a middle school boy who doesn't know how to talk to girls and pulls their hair for attention. Fuck.

"You look like someone kicked your kitten," Colin says, walking into the room.

"*Are we getting a kitten?*" Emmett shouts as he races in.

Colin and I both look at him, trying to decipher what's happening in his head. He's impulsive, but damn, that was a jump even for him.

"No, Emmett, we're not getting a kitten," I tell him gently.

He frowns before walking away muttering, "Spoilsport."

Colin smiles and giggles a little. "I love that motherfucker."

"Me too." I return his smile.

Colin moves to the couch with me and sits so we're almost touching.

"Wanna tell me about it?" he asks.

Staring at my phone for a moment, I think through what I want to tell him. Colin is well aware of who Danika is, and that Emmett and I want her, so I wouldn't be saying anything new. He's been supportive the few times we've mentioned it, and I really want to introduce them. Maybe that's part of my indecision.

"Danika said I can message her and set up a coffee date, but I can't make myself do it. I get too nervous," I say slowly.

Colin hums but remains silent. I let the silence stretch as he thinks and I continue to avoid. The more I avoid, the more frustrated I become. Feelings of inadequacy start to take hold and that pisses me right off.

"You're not usually one to get so nervous," Colin comments.

"No, I'm not," I agree. "I'm just gonna fuckin do it!"

Colin throws both arms in the air. "Do the thing!"

Bolstered by my own quiet introspection and Colin's gentle nudge, I grab my phone and pull up my messaging app.

Me: Hi, Danika, this is Jonah. How are you?

Of course, there's no immediate response. For some reason I assumed she would reply right away and tell me to go fuck myself. Somehow, I don't see that being her style. If she's not interested, I'd say she's more likely to ghost me or decline me in a painfully polite manner. Colin's hand reaches out to grab my phone from my hands and he turns the screen off.

"Good job, Alpha," he says softly.

My eyes meet his, taking in his gorgeous face, and brown, curly hair tied back but still escaping his hair tie. Colin has always been a bit of a wild child; he loves to support other people and goes with the flow easily. When his preference of supporting people conflicted with "family duty," he walked away and I scooped him right up. Emmett took to him immediately, and when Colin accepted him right back, it was magic. The three of us fit together perfectly, our odd shapes making a perfect puzzle.

Unable to resist, I reach up and take his hair out of the ponytail he was trying to contain it with. The softness of his curls is a comfort I never knew I needed until I touched them for the first time. My fingers glide through the silky locks, and Colin closes his eyes, savoring the feeling. Peace fills me when we sit like this, the intimacy in both of us being completely unguarded soothes my rough edges. The two of us savor the simple touch, existing in a moment only for each other. My soul feels incomplete, and I know Colin is one of the pieces that will fill the void. Our odd-shaped puzzle is just waiting to be filled.

Then my phone buzzes, breaking the silent spell we've woven over ourselves. Colin's eyes snap open with excitement and he pulls away from my hand.

"Well?" he asks impatiently, gesturing to my phone.

Biting my lip, I pull the phone screen up so I can see it.

Danika: Hi, Jonah, it's nice to hear from you.

Me: Same! I'm glad you replied to me.

Danika: Of course!

I look over at Colin, my nerves getting the better of me. Doubts pop up in my head about actually taking her out. I know Emmett and I like her, but Colin hasn't met her yet. Is he really okay with this? We need an omega for a pack bond, but everything seems sudden in this moment, overwhelming and complicated when it shouldn't be. Colin just smiles and nods his head to my phone, nothing but calm and reassuring.

> Me: Is there any chance for me to take you out for coffee some time? Or something else if you don't like coffee?

> Danika: I'd love a coffee date. I can't function without my bean juice. ☕

> Me: Glad I'm not alone in my addiction

> Me: Are you a morning person? Could I take you out in the morning this week?

> Danika: Sure, maybe Thursday or Friday?

> Me: Thursday sounds great. I'll send you the location of my favorite coffee place. Is 7:30 too early?

> Danika: It's perfect. See you there.

Colin's grin is wide when I bring my attention back to him.

"Look at you, my smooth Alpha, makin' dates and stealin' hearts," he teases.

Laughing, I push him over.

"Should we tell Emmett?" Colin asks as he rights himself.

"We probably should, but I'm worried he's going to get his hopes up. I don't want him to deal with heartbreak again if this doesn't work out." A large sigh escapes me.

"Well, tell him about the date, but you don't have to tell him when it is or anything. That might help if he's not obsessing over the specifics of the date."

I nod. "Yeah, I think I'll do that. Maybe at dinner tonight? What's for dinner anyway?"

Colin gives me a look of mock offense. "Whatever you can make yourself, you freeloader! I am not your personal chef!"

"You may not be my personal chef, but you are mine," I say softly, one eyebrow raised at him.

He tries, and fails, to keep a straight face while backing up a bit on the couch. I follow him, prowling at what is now my prey. His eyes light up in excitement.

"Who says I'm yours? Maybe I belong to someone else!"

The jab would sting if I didn't know any better. However, I am well aware that he is fully mine and Emmett's, just as we are fully his. Instead of replying, I pounce on him, making sure he doesn't hit his head on the arm of the couch as my body covers his. The scent of summer nights and bonfires fill my nose as I drag it up his neck before landing a soft kiss on the tip of his nose. He launches up to nip at my lips before I can fully pull away.

"Brat," I chastise him.

"You love it."

Colin moves his hips up just enough to tease me with the bulge he's sporting. My own pants are tight, my dick desperate for his heat, my eyes drinking all of him in and wanting to see him as he writhes before I make him come. I press against him, turning the tease into full on pleasure as we both groan softly. One of my hands holds both of his above his head, so he can't stop me as I pepper kisses around his face and neck before I take his lips gently. There are times that we're both so frantic that we can't wait, but in this moment, I want to savor him.

Our kisses are soft but sure, and before I can even lick his lips, he's opened his mouth to me. We're so in sync that we can tell what the other wants before asking, and our tongues meet and tangle, letting the feeling of each other fill the moment. My jeans are a little painful now with how hard he's making me. I need to be in him, doesn't matter if it's his hole or his mouth.

My movements start to become more frantic, the sexual tension between us rising, driving us higher and higher. Colin starts to let out small whimpers, his sign that he needs to be fucked. It's so damn hot that I drive him a little higher just to hear his noises. He pulls his head back with a gasp, one of his legs wrapped around my hip as we grind into each other like horny teenagers.

"Where am I fucking you today?" I whisper in his ear.

His breathing stutters when I drag the tip of my tongue along the shell of his ear.

"My ass," he finally breathes out.

"I'm not sure I have the patience to prep you," I warn.

He moves his hands, silently asking for permission to move fully as I continue to kiss his neck, licking and nibbling at him as if he's my last meal. Colin reaches behind him and snags a small bottle of lube from the end table.

"I don't need prep, just this. Please, please fuck me." His eyes are full of desperation and longing.

Smirking, I nip the spot where his neck and shoulder meet, mocking an actual pack and mating bite. He shudders in pleasure before I ease back and unbutton my pants, nodding at him to remove his. Quickly, he rids himself of his pants and lays back down, spreading his legs for me. The sight of his hard, flushed cock makes my mouth water, and I can't help but lick a strip up it before taking him deep in one suck.

He moans through the catch in his breath, hips trying to follow me as I ease back off so I can get my own dick lubed up. My pants are lowered just enough for me to fuck him, and I know that means I'll get the lube on them, but I don't care at the moment. My dick is weeping for him. My fingers gather the pre-cum leaking from me, and I use it to rub around his tight hole. A low moan of pleasure escapes from him as I push gently, trying to get my mark on his body, even if it's just my scent.

My hand moves away from him, and I open the travel size bottle, dribbling half on me and half on Colin. Throwing one of his legs over my shoulder, I line myself up and push in as I lean back over his body. As much as I'd like to go slow, I can't make myself do it, so I settle for steady as I push my way into him. The tight ring of muscle makes my eyes cross as his body squeezes me before letting me in. Our eyes meet once I'm buried in him.

"Are you okay with all this?" I blurt out.

"Yes. If you guys like her, I know I will," he assures me, not missing a beat.

"I love you so much."

"I love you, too, Jonah. I'd love you more if you start moving, though."

I chuckle and ease out a bit before slamming back in, mindful of my knot swelling. We've trained him to take it, but now isn't the time.

"Is this what you wanted?" I coo at him while he moans.

Picking up a rhythm now, words continue to flow from me, the knowledge that he's fully on board with this ramping up my own desire.

"Do you need your alpha to put you in your place? To fuck this tight hole until you forget where you end and I begin? I can't wait to see your face when you come and watch you spill all over yourself, you dirty beta."

Colin writhes beneath me, moaning and whining incoherently, begging me not to stop. His hands pull his shirt up enough so he doesn't spill on it.

"That's it, show me that body. Show me what's mine, what will *always* be mine. I'm gonna fill you with so much cum it'll be leaking out of you for days," I snarl.

My rhythm picks up, and I move so I can jerk him off while still watching his face.

"Oh fuck," he whimpers.

Eliza Jonas

"Show me, show me what I want to see. Give it to me, beta, give your alpha what he wants!"

Just as I'm ready to combust, Colin spasms around me, cum shooting out of him to land on his abs and chest. Between the sight of him below me and his muscles squeezing me rhythmically, I slam in one more time as far as I can go before grunting while my own release takes over. It feels uncontrollable, like I'll never stop releasing into him, but then it subsides and I resist collapsing on him. Instead, I lift the hand that was on him and lick off his cum, maintaining eye contact as I do. Then I pull him up and slam our mouths together.

"One of us really should make dinner," Colin says once I release him.

"How about we order out?"

"Sounds perfect."

Chapter 9

Danika

My skin feels tight, like I don't quite belong in it. Maybe I changed bodies last night before waking today. It would track. My stomach is doing backflips, my hands are jittery, and there's a restlessness under my skin. I know it's not my heat, I just had one before my art show. Not that I remember it, better living through drugs and all that. Refusing to touch anyone means I go to my omega specialist and have them knock me out and monitor me for the duration. The only downside is feeling almost hung over the next day.

Determined to be mature about this, I shake off my internal monologue before literally shaking my hands to dispel some of the nerves I feel. Looking at building, I notice that it's more modern than where I normally go. The café is the bottom level of a moderately sized office complex. Nothing intense, but still bigger than I'm used to. The sign above the door reads Wake Up and Grind. The interior is fairly open with grey walls and plenty of plush seating. I take a large breath and steel my spine before I open the door. My eyes scan the room, but I don't see Jonah here yet, so I go to order my own coffee. This girl isn't waiting for her caffeine.

The guy taking orders is tall with black curls pinned up and fighting to be free. There's a scar through his eyebrow, and he could easily be scary, but there's a pleasant smile on his face while he talks to customers. When the woman in front of me gets to the register, his eyes light up, and he leans over the counter. She giggles and leans in for a kiss, which is adorable. He directs her to the other end of the counter without taking her order, and she plants one more quick kiss on him before walking over. There's a deep longing in me to be confident enough for that kind of interaction. What would it be like to be with someone and interact so naturally?

"Can I help you? Unfortunately, my omega is taken," the man says.

It's then I realize that I'm staring at her, and snap my eyes back to him, feeling warmth infuse my cheeks. Thankfully, he doesn't look angry, just amused.

"Sorry! I didn't mean to stare. You guys are cute. Uh, can I have a large caramel brew?"

"Sure thing." He smiles. "Anything else in it?"

"No, just leave it black like my soul," I quip without thinking.

He chuckles as he inputs my order. "Two dollars, and compliments on your humor." He grins.

I hand him the cash and smile through the flush I can still feel on my face.

"Thanks," I tell him as I move to the end to collect my drink.

My coffee comes out quickly, and I dump some of the sugar that's out into my drink. I do like it black, but I need it sweet, so maybe it's more of a dark grey situation. Turning, I see Jonah opening the door, eyes searching the café. We smile at the same time, though his falls a bit when he sees I already grabbed a coffee. I meet him at the end of the line.

"I was gonna buy you a coffee. I'm so sorry I was late!" he says.

Waving him off, I reassure him, "No worries, I just wanted my caffeine immediately. Mind if I grab a spot?"

"Sounds good, be there in a minute."

My mouth is still stretched in a smile as I find a spot away from the other patrons. There's not much privacy, but there's also no bad spot to sit in. The designers really put some thought into this place. True to his word, Jonah sits opposite me in almost no time. His scent wafts toward me, and I can't help but close my eyes briefly as I get a hit. You would think I wouldn't be able to smell him in a coffee shop, but there's something just slightly different about Jonah's scent. There's no putting my finger on it, but I can distinctly separate the overall coffee shop smell from his.

"Thanks for meeting me here, it's my favorite coffee place."

"Yeah, sure, no problem! It's a really nice café," I reply.

Silence overtakes us as we sip on our drinks, and I can't help but let my eyes wander about the shop. The longer this silence goes, the more fidgety I get. There's an air of awkward that's rising now and I'm not sure how to break it. Restlessness gets the best of me, and my knee starts bouncing as I bite my lip.

"Well, this is sufficiently awkward, isn't it?" he quips.

His comment startles a laugh out of me, and he chuckles along.

"Sorry, I haven't done this before," I confess.

"It's been a while for me, too. The last time I tried to date someone was probably Emmett, but that was mostly going from friends to more. When was your last date? We can feel out of practice together." He smiles kindly.

"Um. Never." I shrug.

His brow furrows. "You've never been on a date?"

"Nope."

A smile slowly spreads across his face. "I get your first one. That's pretty awesome."

That damn flush starts up again and I can't maintain eye contact. A shy side I didn't realize exists has fully taken over. There's a hint of embarrassment building, but I can hear Sophie in my head telling me not to be embarrassed over this. *You don't need to apologize to anyone! It's been a while since you tried something new, just enjoy it!* Okay, Brain Sophie, easier said than done. Although, he hasn't teased me for it yet, so maybe not as bad as I feared.

"So, um, how long have you and Emmett known each other?" I ask, pushing past my initial shyness.

"We actually met in high school. He transferred in during our senior year, which is hard enough as it is. Then throw in someone as different as Emmett and you have a recipe for being an easy target. He captivated me from the first moment I saw him, though."

"I can understand that. He's got something ... something I can't quite put my finger on, but it draws me in. Makes me want to get to know him. What was the first thing that caught your eye?"

Jonah grins as he answers. "He had this huge, out-of-control afro at the time, and I remember just staring as he walked or talked, because it would gently bounce or sway with whatever he did. I don't know why that's what got me, but I loved seeing it."

I laugh with him as he chuckles in remembrance. They sound like a naturally matched pair. I doubt there was much time between when they met and when they decided to be pack.

"That sounds like fate," I tell him.

"Sometimes it feels like it, definitely. How about you and your emotional support Sophie?"

He surprises me with reliving her title from when I introduced her and I can't help the boisterous laugh that escapes. I'd almost forgotten I said that.

"Well, I've known her for seven years, and while the title was a joke, I'm not sure what I'd do without her. We actually met at an Omega Heat Clinic, sitting in the waiting area."

There's a flash of ... something in Jonah's eyes, but I miss it and find myself feeling almost guilty for having been at a Heat Clinic. There are several options they provide to omegas, but one option is spending heat with alpha volunteers. I've never taken that option, but Jonah doesn't know that and I'm not sure I'm ready to tell him that yet.

"She took one look at me, declared us friends, and hasn't left my side yet," I continue, leaving out a few details in the process.

Some tension leaves Jonah's shoulders, and this time when

silence falls, it's not long and awkward. There's peace in it, and we just quietly observe each other. The door chime rings intermittently as people come and go, but there's an understanding between us that it doesn't matter. I don't think anyone has ever looked at me quite the way Jonah does. There's definitely heat there, but there's also something more. Almost like he really wants to know who I am, not just what's between my legs.

"I'm glad I came today," I confess.

He raises one brow. "Were you considering standing me up?"

"No, but I thought about canceling." I huff a laugh.

"Well, knowing now that this is your first time, I don't blame you. It's a lot to go out of your comfort zone. I'm really glad you did though."

"Yeah?"

"Definitely." He smiles widely at me.

Movement from the window on my left catches my eye, and I can't help but turn to see. There are a couple tables between us and the windows, but that doesn't hinder my view of Emmett leaning up close to the window, waving frantically at us. His grin is adorable, and I can't help but grin back at him. Jonah, however, groans and places his hands on his face.

The door chimes as I turn back to my date.

"Are you okay?" I ask.

Jonah lifts his face and glances to where Emmett walks in.

"I'm fine, but I was hoping not to bombard you with more than one of us at a time," he confesses.

Well, there goes my heart. My stomach explodes in butterflies, and I can feel my insides go gooey from his words. He noticed my reaction to crowds and wanted to accommodate that. How did I manage to meet an alpha who is so considerate? I thought they didn't exist. There's no time to reply as Emmett reaches us and plops down next to Jonah, across from me.

"Well look who I found," he says cheerily.

"Hi, Emmett." I smile.

"Hey there, Stargazer. Fancy seeing you two here!"

"Hey, babe," Jonah replies.

He grabs Emmett's hand and places a kiss on his cheek.

"I was attempting to not overwhelm our girl with more than one of us at a time," he explains.

Emmett nods like that's obvious. "Of course you are. I waited thirty minutes before following you, so I think we did good."

"We?" Jonah asks.

"Of course! I can't take *all* the credit for being amazing. I do think I deserve a cookie though, brb."

Emmett stands and is off for the line to order himself a treat. I can't help but look at Jonah, absolutely astounded by the two of them. Jonah, for his part, is a mixture of confused and affectionate as he watches Emmett for a moment before turning back to me. We burst out into giggles, and I feel one of my walls crumble just the slightest amount. A feeling of ease and belonging fills me from my toes through the top of my head. In all my life, I can't remember feeling so certain that I belong with the people here with me.

As the realization washes over me, cold prickling follows along my spine. Comfort isn't a feeling that I understand. I understand feeling safe, seen, sane, and even loved a bit. I don't understand the comfort rolling through me, and unease fills me as the prickling sensation continues to swamp me. I shove the feeling down as deep as I can and try to take deeper breaths. New feelings aren't bad, right? It's okay to feel like I belong and be comfortable.

"What's wrong?" Jonah asks.

My head jerks up from where my gaze drifted and stuck to my coffee cup. I meet his eyes, full of concern, and realize that Emmett is walking back toward us.

I brush his question off, "Oh, nothing. Just got lost in thought."

I'm not sure he believes me with the look I'm getting right now, but that's okay. As long as I don't have to explain anything, then I can make it through this. I can't imagine people want to hear that their date is having a small panic attack during their time together, especially if it's triggered by good feelings. They don't need to know where my broken bits are.

Emmett sits down, completely oblivious to my spiraling emotions, and smiles at the two of us.

"Gertie wanted her own cookie, but I told her no. She already had a treat today and she needs to eat more balanced," he says.

"Gertie?" I ask.

They both freeze for a moment, and I wonder if I've asked something too personal by inquiring about the name. Who the hell *is* Gertie and why are they out with me if they have a woman?

Settle down there, tiger. She could be part of their pack or family. She might not be their omega.

My mental pep talk helps any rising emotions to settle, and I look at the two of them, waiting to see if they'll answer. There's a silent conversation where Jonah shrugs and Emmett nods. Emmett then reaches into the breast pocket of his polo shirt and pulls out a tiny, furry ... thing.

"Gertie, this is Danika. Danika, this is Gertie. She's my Sophie!" he says brightly.

Staring at the small fuzzball for a moment, I can't figure out why there's any relation to Sophie.

"Um, is she asleep? She's not moving ... and she's your Sophie?" I'm so confused.

Emmett just smiles brighter. "Oh! She's taxidermized. I had that done when I was ten or so. You have an emotional support Sophie, and I have my emotional support Gertie."

Things finally click into place as I remember that I had introduced Sophie that way. My head tips back in a boisterous laugh, and I think about how I haven't laughed this much in months. At my insistence, Emmett explains her full story, and I get caught up in the moment with them. Maybe these guys are better for me than I want to admit. If nothing else, I hope we can be friends. That would be nice.

Chapter 10

Emmett

As I wipe this animal one last time, I realize that I need to clean my taxidermies more often. Poor guys and girls are way dustier than they should be. I vow to do better by my beauties as I place the squirrel back on her shelf with the chipmunk. They're in the midst of a torrid love affair and who am I to get in the way?

"Gertie, do you think I'll get to be part of a torrid love affair someday?"

She just stares at me with her beady eyes, and I sigh.

"I suppose not. It is a lot of drama, to your point. I'll settle for pack life if we can get Danika on board," I tell her.

Crashing Jonah's date the other day wasn't planned, but it *was* a temptation that I couldn't resist. He and Colin informed me of the date with no details, and I understand why. I don't really care, but I understand. When I saw them in the café, looking so natural together, I couldn't bring myself to walk away. A desperation welled up inside me, and I followed the pull to them.

I know Jonah was a little annoyed, but I'm so lucky he's mine because he understands me. Even when he's annoyed, he never makes me feel like I'm unwanted. Danika seemed to light up when she saw me, and I've got her smile etched into my memory. I wonder if I could get it tattooed on me.

My alarm goes off, startling me out of my thoughts, and I turn it off before cleaning up my workstation. Then I grab Gertie and we head out of the house. Jonah scheduled a new exhibit for the gallery, more of a long-term situation. So I have my work cut out for me. We have not set up for a long-term display in a while, so there's a fair amount of work to do.

Once I'm buckled into my car, the passenger door opens, and I let out a very manly grunt of surprise.

"Ow, could you scream any higher? I think you burst my eardrum," Colin says, settling into the seat next to me.

Okay, maybe my scream was a little high-pitched.

"What the hell, man?"

Colin looks up, surprised. "Oh, I thought you heard me say wait up. Did you not?"

"Clearly not."

"Oops, my bad. Anyway, I need to go to the gallery, too ... so I figured save the gas, ride with Emmett." He shrugs.

"Ha-ha, nice. Save some gas, ride with Emmett," I reply, emulating the tune of the song.

Colin chuckles along as we head to get some work done.

Colin has been done with his tasks for a while now, and even though he's offered to help me, I'm too stubborn to let him. I know what I'm doing, and I'm an alpha, I can take care of this so he can rest. Colin does so much for Jonah and I, and I hate asking him to do more than is needed

"It would be faster if you let me help," he sing-songs again.

I finally get the frame supports in the position I want, the last thing I needed to do.

"Joke's on you, I'm done." I stick my tongue out at him.

Colin grins in reply. "I can think of some good ways to use that tongue of yours."

"Is my beta feeling sassy today?" I purr, stepping closer to him.

"Can't be helped. I've been watching my hot as fuck alpha doing physical labor for a while."

We chuckle, and I help him up from his seat on the floor. Instead of letting him go, I pull him closer and use my other hand to bring his head close to mine. My lips massage his gently, showing him how he calms me and how enraptured I am with him. Colin is fucking gorgeous, and the fact that he was willing to stick around with all my oddities made me fall head over heels. Guys can be head over heels, right? We don't usually wear heels, unless there's drag involved, but there's no reason we couldn't.

Colin pulls away and assesses me.

"Where'd you go?" he asks without judgement.

"Can I say I'm head over heels if I never wear heels?" I ask.

He chuckles at my statement, one hand running gently down my cheek. "I love your brain. You can absolutely be head over heels without wearing heels. Everyone has a natural heel, so it counts. If you want to wear heels, we can go shopping."

My heart melts for this man. That warm, wonderful gooey feeling takes up residence in my chest, and all I want to do now is snuggle with him. We smile at each other for a moment before I run my nose up his neck, arching so he can do the same.

"I love how we smell together. It's like a quiet cabin out in the woods somewhere," he says.

"Totally agree," I reply.

We pack up any tools laying around, then hold hands as we leave and hop into my car. I don't let him go the entire ride home, and it continues to settle that piece of me that's always doubting. Is this going to be the day he's done with me? He says he never will be, but what if it happens? I wouldn't blame him. I think Jonah only keeps me around because he feels bad for me for some reason.

Don't get me wrong, I will take whatever I can get from both of them, but the doubts never really leave. It's hard to believe that they're unfounded most days. For a while, I had this taxidermy owl named Sir Hoots. He was very regal. However, he always looked at me like I was about to fuck something up, and I swear he told me at least twice that the guys are only with me out of pity. Jonah made me get rid of him.

When I pull into the driveway, I retake Colin's hand the moment we're both out of the car.

"Movie and snuggles?" I ask.

He grins openly. "Absolutely."

Just like that I feel reassured, and Gertie is definitely saying "told you so" to me in her head right now. Honestly, she's a bit of a brat. She's always been there for me, though, ever since I found her in a pawn shop when I was ten.

Jonah walks by the living room just as Colin and I get settled and stops to look at us. His eyes roam over both of us, a smile tugging at his lips.

"Well, you guys look cozy," he says.

"You could be cozy with us, Alpha," Colin informs him.

I flip up the blanket on my other side and pat the couch, hoping he takes the hint. Jonah's eyes flick back to Colin for a second before he smiles and takes his designated spot, scooting in nice and close. His long arm wraps around me easily and touches Colin's shoulder as well.

"Should we order out for dinner?" Jonah asks.

"I'm good with it," I reply.

Colin gives a thumbs-up and a nod, keeping his eyes on the screen. Glancing over as Jonah opens his phone, I catch the last app he had open and snag his phone to take a look. Sure enough, he had a social media app up, with Danika's face on it. She's giving the camera an exasperated smile, and it's the cutest thing. There's a shift on my other side, and I can feel Colin lean in.

"That's her?" he asks.

"Yeah."

He and I stare at her picture for another thirty seconds before Jonah takes his phone back. In unison, we pout at him.

"I can't order dinner without my phone, guys."

I huff, "Fine."

"Dude, I know you said she was gorgeous, but hearing and seeing it are two different things. She's absolutely stunning. Now I'm a little jealous," Colin says.

I wrap my arms around him snugly.

"No jealousy, only love," I state.

He relaxes into me, and Jonah pulls both of us into him. We only break when the food comes, then we go right back to our snuggle pile, picking something new to watch. My soul continues to settle as the three of us exist in harmony. Despite my obnoxious doubts and concerns, I know this is where I belong. With these two men, and hopefully adding one woman. Maybe she'll be a match for one of us. Wouldn't that be wild?

"Do you think she would be up for a group chat?" I ask into the quiet of the room.

"What?" Jonah asks.

"Danika. Do you think she'd want to?"

He hums for a moment, thinking it through, and Colin turns a little to watch the interaction.

"It might be too soon, but I can ask her. She and I haven't texted a ton, but I don't know if that's because she's a little shy or if it's a different reason."

"That's fair," I tell him.

Jonah goes to settle back in his spot, when he notices I'm still watching him. As much as I want to fully relax back into his embrace, I can't figure out why he's not asking her. He just said he could.

"Now?" he asks.

"Duh," I reply.

Jonah leans in and nips my nose. "Brat," he mutters.

His phone appears, and I see him pull up the messages she has with him. He's right, the conversation looks short, almost like business transactions. Slowly, with the phone in one hand, he gets a message typed out and sends it off. Jonah meets my eyes before putting his phone down.

"You're not going to be able to relax until she responds, are you?" he asks.

"Duh," Colin chimes in this time.

I turn to smile at him. "You get me."

"Always, babe." He pulls me down for a quick kiss.

The two of us then turn and look at Jonah expectantly. His brow furrows.

"What? I can't control when she responds!" he protests.

At that moment his phone pings with a notification.

"Are you guys psychic or something?" Jonah asks, brow raised.

"What did she say?" I ask.

After opening the thread, he reads her response with a small smile on his face.

"She is open to it, but she's worried she won't be active enough for us."

I scoff, "Well that's just silly."

"There are three of us and one of her. I can understand why she's a little hesitant," Colin adds.

"Good point."

Jonah starts a new chat with the three of us and Danika.

Jonah: Hey Danika

Danika: Oh, hi Jonah. Emmett too I suppose?

Eliza Jonas

I quickly pull my phone out.

> Me: Hey Stargazer

Danika: Hey ☺

Jonah: Colin's here too, but he doesn't have his phone.

Danika: Colin?

I look over at Jonah, alarm rising within me as I read her question. Shit, this is going to be really awkward, isn't it?

"Jonah, we *did* tell her about Colin, didn't we?" I ask.

Jonah looks at me and Colin like a deer in headlights. Sighing, Colin rubs his eyes before digging in his pockets to pull his phone out. I'm pretty sure he mutters, "Oh, alphas," under his breath. Hopefully it's an endearment, but I suspect it's not.

Colin: Hi Danika, I'm Colin. I'm the beta of the group. I'm sorry if these hard-headed alphas caught you off-guard with this chat. If you're uncomfortable, I totally understand and can step out of the chat for now.

Danika: Oh, no, they didn't mention you. Are they trying to hide you? Blink twice if you need a rescue.

Colin bursts out laughing, before typing his response.

Colin: 😵 😵

Danika: 🛏

Jonah: Emmett, I think we're getting ganged up on.

Me: I'm okay with this situation. Stargazer and my beta can gang up on me any day.

Colin: Masochist.

Me: correct.

Me: Danika, can we interest you in a second date?

Danika: That sounds lovely.

Colin and Jonah become background noise as I make plans with Danika. Dozens of ideas fly through my head, thinking through what would be a good option for a date with her. Would she appreciate a painting event since she paints, or something totally different? Maybe a walk in the woods? The options flicker through my head rapidly, making it hard for me to nail a single one down. I reach up and pet Gertie as I think through what would be fun, yet let us talk.

Inspiration hits as I feel Gertie's soft fur, a desire to share part of me with my stargazer. There's a taxidermy museum in a town near here, and I bet it would be perfect. I would be happy to explain things to her, and it should be quiet enough for us to chat with each other. Maybe even a corner for me to kiss her in? I'd have to be careful about prying eyes, don't need to traumatize the animals. I can't imagine all the things they've seen.

My stomach swoops with butterflies as we make plans, and I bite my lip, giddy with excitement. It's going to be great having her all to myself. Maybe she'll tase me again, we can re-create the moment we met. That moment is going to live rent-free in my head for the rest of

81

my life. She took me down like an avenging angel, then saved me all in the same moment. I should probably ask the guys if that's weird. It's probably weird. Maybe she'll be into roleplay and we can re-create it there; she'll nurse me to health, and I'll thank her enthusiastically.

Chapter 11

Danika

Thoughts plague me again today, spiraling about the men I've been talking to, what my plans are for my next show, and what paintings I should sell as prints on my website. So many possibilities and options are making me crabby. Can't everything just be straightforward? Although, I suppose if it was, I wouldn't have much inspiration for my work.

I lean back from my canvas, eyeing my sketched-out plan, and decide it's ready to go. The color palette hasn't popped in my head yet, so I grab every color I have. Better to be prepared than have to stop my flow and grab new colors. Once I have my brushes and paint, I get to work.

The intent behind this one sits in the back of my mind as I try to puzzle it out. Adding paint and vibrancy is almost automatic for me, but I can't quite grasp why this one feels important enough to capture. It's the feeling of surprise, embarrassment, exposed, and a little betrayed. Not horribly so, but enough that it's stuck with me. Balancing those emotions is tricky, because I don't want any one particular emotion standing out over the others.

My stomach feels a little unsteady and a sense of unease spreads through my body, giving me a feeling of tightness in my chest. It's not quite anxiety, but it sits there nonetheless, and if I weren't absolutely sure my door is locked, then I'd almost think someone is watching me. The feeling grows, and now all that's on my mind is someone outside, crouched in the bushes, looking at me as I paint. Nerves spread through me, and my feet start bouncing until I finally give in and look behind me through the windows.

Nothing. Nobody's there, there's no movement in the bushes, it's totally normal out there.

"You need to cool it, Danika. Paranoia never helped anyone," I mutter to myself.

My phone rests on a stool next to me, set on Do Not Disturb with a few notification exceptions applied. Otherwise, the silence of the room is only broken up by the sound of my brushes against the canvas. My emotions bleed into the painting as I go, allowing me to think through the situation I've found myself in. I'd never considered a smaller venue before, but after a lackluster event, I decided it might be worth trying something solo.

Jonah's gallery called to me by name alone. Colorful World. It sounded like the perfect place, and when I talked with Jonah, something felt right about it, so we went through details and made an agreement. In hindsight, maybe it was too perfect. Now I'm somewhat entangled with him and his ... pack? He said that he and Emmett are pack, but never mentioned this Colin guy. He seemed almost embarrassed for Emmett and Jonah when he introduced himself, so I let myself be playful with him. Was that the right choice?

A need to fidget rolls through my body, little urges of moment pushing at my muscles, and I lock down on any additional movement so I don't smudge my paint. I can fidget later. Right now I need to focus on paint therapy. This one is another mix of traditional paint and UV light, so I focus on getting the regular paint layer down first.

Neither Jonah nor Emmett told me about Colin, and they've definitely had the opportunity. Does it mean they are ashamed of him? Or am I just a passing amusement to them? I have no desire to be someone's plaything; I've managed just fine on my own for fifteen years. There's not a hole in my life that needs an alpha or a pack to fill it. Sighing, I finally admit to myself that I should really just call them. Or one of them, probably Jonah. Somehow, I doubt they will give me the run around.

The canvas in front of me begins to show my two subjects, a man and a woman. They're leaning against a wall with a generic background, gazing at each other. My goal with this one is to show that initial adoration and trust one gets in a new relationship, then use the UV to show her hurting from a betrayal with him asking for forgiveness. This one won't be extreme, but that's the point. So often we have extreme emotions and reactions, that the little ones get overlooked. It can be just as painful sometimes as the large emotions.

Now that I've decided not to be stubborn, I'm anxious to make the phone call, to get resolution on these emotions. Clearly we're not in a serious relationship at this point, but making assumptions doesn't help anybody here. God, it's been years since I've had a real conversation with an alpha. Even then, most of the conversations weren't exactly pleasant.

What's a pretty omega like you doin here?

All omegas want a knot, don't deny it.

You asked for it with that dress.

You just wish I had taken you home.

You're just a warm hole to fill for right now. I've got better at home.

My breathing stutters as my memories swirl in my head; all the men who have taken me when I didn't want them press in and demand attention. I swore to myself they wouldn't get a moment more of my life. I drop my paint brush, snag my phone out of habit, and leave my studio space. Shaking has taken over my hands and body, and nausea builds up in my stomach, while the room starts to spin.

Stumbling, I make my way to the toilet, collapsing as my stomach empties itself. I try to tamp down the memories and voices, but my memory has decided to go rogue, and I can feel phantom hands roaming my body where I never wanted them. That feeling of fear when I woke up in the woods the first time echoes in me. I don't understand what I've done to have to keep these memories.

A buzzing starts up on my ass, confusing me for a moment, until I remember my phone is tucked in there. With no idea who is on the other side of the phone, I make an effort to gather myself and lean back from the toilet. I accept the call without looking at the screen.

"This is Danika Hart," I give my professional phone answer.

"Danika, hey, it's Emmett."

Shit, I don't know if I have the capacity to do this right now. He isn't my past alphas, but it's hard to separate in the middle of a panic attack.

"Oh, hey, Emmett."

"I know we just decided on our date, but I wanted to ask you a couple of questions," he explains.

"Uh, I guess, but I can't talk long," I try to defer him.

He pauses for a moment before replying.

"Are you okay? You sound ... off."

"Oh, yeah, just busy." I try for a chuckle, but it might come out as a hysterical giggle.

"You're not okay, I can hear it. What can I do?"

His voice is so gentle and calm that my throat tightens and my eyes burn.

"Nothing, right now. Just a rough moment. Can I call you later?" I manage to say.

"Yeah, that's fine, Star. Take care of yourself, you're amazing."

I manage to choke out a goodbye before I curl up on myself and let the tears come. My tears help to cleanse my mind, letting out all of these emotions in the sorrow I'm stuck in. When I finally take a deep breath, I find myself curled into a ball on the floor of my bathroom. There's a small voice in the back of my head noting that it's impressive that I can fit my tall frame in the small room like this.

A notification chimes on my phone, noting my video doorbell has picked up movement, before I hear the doorbell itself chime. I wasn't expecting Sophie today, but I'm not mad that she's here. When I open the app on my phone, I'm absolutely gobsmacked seeing Emmett on the porch. He has a large bag with him and Gertie faithfully in his front pocket. My lips turn up ever so slightly, and I gather myself up off the floor and plod to the front door.

I open the door just enough to see him, not caring about how puffy my face is or how red my eyes are. There's no hiding it at this point, and Emmett's so sweet that I can't bring myself to tell him to go away in the doorbell app. His eyes race over my face, noting my current state, before trying to look at what he can of my body, concern evident on his face.

"I know we don't know each other well, and I know you didn't ask me to come over, but I couldn't shake the need to at least bring you a few things," he says, a note of anxiety threading though the words.

"How do you know where I live?" I sniffle.

Emmett pauses and looks down at Gertie, then back to me.

"I might have done just a wee bit of internet stalking. I hope you're not mad, but I understand if you are. I probably should have asked Jonah or Colin if it was weird to do this." He frowns at himself.

The giggle that escapes me surprises us both, but his face transforms into a warm smile.

"What's in the bag?" I can't help but ask.

Nobody except Sophie has brought me any kind of gift, and my inner omega is pushing me to look in the bag and hoard it all.

"Chocolate, chips, an angry coloring book, and a fuzzy blanket," he states proudly, holding it open.

New tears threaten to escape, and I open the door just a little bit more. The move is instinctual, and I'm just going with what feels right at the moment.

"Thank you. I don't think anyone has ever done something like this for me," I admit.

"I'm happy that I get the solo award for that because I can brag to the guys, but it breaks my heart that you've never had this before," he replies.

When I sweep the door open all the way and gesture to him, he takes the invitation and steps inside. He stands a few feet into the house, looking around the living room that my front door opens to.

"This is super cute. Gertie says she approves, too," he tells me.

"Well, thank you, Gertie." I clear my throat.

Emmett startles and hands me the bag of goodies, almost shoving it toward me. A smile takes over as I move to set the bag on the small coffee table I have and start to dig into it. The blanket is the first thing I grab and it's blissfully unscented, which makes me so happy. I don't have to worry about residual scent from people I don't know. The snacks in the bag call to me, and I bite my lip before turning to Emmett.

"Um, would you want to, uh, stay and maybe snuggle for a bit? No skin contact."

His answering smile is blinding. "Absolutely, Stargazer. Gertie and I will happily snuggle by your rules."

I do a small happy dance before disappearing, taking the few steps to my room to grab an old, oversized hoodie to wear. Jealousy alights in Emmett's eyes when he sees the clearly too big hoodie on my body.

"I bought it because I wanted to feel small. It never belonged to anyone else," I tell him.

"Oh, I didn't mean to ... I mean, you don't have to tell me if you don't want to. You don't owe me any explanations," he says.

I shrug. "I wanted you to know."

His shoulders relax, and I direct him to sit on one end of the couch, against the armrest. Then, I grab the blanket he brought me and settle in next to him before covering us. While I'm technically sitting on the couch, I've thrown my legs over his and curled my body into his chest, resting my head in the small hollow of his shoulder. Emmett carefully lifts my hood over my head and then rests his cheek on top of my head. This man is going out of his way to ensure he follows my rules, and I can feel my heart soften for him.

Chapter 12

Emmett

Sitting here with my stargazer in my arms, a peace has settled over me that I've not felt before. She's tucked her body close to me, while still ensuring our skin isn't touching. My hands exist firmly on the outside of the blanket. The urge to fully envelop her drives at me, so I finally give in to the need and pull her hood up just enough so I can lay my cheek against the top of her head.

It probably wouldn't have been skin on skin through her hair, but I'm not taking any chances. The raw pain on her face when she opened the door cracked my heart almost in two. Gertie and I agreed that if we ever come across someone who has hurt her, they're not going to be breathing long. When she answered the phone earlier, it was obvious that she was not okay. My heart and brain warred with each other for all of thirty seconds before I left the house to gather supplies for her.

Now, I'm so fucking glad I did. My girl needs someone more than I think she realizes. I'm happy to be that someone, and I hope that I can be that for her for a long time. She does have her Emotional Support Sophie, but I doubt she's as comfortable to cuddle with as I am. Part of me hopes she falls asleep so I can hold her for hours. It feels right to have her in my arms, solidifying my need to have her. She'll be a bit skittish, kind of like the mice I have at home, but they warmed up when they moved to sit with my squirrel and chipmunk. I suspect they're secret voyeurs.

Maybe my stargazer is, too. I can just imagine her, face and chest flushed pink, wide eyes, chest moving quickly with her rapid breaths, and slick soaking through whatever she's wearing. All while Colin's dick is buried in Jonah's throat and my own is being caressed with Colin's hand. The image in my head causes a warmth to rise, low in my belly, and my pants are suddenly feeling tighter at the zipper. Shit, now I am actually being a creeper; hopefully she doesn't mind. I have no problem with her feeling how turned on she makes me, but I don't want her to run away with nerves.

"Emmett?" she whispers.

"Yeah, Stargazer?" My voice matches her volume.

"I might be a little broken."

"We're all a little broken. We just gotta figure out how our pieces fit together again."

She snuggles in closer, but I'm not sure that there's actually a possibility that she can be any closer. My arms tighten in response anyway, trying to make her feel as secure as possible.

"What if I can't put them together? What if they don't match anymore?"

I hum. "Then I think we make a new design with the pieces. Maybe even use other people's pieces to help fill any holes."

She goes quiet again, and after a few minutes, I realize she's gone to sleep. Her body is totally lax against mine, and I'm pretty sure there's a light snore coming from her. Fucking adorable. If I were a cartoon, I'd have literal hearts in my eyes as I gaze at her, what limited view I have from how close she is. Danika's body feels so *right* in my arms, and I know that I'm never letting her go. Even if we aren't a match, she's mine and I'll fight whoever I have to so I can keep her.

When I get home after spending a little time with Danika, my heart feels battered and bruised. Some of it was having to leave without her, and some of it was knowing how deeply she's hurting. Something I don't think she ever would have shared unless I had caught her in that vulnerable moment. She's had to be so strong on her own, that I think she needs someone to hold her up so she doesn't have to be.

I can hear Jonah and Colin yelling and excited; my mood lifts at the sound, knowing what it means. Sure enough, when I walk into the living room, they're on the couch playing Overcooked. When the three of us play, it's absolute chaos and the most fun game I've ever tried. Today, though, I just want to be near them and soak up their presence. My body flops onto the couch, and I grab a blanket to wrap myself up in. There have been a few times where I've wondered why I didn't present as an omega, but the fact is that I didn't and I crave softness and cuddles at times. Okay, fine ... I may take any opportunity given to cuddle, but that's out of alpha obligation.

I swear I can hear Gertie laughing at me.

There are frantic shouts as the level comes to a close, and I chuckle softly when something catches on fire on the TV. Colin starts shouting about the fire extinguisher while Jonah tells him the orders are more important. Amid the chaos, the level ends and both of my men lean back, laughing.

"Oh my god, I love this game." Jonah chuckles.

"Seriously, it's the best," Colin agrees.

When the laughter dies down, they both turn to look at me on the couch behind them. I smile at them from my blanket wrap.

"I feel snuggly," I tell them.

Colin stands. "Dog pile!"

The two of them immediately pile on top of me, burrowing into my blanket and grabbing any other throw blankets they can find. Laughing at their efforts, I do my best to help them get comfortable in our dog pile, ensuring we all have a blanket on us. We end up in a "me" sandwich with Jonah and Colin bread; Jonah spoons me from behind and Colin lays facing me. We have a deep couch, but not quite deep enough, so they're both a little on top of me, and it's strangely calming.

"What's up, snuggle bug?" Colin asks.

"I went to visit Danika," I confess.

Jonah nuzzles his nose closer to my neck, taking in my scent. "How did it go?"

"I don't want to share anything she's not comfortable with, but she is definitely not okay. We'll need to be gentle with her."

Colin lands a kiss on my forehead.

"I'm glad she had you, then, today."

"Me? I'm the crazy one," I scoff.

"Doesn't matter if that's how you see yourself, you have the biggest heart, babe, and I'm glad she got to see that," Colin replies.

We lapse into comfortable silence, occasionally scent marking each other and savoring the feeling of our bodies laying together. Once in a while we get to do this in bed, but often we're on the move, talking to potential artists, cleaning the gallery, doing maintenance, all those little details that get looked over. Even though we're not in our big pack bed, this is so cozy and comfortable.

"Can we just steal her?" I ask.

"No!" Jonah chuckles.

"Spoilsport," I mutter.

Eventually, our dog pile breaks because none of us want a golden shower. Colin heads into the kitchen to get some dinner started, and I make my way downstairs to my taxidermy room. Yes, I do have a room dedicated to my animals. I've cleaned them all recently, so I make the rounds to say hello and hop on my laptop to see if there are any new guys that need saving. Some of the animals I have in here, I've actually done myself, but I also look to see if any are being sold off or discarded. I refuse to leave them homeless.

There's nothing I can find today, which will make my wallet happy. Thanks to Colin, our pack doesn't have to worry about money, but I try not to over-spend. Unless there's an animal that *needs* me. You can usually see it in their eyes. Maybe I should start on one of the hides I have in the fridge. I prepped and preserved two of them recently, so I'm sure they're ready to go and I think I have the proper eyes to put on them.

Opening the mini fridge I keep in the closet, I grab the bag on the higher shelf. She's a gorgeous specimen, her fur dark and rich in color, and I bet in life her milkshake brought all the boys to the yard. I have a form ready to go for her, so once I unroll the skin, I slip her on the form and start to smooth things down and make sure it looks fairly life-like. I fish around for the extra eyes I keep and dig through them to find a beautiful brown for her. I also grab my needle and thread before turning back to my gorgeous girl and flipping her belly up so I can sew her closed. As I'm working, I hear my phone ping with a new message.

> Stargazer: Thanks for today, Emmett. I'm sorry you had to see me like that.

> Me: It was a privilege to be there for you, but I'm sorry if it made you uncomfortable.

> Stargazer: You're so sweet. My emotions started evening out once you arrived, so it was really nice to have you with me as I calmed. Thank you.

> Me: Of course. Please use me again if you need me 😌

> Stargazer: 😌

> Me: Are you still up for a date soon?

> Stargazer: Is that what we're calling it?

> Me: Absolutely

> Stargazer: How can I argue with confidence like that?

Me: free tomorrow?

Stargazer: For you? I will be

I abandon my girl and run upstairs to squeal in excitement. When I don't easily find Jonah, I race into the kitchen and grab Colin from behind.

"She loves me!" I exclaim.

Colin chuckles. "What? What are you talking about, Alpha?"

Fuck, it's sexy when he calls me that. I can feel myself start to harden just from his words, so I rock my hips against his ass.

"You tryin to drive me crazy with your words, Beta?" I croon.

"I wasn't, but now I'm seeing the benefit of doing that," he admits, somewhat breathless, as he grinds back into me.

His ass feels divine, and I can just picture bending him over the counter in here and sinking into his tight heat. I will make sure he's on edge the whole time, changing up my pace before wrapping my hand around his hot, hard length. My teeth will ache to bite him, so I'll run them gently over his neck and he will start to keen for me. I won't let him come, but I'll stuff him full of mine before sinking to my knees in front of him and letting him face fuck me until he comes down my throat.

"Babe? I'm really not going to get anything done if you keep that up."

My brain snaps back to the moment, and I realize that I'm grinding on him now, one of my hands rubbing him outside of his pants. My body protests, but I slowly stop what I'm doing and place my forehead on his back, breathing hard.

"Sorry, I got distracted," I admit.

Colin turns and looks at me with a smile. "I can feel that."

Leaning forward, I nip his nose. "Beta brat."

"Just for you," he says softly.

I grin at him with a dopey smile before he breaks our spell.

"What were you saying before we got distracted?"

How could I let myself get so distracted? I need to let the world know that my stargazer loves me! Stupid, sexy beta in front of me; I love him so damn much.

"She's in love with me! My stargazer!"

Colin gives me a confused smile. "Did she say that?"

I feel some of my excitement deflate, and my shoulders actually feel like they've drooped down. When I read the messages, I was so sure, but she didn't actually say that, did she?

"No," I mumble.

Colin's hands land on my cheeks, forcing me to look at him. His eyes are painfully understanding and full of love and affection. Why does he have to be so wonderful? He could easily just tease me over it.

"I am sure she *will* love you as you get to know her, but make sure she says it, yeah?"

"Why do you have to be so smart?" I whine at him.

"Not smart, just protective of your heart."

Chapter 13

Danika

After Emmett left, I went straight to my studio space to clean up whatever mess I'd made. Thankfully, my brush didn't catch the canvas when I dropped it, and the paint was still wet. It wouldn't be too hard to clean. Plus, I hate when I ruin my brushes. The new ones always take ages to feel like they actually belong with me. Weird artist quirk, right? For some reason, though, I find a little personality in each of them, and it takes a while for the brush and I to gel together.

Once my brush is clean, I look at my canvas and decide it's a bust for the rest of the day. My heart is still tender from the memories that assaulted me, my head is fuzzy, and I feel absolutely worn out. While my mind is done for today, my body isn't and I'm itching to get some cleaning done. I start with the bathroom where I was sick and deep clean that room before doing the same to the kitchen. If it's clean, it's okay. Everything is fine when it's clean. After my last swipe of the cleaning rag, I sit back on my heels and survey my kitchen. Perfect. Not a speck of dirt to be found.

There's sweat on my brow, and my body feels like I've pushed it in a heavy workout, but now that the kitchen is clean, I can't stop staring at the living room. Who knows how many dust bunnies are under that couch? I should look—I can't have anything dusty or dirty, it's just not allowed. My fingers itch to find every speck of dust and get rid of it. Needs to be clean.

Without warning, I startle when a hand lands on my shoulder and shakes it gently. Screaming, I whip around to see who the hell got into my house. It takes me a moment to recognize Sophie standing in front of me, her face full of confusion and concern. My hand covers my heart, and I let myself fall onto my back gently.

"What the fuck, Sophie?" I hiss.

"What the fuck me? What about what the fuck *you*, Dani? I've been ringing the doorbell and knocking for ten minutes. Then I called your name like twenty times, and you gave zero response. I thought you were having a fuckin' seizure or something!"

My eyes take her in as I push up on one elbow to better see her. She settles down on the floor in front of me, holding out her hand for me to grab, which I do and drag myself up to sitting. Sophie looks around the room, noting the disarray and cleaning products strewn about the room. There's a platter that she set down next to her, and now she grabs it, uncovers it, and hands me the whole thing full of double chocolate cookies.

"What happened? Haven't seen you this scared in a while," she says to me.

The platter sits on my lap, full of delicious sugar, and I stare down at it, attempting to find words to explain my mind. I've had two other meltdowns like this, and I've managed to defer her in the past, but this time I never heard her ringing the bell. Before I could at least hear the bell and ignored it, but someone could have come in and robbed me and I'd never know. Maybe it's time to tell someone.

"You know why I left my home at sixteen, right?"

"Duh," she says with a smile.

"You know that when I moved to the city ... I was homeless for two years." I say, grabbing a cookie.

"Jesus, I still don't know how you survived. The amount of disgusting alphas in the city ..."

A small smile tugs at my lips, and I take a large bite of cookie while I think.

"Before I left for the city, I used to be so shallow. God, I was so fucking shallow. I thought everything revolved around me, and life was good. I was one of two omegas in town. I had everything in the palm of my hand. Then he took it, and when I moved to town, people kept taking it."

Sophie's eyes go glassy, and I can hear her breath stuttering as she tries to keep it together in front of me.

"The first time was my own doing—I saw an omega offer her heat for cash. I needed cash. So ... I did it. They paid enough that I could get suppressants for my heats over the next two years, but all they did was dampen them. I could manage though. The rest of the time, alphas and a few betas just took. I wasn't in heat, but I was an easy target."

Sophie opens her mouth to speak, then closes it and repeats the action three times before moving her body around and sitting next to me. Instinctively, I let my head rest on her shoulder, and she responds by running her hand through my hair.

"I wanted to call Jonah today, then kept thinking about how my casual alpha interactions have been ... not great. Then the hands were all I could think of, and Emmett called while I was trying to stop crying. He surprised me by showing up and just ... holding me. Now we're here."

Sophie hums.

"Now we're here," she repeats.

I close my eyes, and she continues to run her fingers through my hair.

"I don't know what I'd do without you," I whisper.

"You'd be way less cool, that's for sure," Sophie quips.

We break into giggles, and I wrap my arms around her, which she reciprocates. Sophie helps me put the living room right again, and we spend the rest of the day watching trashy TV and snuggling.

Pulling up to the address that Emmett gave me, I'm both incredibly surprised, and not surprised at all. I should have known since he carries Gertie around. The sign reads Blackford Museum of Taxidermy, also advertising other displays and exhibits. A smile tugs at my lips and warmth spreads through me when I see him standing near the entrance, waiting for me.

"Hey, you," I greet him as I approach.

"Stargazer!" Emmett opens his arms to hug me, then realizes what he's doing and puts his arms back down, stiffly at his side.

"Sorry," he mumbles.

I shake my head with a smile. "It's fine."

Instinct pushes at me, and I almost grab his hand, but I catch the thought before my body can move and keep my hand to myself. I'm not ready to know, and I'm not sure if I ever will be. So I smile brightly and follow Emmett through the door. He pays for admission, and we begin our date of looking at stuffed animals. I giggle at the thought.

"What are you giggling about over there?" he asks with a smile.

"I just thought of all these as stuffed animals, which isn't wrong, but then all I can think of is teddy bears." I giggle.

Emmett lets out a chuckle. "You're not wrong there."

The museum is split up so different types of animals are grouped together—woodland animals together, desert, pets, all set up in some sort of scene that fits. As we move through the pets, I'm a little sad to see how boring it is. The dogs are mostly sitting, cats laying alert, a few birds sitting in cages.

"Do you know how much opportunity they missed here?" I complain.

Emmett just shakes his head and waits for me to continue.

"They have these dogs sitting here nicely, when they could have set up for a poker game. The cats are all laying nicely instead of poised to pounce!"

I move to a shelf where one of the cats are, and put my hands up under my chin like paws and stare at the cat with narrowed eyes. Emmett laughs and finds a dog standing, where he promptly goes to all fours and lifts his leg like he's peeing on the other dog. Laughing, I grab my phone and scramble to get a picture.

"Did you just take a picture?" he asks.

His tone is teasing but he's working hard to keep a serious face. I school my expression into a slightly aloof indifference.

"I don't know *what* you mean." I sniff, trying for a haughty demeanor.

Emmett walks up to me and stands in my space, but not close enough to touch.

"Oh, darling, you're in for it now," he purrs.

A shiver snakes down my spine, and I want to poke at him some more to see where he ends the playtime and starts the fun time. Although, that would mean touching and we can't exactly do much at the museum without being arrested. Butterflies erupt in my stomach, and I work to keep my breath steady. He winks at me before turning to head to the next exhibit.

"Fuck me," I murmur to myself, breath shaky.

"That's for next date," Emmett calls back.

How the fuck did he hear me? Sneaky, sharp-eared alpha. Smirking, I follow him to the next room where we continue to critique each set up, and pose in a weird position with each animal. Obviously, no touching of the animals, but it's fun to play around like this; just light and carefree. It's okay to be as silly as we want here, there's no rules on having fun. Just don't touch the animals. Emmett makes a point to educate me on the animals he knows, and explains the process of taxidermy to me. It's a hard pass for me on that hobby.

"So did you do Gertie yourself?" I ask.

"No, Gertie was my first one. I found her at a pawn shop, poor thing. Took her in and started learning all I can about taxidermy. I did my first one on my own in late high school. My parents never quite knew what to do with me, especially once I started getting more animals, but they bought me supplies and let me give it a go."

"Sounds like you have awesome parents." I smile at him.

He returns the smile. "Yeah, they are pretty great. We don't understand each other much, but as long as I'm happy, that's all that matters to them."

An ache appears in the center of my chest, and my thoughts turn to my own family. Longing spreads through me at the idea of a supportive family, even if they didn't understand me. Emmett's parents sound like they were always supportive of him, and I hope he recognizes how special that is. My desire to have parents who care threatens to weigh me down, sorrow and pain heavy on my heart. I refuse to let it, though. They don't get to interrupt my date with Emmett.

"Where'd you go?" he asks, interrupting my spiraling thoughts.

"Oh, sorry, just thinking of something. Anyway, tell me about this grizzly bear."

He obliges my topic change, and I insist we have to pose like the grizzly. I go first and stand as tall as I can, holding my arms up and away from my body a bit, curl my fingers into claws, and put a snarl on my face. Emmett is cracking up laughing but manages to get a picture anyway. At first, I was worried they'd all be blurry. I shoo him over to the bear and have him do his version. It's much the same, but Emmett also rounds his back slightly and lowers his head as well. It's much more menacing, but it's also Emmett, so of course you can see the laughter in his eyes as I take the picture.

As we approach the end of this area, there's a fake cabin scene to showcase the forest squirrels and smaller land mammals. The fake cabin front is a façade attached to a wall, and a few feet away, there's a fake fire surrounded by benches. Dread clenches in my stomach, and I start to feel a little clammy. I don't do fires well anymore. Even when I was homeless, I refused to light a fire to keep me warm. The one time I joined a circle of people at a barrel fire, an alpha decided he deserved access to my body. So, no, no untamed fires for me. I think if it were in a fireplace, it wouldn't upset me, but I can't say for sure. All I know is when I see one, my mind screams danger and insists I run.

Knowing how much is on display here, I resist the urge to run, but my feet can't stop backing away from it. Even if it's fake, my stomach churns and any food I've had today threatens to make another appearance. My breathing increases with speed, but I don't even catch that since I'm focused on making sure the fire isn't close to me. If it's not close to me, then nothing bad will happen.

"Hey, Danika, are you okay?" Emmett blocks the view of the fire, and I snap out of my flight response.

"Shit, um, yeah, I'm okay. I think ... I think I'm ready to go home, though. This was really amazing, and I'd love to see you and Jonah again soon. Maybe Colin, too," I blurt out.

"Yeah, we'd love that." Emmett smiles.

"Okay, great. I'll, uh, I'll text you! Yeah, text you. Okay, um, bye." And I run like the coward I am.

Could I have explained the situation to him? Absolutely. He would understand, I can just tell he would. But that would mean remembering things that I've worked hard to push down in the back of my mind. I can't open that bottle of trauma, I just can't. It will stay pushed down and I'll just ... get over it.

Easy.

Chapter 14

Colin

"F uckin' screw, *go in.*" My screwdriver finally grips the screwhead and I'm able to get the last few turns done to ensure the camera is installed properly.

"All set?" Emmett calls up.

"Yep," I say as I climb down the ladder.

When I'm on solid ground again, I grab my phone to check the feed on the camera's app. Camera is online, video loading … and there, a beautiful view of Emmett flipping the camera off with my own back to the camera.

"Looks good," I tell him.

Emmett nods and moves to the ladder, packing it up, and I follow him as he walks around to the back doors. We could go in the front, but the entire front of the space is glass windows and it makes me nervous. So, we go through the back to keep the gallery safe. The box of old security cameras is on my desk, and I re-check to ensure all are accounted for. It was time for a refresh. All our cameras were at least three years old, so I informed Jonah we need new ones. Thankfully, he doesn't question me on this stuff.

"I may float the idea of indoor motion sensors to Jonah," I tell

Emmett absently as I ensure the video feeds are running the way I want them to.

The last thing I want to deal with is customer service, so I make sure all the settings are accurate and that the videos are being backed up the way I want as well. Emmett sits on my desk and swings his legs like a kid would.

"You think he'd go for it?" Emmett asks.

Thinking it over, I hum with indecision. Truthfully, I don't think he will, but I tend to be hypervigilant when it comes to my alphas.

"No, he'll see it as over the top," I confess.

There are cameras inside of the gallery, ensuring we can see from every angle, that way nobody can hide their face if they do something nefarious. We've never had a problem with it, but like I said, I'm not leaving anything to chance with my alphas.

"Okay, I think that's as good as it gets right now. If they break in, we have the alarms that will go off, we'll catch the movement outside, and we should be able to see them," I list out.

"Do you really think this is all necessary?" Emmett asks. "It's not like we're in a bad part of town."

Pushing up from my chair, my legs take me to where Emmett's sitting, and I move his legs so I can stand between them. My hands cup his face and pull him close so that I can land a peck on the tip of his nose. His answering smile is slow and full of mischief and love.

"Need I remind you that I'm almost more protective of you two than you are of me? There's *two* of you to watch after and just one of me. So nothing is unnecessary to try and keep you safe."

Not giving him a chance to respond, I lean in closer and meet his lips with mine. We merge together naturally, and I savor the feeling of his lips on mine. Instead of bantering with him on which of us is more protective, I let our bodies talk. His hands land on my hips, pulling me as close as he can, our chests touching and my hands migrating from his face to hold the back of his head and his upper body close to me. Our tongues play, each of us trying to tease the other into a frenzy.

Once our breathing is heavy, I pull back. I absolutely want to fuck him into a blubbering mess, but this isn't the time or place. I mentally scold my dick and tell it that good things come to those who wait. I'm not sure it believes me, but I'm well aware that Jonah wants us present today, not fucking in the security video room. Unable to resist, I lean in and nip his ear.

"Later, baby, I'll rip off all your clothes," I taunt.

"Don't threaten me with a good time." He grins.

We both adjust, trying to make our raging hard-ons less visible, and walk out of the room together.

"Have you considered letting your hair loose? Doing an afro again?"

Emmett hums. "I haven't thought about it, but I suppose I'm not opposed to the idea. These locs took a long time to get right, though."

"Whatever makes you happy. I just like being able to run my fingers through your hair. If you prefer it differently, then do that," I encourage, not wanting him to feel like he has to change anything because of my preferences.

The gallery is open today and we can see plenty of people milling about, looking at the art and chatting to each other. People watching is always a good time for me, and if I can get Emmett interested, it's an absolute riot. He's finicky about who he'll watch, though, and sometimes I just watch with my own mind at peace.

We have a few students today; it's easy to tell which customers are the students. They look in a group and talk about each art piece in depth as they go along. I'm not sure how much merit truly lies in artistic vision and the use of composition, but I can tell which art pieces are made with feeling. Those ones call to me the most, like they have secrets they want to share. There's beauty in carefully composed pieces, but it's not quite the same as ones made with emotion.

As I watch, my nose picks up a new scent, a strong whiskey. The kind that almost burns your nose instead of being soothing and nostalgic. That scent beckons me, but I'm not sure why. I don't particularly like the scent, but it feels like something I need to figure out. After scanning the small crowd, it's not hard to find him.

He's tall, giving out alpha vibes without trying, and his hair is mussed like he can't stop playing with it. His light brown eyes survey the room, like he's not quite sure what to look at. While his steps are hesitant, he gains confidence as he inspects at each art piece. It's clear he's searching for something specific when I see him checking the artist name instead of the painting. Maybe I should put him out of his misery and lend a hand.

"Hi there, how can I help you?" I ask once I reach him.

He startles when he realizes I'm addressing him and not a different customer.

"Me?" he asks.

I smile. "Yes, you seem to be looking for something specific."

He grimaces. "Am I that easy to read?"

"No, I just know the look of someone searching. My alpha owns the gallery, so I see it a fair amount."

"Oh, right." He nods like that's an obvious statement.

I remain silent, waiting to see if he has any questions. His eyes dart away from me, and he chews his lower lip gently before coming to whatever decision he seems to be wavering on.

"I heard an artist got lots of attention when she had her art here. Is there any chance y'all got a few paintings for viewin'?" he asks, a southern drawl making itself known as he relaxes into the question.

"Do you know the name? We've had a few good artists come through." I'm pretty sure that he's asking about Danika, but for some reason I want him to say it.

"Uh, yeah, she goes by Danika," he hesitantly says.

I can't help the smile that comes to my face; it's essentially reflexive at this point.

"We were able to keep one. Her art is special. You see the painting, but to see the full image, you need a UV light. It's too expensive for us to keep the display full time, but we hope she shows here again. I'll show you how the UV wand works," I explain.

We reach the painting, and I explain how the wand works, demonstrating how to angle it and sweep over the painting to better see that side of things. We have the painting in the shade so it's easier to see the difference. The one he's looking at depicts the bust of a woman, looking over her shoulder. Her hair is flowing in the direction of her face as if she's walking into the wind while looking behind her.

Once the UV light is passed over the image, it reveals a mirror image of the woman. Instead of an image of a woman looking thoughtfully behind her, the second image shows two women longingly looking at each other. Their faces are almost the same but there are subtle differences between them. The noses aren't identical, one face is rounder than the other, and the second woman has the tips of her fingers resting lightly on her lips. Like she's reminding herself that they're there.

I step back to let the patron have his moment, watching as he looks with a blank face, seeming to be unsure how he should react to what he's seeing. He stands at that painting for ten minutes, looking at it without the light, then with it over and over again. Eventually, emotion starts to show through on his face, and I'm not sure if he's breaking whatever stoic façade he adopted or if I'm just understanding them now.

Once he finishes looking at the painting, he places the UV wand in its holder and walks over to me. He rubs his mouth with one hand as he thinks over his words.

"She gonna show again?"

I shrug. "I know my alphas would love her to, as would most of us, but there's nothing specific lined up."

He nods, lapsing back into silent thought.

"She sure is somethin' special, ain't she?" he says, almost to himself.

"It seems so," I reply, acknowledging my own longing to actually meet her.

There's an awkward silence, where he seems lost in thought, but I'm ready to move on to whatever task Jonah has next for me. Social niceties that have been drilled into me as a kid have me waiting, though, wanting to ensure the patron is satisfied with whatever service I've provided. Finally, he puts his hands on his hips and nods to himself.

"Thanks, I'll get outta y'alls hair."

He walks away before I can respond, and I can definitely put that in one of the more awkward interactions I've had at this gallery. Turning, I search out Jonah and find him at the front "desk" we have. It's mostly for appearances. On exhibitions where we do sales, we put out a tablet for payment transactions, but it stays empty otherwise. So, naturally, Jonah has a big folder of paperwork and his laptop in front of him, working away.

"All work and no play ..." I taunt him from behind.

He turns and growls, "Makes an alpha awfully cranky."

The scent of coffee intensifies and sweetens as he speaks, and now all I want is him. My mouth remembers the feel of his hard length on my tongue and the feeling of when he chokes me going deep into my throat. My dick hardens as my body remembers how his feels against me, and if there weren't so many people here, I'd get down on my knees and show him how much I love him.

Instead, I lean against the arms of his chair, caging him in gently, hoping that this isn't too intimate to do while we have a building bustling with people.

"Maybe I can help you wind down after we get home tonight. You look like you need to take some control," I murmur, giving him a sassy wink.

His lips curl up in a smile, even as he tries to look grumpy.

"Better watch out, Beta, I'll be taking you up on that," he quips.

"Anything for you," I purr before straightening up. "I wanted to see if you need anything else done before I head home. I think I got it all, but checking in."

Jonah shakes his head. "Nah. Even if you missed something, I don't have a list in mind right now. Head out and do your thing until I get home. Then you have a promise to keep."

We stare at each other for a moment, heat burning within both of our bodies, before I step backward. Normally teasing is more of Emmett's thing, but I can't help the sassy air kiss and wink I toss his way before turning and heading for the back door. Pun absolutely intended.

Chapter 15

Danika

While I have immensely enjoyed having the guys in a group chat, Colin and I ended up making our own. Just the two of us. It started as a joke after Emmett and Jonah got caught up in their own banter, but soon it became an everyday thing. I enjoyed messaging him to say good morning and ask what he's eating for breakfast. When it's early afternoon, I look forward to seeing what ridiculous meme or gif he found to send me. It's ... well, it's comforting, which I never thought I would feel when it comes to interacting with a guy who's into me.

There's a small lake near my cabin, about a five-minute walk, so after packing myself a thermos of coffee and grabbing a couple of muffins, I sling a camping chair over my shoulder and take a walk. That's how I find myself sitting near a lake, in the woods, and smiling like an idiot while I text this beta. Nature around me fills me with the feeling of possibility. Squirrels jump from branch to branch, flying through the air, relying only on instinct and dexterity to get them safely to their tree of choice. If one element is off, or their judgement is ever so skewed, they'll fall to the ground and miss their shot.

The quiet rustling of the trees marks the light breeze I can barely feel from the ground. The gentle sway is hypnotizing, letting the sun peek through the leaves as they are pushed to and fro. I fill my lungs with a refreshing breath of air, and savor the smell of dirt, wood, and whatever it is that makes a lake smell amazing. I have no idea if there's a word for it, but I swear it has its own smell.

My phone pings gently, almost as if it is sheepish to break the silence around me. Picking it up, I look with a grin.

> Colin: Breakfast of champions today

He sends me a picture of his eggs, toast, and bacon.

> Me: You might have me beat there. Although you're missing something really important.

I send him a picture of my travel coffee mug sitting atop my knee, which is crossed over the other.

> Colin: Your lovely legs do look delicious today

> Me: Hmmm I don't think those are on Chef Colin's menu. Something about cannibalism not being ethical.

> Colin: 😅 true, but I wouldn't share those legs with anyone else. Maybe the alphas if they ask nicely.

He's been expertly walking that line of flirting but not pushing things. It's a surprisingly delicate balance, and he's managed to express his interest in me without me feeling like he doesn't care what I think. You'd be surprised how many betas don't care what an omega thinks. Everyone blames the alphas, but the betas can be almost, if not more, dangerous.

> Me: Just promise me that if you eat my legs, you do so ethically and let Emmett keep them to taxidermy.

> Colin: OMG we could make our own leg lamp!

My loud laugh startles whatever birds were nearby, and I hear a mass fluttering of wings taking off. Oops.

"Sorry, birds," I call after them.

I can't help the additional chuckles that spill out of me as I think on his *A Christmas Story* reference.

> Me: That, my friend, is a solid plan. Take pictures for me.

> Colin: Absolutely. You'll have a wheelchair, so you can come see it yourself if you'd like.

> Me: LOL, I appreciate how well thought out this is

> Colin: I live to serve.

My phone is quiet for a moment before he continues with his thoughts.

> Colin: So, I know you've met Jonah and Emmett, but do you wanna meet up some time?

> Me: I think that could be a lot of fun.

> Colin: What are the chances of getting you over here for dinner tonight?

Originally I had assumed Colin and I would do our own thing when we eventually met, but I really enjoy the idea of seeing him with

Jonah and Emmett. It will be nice to see the three of them together. Maybe it'll help my general nervousness, too. It feels fast, to make plans for today, but before I had my recent meltdown, I'd decided to try.

Of course, then I spiraled and had a massive breakdown. Trauma, what are you gonna do?

> Me: That sounds fun, actually! What time?

> Colin: Is 5 ok? I'll do my best to entertain you.

> Me: I'll be there 😊

Plans made, I let myself enjoy the quiet morning for a while longer. When I finally pack it in, I head straight for my art room. The sun is out today and it's perfect lighting for my canvas of the man and woman; it's coming along nicely, and I'm looking forward to adding the UV alternate image. Sometimes I stock up several UV paintings at once, so I can set a nighttime work schedule, but who knows how I'll handle it this time. Future me makes weird decisions sometimes.

When I finally surface, I make a beeline for my bathroom, realizing that I'd forgotten to set a bathroom alarm. Again. Sophie would yell at me about it, saying something about my kidneys. A smile comes to my face as I think of her as a mother hen, a warm feeling spreading through my body as I remember all the times she's done that for me. Thankfully, I enjoy when she tries to mother me, and she understands I may or may not listen, so it works out for both of us. She gets to feel like she helped, I get to feel like someone cares, and we both understand there's no pressure to follow through on some things.

Past me must have been in a hurry this morning, because I find my bag full of muffin crumbs and my empty thermos by the door. Good thing I don't have a dog; I'd feel bad if one ate the chocolate treat leftovers. I'd love to have a pet, but I leave out too much food to have a dog, and could easily ignore it if I'm in the zone painting. With a cat it would be less maintenance with the animal, but I'd be too scared of the cat ruining my art room. No, for now it's easiest to just have me. I'd never felt particularly lonely, since being alone has been my preference, but lately I've wanted more company. Not bad enough to really act on it yet, but the fact that I'm willing to go to the guys' house today signals a need for human companionship. Maybe I could consider them my pets. Can omegas do that? I'll have to look into it.

I rinse out the dishes and check the time, noting that it's already four p.m. and yelp at the time. My body is covered in paint splatters, and I'm wearing the loungeist lounge clothes ever. While comfortable, I'd rather not look like a hot mess when I get there. I shower quickly, rubbing softly but firmly at the paint on my arms, my skin feeling relaxed after removing the tight, dried paint on it. It almost feels like I'm removing a facial mask, but I doubt there's any skin benefits to covering oneself with paint before washing it off.

The weather is a weird mix of too-hot and too-cold. If I wear too heavy of a coat or sweater, I'm going to overheat, but if I go too light, I'm going to be way too cold. The joys of living in the northern part of this country. I finally settle on a light sweater and some jeans, grabbing a light jacket on the way out. Just in case.

Once I've settled in my truck, I input the address that Colin sent, and set my phone in its dash mount. The drive is peaceful, despite the traffic on the road, since the app I use for navigation avoids highways and instead guides me through scenic side streets. Eventually I'm taken into a well-established neighborhood. A smile appears on my face as I take in the large trees providing shade to the houses here. Each house is a little different, and there's plenty of space between each, making it a comfortable mix of space and people. If I ever decided to live near people again, this would be an amazing neighborhood to live in. However, I've established in my life that most people suck, and I'd rather not live near any.

When I pull into the driveway that matches the address I have, my mouth hangs open. I park my truck in the long driveway, and insecurity roars through me, making my hands shake and head swim.

Their house is stunning! It's two story with a gorgeous front porch hosting a bench swing. I can picture sitting next to Jonah on that swing, holding hands and enjoying a quiet evening together, content in our silence and each other's company. My mind switches to picturing Emmett running up the porch steps to race home and burst in the door with his unending enthusiasm. The house has to have at least four bedrooms with its size, likely more. There's an understated wealth I can sense, and I'm not sure how comfortable I am with that.

I'm not going to judge them for it, they seem like great guys, but what in the world would people this wealthy want to do with me? Overweight, clearly overly frugal, not much money to speak of, and driving an older truck that is probably two years overdue for a carwash. My teeth clamp down on my lip as indecision takes over. Should I really leave the car and go in? Maybe they haven't seen me yet. I could probably still bail or make it look like I have the wrong house. Then again, most people turning around wouldn't park this close to the house, they'd stop at the end and back up. My stomach feels like someone left rocks in it, and just as I'm about to move into reverse and bail, the front door opens to Jonah's easy smile. He holds up a hand in a soft wave. *Shit.*

Relenting to the fact that I can't escape, I turn my truck off and take a deep breath. I can do this, right? It'll be fine. Emmett and Jonah are great, and I've loved texting with Colin. None of them have judged me for my lifestyle or how shy I am. These are good guys, I know it deep down, so I keep that mantra in my head as I step out of my truck. Jonah walks to the bottom of the steps as I approach, his smile never wavering.

"I'm so glad you came," he says when I'm close enough.

"Uh, yeah, me too. It's good to see you." My words are awkward and stilted.

His brow furrows. "You okay?"

"Nervous," I admit with a large breath.

"Totally understandable. Hopefully, we can chase that away." He smiles.

I nod. "Let's do this."

His scent of coffee hits me, and my muscles ease from the tension I was holding in anticipation. Okay, fine, they were tense in borderline terror from meeting a new person, but I'm going to live in my own reality over here. Before he can turn, I lean in and take a deep inhale, wanting more of his comforting scent. As my muscles continue to relax, filling my body with peace, I hear a low rumbling. Oh, my omega and I both like that. I wonder if I can record that noise once I figure out where it's coming from.

Belatedly, I realize my eyes are closed. When I look again, I realize my nose is inches away from his throat, and he's purring for me. Heat rushes through me in embarrassment at my hussy behavior. I basically just invaded his personal space and took his scent in like he's my mate. Or match. Shit, no, not a match, can't have that. That's too much, I can't handle that level of relationship. My feet stumble back, my cheeks feel like they're on fire, and my body wants to curl in on itself and hide.

"I'm sorry," I rasp.

"Baby girl, you have nothing to be sorry for. I loved it, and my alpha loved it. I couldn't help but purr for you." His voice is like gravel.

Looking into his eyes, a different heat fills me, one that has nothing to do with embarrassment and everything to do with the wetness gathering between my legs.

"Let's head inside before my alpha takes over and breaks all your boundaries. I want to be respectful, but damn it's hard when you get close."

I shuffle back and forth, uneasiness popping up again, but Jonah seems to sense it and reassures me.

"Dani, I would *never* break your boundaries. It might be difficult, but both my alpha and I want nothing but pleasure for you. We want to respect you and treat you like the queen you are."

I smile at that and meet his eyes, where only sincerity shows.

"You're a pretty great alpha," I tell him.

He preens ever so slightly before turning to open the door and gesture for me to go in. As my feet approach, I pick up on Emmett's comforting leather and whiskey scent as if it's calling to me. My eyes scan the space beyond the front door, and a rush of excitement hits me when my eyes meet his, the caramel color drawing me in with a promise of fun. Then my eyes get caught on wild, curly brown hair and my breath stops for a moment, completely enthralled by the man who owns said hair. His eyes are a deeper brown than Emmett's, and his head sports wild brown curls that seem to resist being tamed. His tresses are gathered in a bun on top of his head, but they're poking out in all directions, as if they need to be seen.

This must be Colin. My lips turn up as I put a face to his name. His face is open and warm, his own lips curved in a familiar answering smile, almost like we've known each other for years. Jonah steps in as well, his hand on the door as we all look at each other. Colin's scent hits me at that moment, but instead of basking in it, cold terror washes over me. My nose is filled with the scent of smoke and fire, permeating my senses like I never left. A reminder of what caused me to run from my home, what I did before I left, both memories I've vowed not to revisit. His scent of campfire throws me straight back there. I can feel my limbs start to shake, the air around me doesn't feel like enough for me to breathe, and all the blood has left my face.

Colin and Emmett's faces twist in confusion, and I see Emmett's foot take one step forward. The terror that held me frozen releases, and I turn, pushing past Jonah to bolt to my car. My hands shake as I try to start the car, but none of them have moved beyond the porch. Tears begin to fall from my eyes, and I push my truck harder than I should to get back home where I wrap myself in every single blanket I can find and bury myself into my bed, with no intention of ever leaving.

Chapter 16

Colin

I've been nervous all day, but the good kind of nervous. My body is jittery with excitement, and I've spent my time doing small cleaning tasks around the house since I can't get myself to stand still. We've talked via text for days now, and this morning I just couldn't take not seeing her. While I'd hoped she would say yes, now I'm thinking maybe this was a bad idea. At the same time there's a visceral need to lay eyes on her. Butterflies are in my stomach at the thought of her, so I suspect I'll feel like I'm on cloud nine when I see her.

As the afternoon eventually turns to evening, Emmett and I find ourselves on the couch, his hands busy with a fidget toy that he's trying to dissect. I look over at him, my heart in my throat.

"She's going to be here soon," I tell him.

"Yes."

"What if she doesn't like me?"

"Then we'll brainwash her."

When his words finally register in my brain, my eyes widen in alarm. "What?"

Emmett looks up at me, confused. "What?"

"You can't just *brainwash* someone!"

"Sure, you can. There's probably a tutorial online and everything."

I lean forward on the couch, my hands covering my face and my elbows on my knees. Maybe this is a terrible idea. Then again, she's met Emmett and was still willing to meet me, so that has to mean it'll be okay. It has to. Our motion sensor camera beeps in alert, and as I pull up my phone to see what triggered it, I hear Jonah call from the other room.

"She's here, I'll go greet her."

Well, there's a little pressure off of me. I don't have to worry about how far to walk to greet her. Or if I should help her out of her car. Would she prefer I stay back, far away? Why is everything so difficult when there's someone I'm attracted to on the other side? Emmett puts his hand on my shoulder and squeezes gently.

"Let's hop up, I'm sure they'll be inside in a moment. Remember: brainwashing."

I roll my eyes as he chuckles behind me, but I'm still admittedly unsure if he is serious or not. You never truly know with Emmett. As we approach the entry space, I hear the door open and Jonah offering for Danika to walk in first. Emmett and I make ourselves known, and I'm pretty sure my jaw is hanging open. She's the most gorgeous woman I have ever set eyes on.

She's tall, her body has perfect curves with some extra, and my mouth waters. I love when a woman has enough body for me to grab, hold, and touch. Her black hair is up in a ponytail, which gives a better view to her deep blue eyes. I feel bare, like she can see all of me, the good and the bad, and I find myself praying that she accepts what she sees. Her scent calls to me, a sweet mint that makes me crave a minty dessert, or a mojito. My head spins with the craving to go to her, to smell her close and hold her to me. Our eyes are connected, and I slowly realize that while I'm drooling over her, she's looking horrified.

The blood drains from her face, and her eyes widen, glancing around the room like she's a trapped animal. A small whine escapes her, but she cuts it off quickly. Emmett makes a small, wounded noise before taking a step forward, as if he's driven to fix whatever the problem is. Unfortunately, all his step does is break her out of her frozen state and cause her to turn and run as fast as she can out of the house.

We watch as she gets in her car and pulls out of our driveway, like her very life depends on it. My stomach bottoms out as it sinks in that she left because of me. She knows Jonah and Emmett, there's no way that she would avoid them to that degree, but I was the new factor here.

My mind searches for an explanation. *Maybe it's my hair, the way I stand ... did I not smile bright enough, was I frowning without realizing? Did I stand too close to Emmett? Maybe she thought I was being territorial about him, or that I was uncomfortable. Did I growl at her without realizing it?*

As my mind continues to race, my stomach feels like it's sinking, weighed down by a massive rock. Somehow, I ruined this for Emmett and Jonah. They could court her on their own, and I can go look for a new pack. My body sweats, and one half of me screams to run away, that it's the only way that my guys will be happy. The other half of my body begs for me to stay, to figure this out together and figure out how to get Danika to be a part of this pack. The backs of my eyes sting as I stand there and war with myself on what I should do. Emotions threaten to drown me, and all I want is to curl up, avoid all of this, and pretend I never invited her over.

"Come on," Jonah says gently.

His hands land softly on my shoulders. I'm steered toward the couch and positioned between my alphas as we sit and cuddle. Emmett curls into my side, and our legs tangle together, making it hard to determine if I'm cuddling him or vice versa. Jonah stretches his arms to try and pull both of us into him.

"I'm sorry," I tell them softly.

"It's not your fault," Jonah says.

"How is it not my fault? She took one look at me and ran like she was on fire."

"There's something more there."

Emmett makes a noise of agreement, but otherwise stays silent, his arms wrapped around me. It's one of my favorite places to be, so I soak up the feeling of comfort and safety in the moment.

"How can you be sure it wasn't me?" I ask.

Jonah lets loose a deep breath. "One of her art pieces from her show was ... emotional to say the least. There's something awful in her past, but I have no idea what it is. Whatever spooked her isn't something you did, whatever it was had to be deep seated with how she froze and ran. Something else is at play here."

I believe that's what Jonah thinks, but I'm not sure if I believe it. Memories of when I left my family re-surface in my head, and even though we're reconciled now, it was rough for me to leave. They struggled with it, too, and I felt like a failure for a while after. That same feeling of shame and regret is pooling in my stomach, the room feels darker overall, and my stomach hurts with the thought that I caused this potential rift.

As if he can read my mind, Emmett places a soft kiss on my temple.

"It's not your fault. We'll work it out together."

Danika

I stay in my blankets all evening. The only reason to leave is to use the bathroom, and I force myself to wait until it's an emergency before I do. Then? I dive right back in. A snarky voice in the back of my head says that my efforts would be better rewarded in an actual nest, so I tell that part of my brain to fuck off and burrow even deeper, or at least I rearrange to feel cozier. I'm not sure I can get underneath any more of these blankets.

The smell of bonfire seems to permeate my skin, and I can't get it out. The scent is lingering like I was scent marked and it's all I can smell. He didn't touch me, and there's absolutely no chance the scent is really in the air, but it's all I can smell anyway. Memories flash through my head as I try to think of *anything* else, but of course that makes them all the louder.

Sneering girls in tight outfits.

The way he looked at me like I was special.

Waking up, scared and half naked.

His soured scent.

Strangers around a fire in the city.

Men who ignored my cries.

My eyes close in the onslaught of memories, and when my throat starts to feel sore, I realize I've been whining for hours now. Shit, how long have I been under these covers? My phone is still in my purse, which got abandoned in the living room. It's fine, I don't need it for anything. If Sophie calls, I'm sure she'll just leave it until I pick up again. Maybe. Hopefully.

It was nice to have some new company while it lasted. The guys were so nice to me, and I hadn't been on a date in ... well, years. I'm not sure anyone has taken me on a date before. It's one of my best memories, both of the dates. Jonah's no-pressure approach was easy to participate in, and he made me smile more than I thought was possible with an alpha. Then I got caught up in Emmett's enthusiasm for taxidermy, seeing it through his eyes of preservation, keeping something good in the world to treasure and savor.

Too bad you can't taxidermy experiences. My brain wanders to the concept of trying to taxidermy coffee and taxidermy-ing a taxidermy place. My whine reduces for a moment as I think, and I actually catch myself feeling amused. The connection that Colin and I forged via text rears its head, and I can't help but smile at all the banter and fun we got up to. Then his smell wafts through the memory and I snap out of it. No, they're not for me, not when Colin smells like that. They'll find an omega without a lifetime of trauma who they like just as much as me.

I still never figured out why they want me. Maybe it's my wounded artist situation. Once again, I think about trying to find a therapist, but the thought of telling someone my past gives me the heebie-jeebies. I didn't even tell Sophie about why I left home until we were two or three years into our friendship. Doing that with a complete stranger? Hard pass.

I'll just hang out in my not-a-nest until I feel like emerging. So, probably never. I live here now.

Chapter 17

Danika

It's day three of letting myself wallow like a little bitch. I've managed to feed myself (mostly junk food) and keep somewhat hydrated, but hiding away is definitely taking its toll on me. There's also my omega nudging at me, saying we're not going to let assholes from our past dictate our future. Plus, she's flashing images of how sexy all three of the guys are. Even the glimpse of Colin had me drooling before I panicked and ran like I was being chased by a murderer. It's actually embarrassing now that I think about it.

I agree with my omega that I'm a badass bitch, and when I take a sniff of my armpit, I realize I'm also rank. Can't be badass and rank at the same time, so I emerge from my cocoon of blankets and drag myself through the shower. I scrub myself enough to get the stink out, but that's all I have the energy for. I need to slowly work back to the idea of shaving my legs. Honestly, I don't shave my legs frequently as it is, but I at least have the idea to do it. Right now, even holding that idea is exhausting. Dramatic? Probably.

There is a full cleansing feel as I get myself washed, though, a freshness that climbs up through my toes and reminds me that I am more than I think. Instead of being dragged down all the time, this

125

cleansing lets me shed all the baggage I picked up and put it back where it belongs. In its own corner, untouched. I picked myself up many times before this, and I can do it again, no matter what the circumstances.

Feeling refreshed and lighter, I make my way to the kitchen and realize I didn't do any grocery shopping in the last week. *Damn.* I pull out a frozen shrimp wonton ramen bowl and nuke that baby up. After settling into my couch with my hot meal, I turn on some baking show. I don't pay attention to which one it is, I just want the noise and visuals. I spear a wanton and shove it in my mouth, humming to myself as I enjoy ... huh, what meal is this? I realize I have no idea what time of day it is, so I reach for my phone only to remember it's not near me.

"Aw, dammit," I mutter to myself once I realize I need to stand up and grab it out of my purse.

My purse is taunting me from the floor, like it knows I don't want to move. Irritation takes over, and I refuse to let an inanimate object take me down, so I push away the feeling and snatch my purse, putting it next to me on the couch. *Take that, purse! You can't keep me down. Emotional trauma? Yes, that can keep me down. Purses? Nope.* My phone sits dead inside of my purse, but I pull it out anyway, dread coiling in my stomach as I consider it and what messages I may have missed. Sophie's probably on her way here to bang down the door. I need to just face the music. So, I dig around my couch for a charger and plug my phone in while I slurp up the last of my meal.

When my phone finally turns itself on, my ears are treated to a slew of beeps and tones, indicating all the messages I've received in the last couple of days. I hadn't expected it to be very many, if I'm honest. And if I'm really honest, it's probably mostly games and news. Hesitation has nestled itself deep in my stomach, leaving a pit there for all kinds of bad feelings to escape, and it's hard not to let that take over. To continue ignoring the world. Bigger than my hesitation, is the knowledge that Sophie won't let me hide away for long, so if I want things to be on my terms, I need to face the music now.

Grasping my phone, I swipe to show all my notifications. There are definitely some app alerts, but I'm shocked to see that the majority of notifications are a mix of Sophie and the guys. Why ... why are the guys sending me messages? Why did they call? I ran like a psychopath, there's no way there's still any kind of interest there. I choose to handle Sophie first, before she bursts in my door, causing additional noise in my brain.

"*Danika!*" she screams into the phone when I call.

I yank the phone away from my ear before replying.

"Hey, Soph."

"Where the hell have you been? I was just about to come over there and pray I didn't find you *murdered* in the *woods!*"

Oh man, she's officially pissed. There's Sophie pissed, then there's actual, officially pissed, which means she gets scared. For some reason when she adds scared to the mix, she gets out of hand with her anger. I was hoping for just Sophie-level pissed.

"Hey, I'm fine. I'm sorry I scared you," I soothe her, picturing our interaction like me trying to coax a hissing cat from under a couch.

She scoffs, unconvincingly. "I wasn't scared. Just a little worried about my best friend."

"Okay, Sophie." I roll my eyes with a small smile.

"Don't roll your eyes at me. I can hear it in your voice. Now tell me what happened before I show up at your door."

I sigh, and she's patient while I try to gather my thoughts. I don't want to go through everything and have her interrupt constantly. So, I tell her about having a quiet morning, texting with Colin again and how smooth and easy everything has been feeling with him. She knows I've been talking with all three of them, so thankfully she doesn't need more information there. Then I tell her about Colin's scent.

"I was completely stunned by how hot he is, and couldn't believe how lucky I was to know all three of them. Then his scent hit me; campfire and wood."

Sophie lets out a shocked sound. "Ohhh, there it is."

"There what is?"

"The reason you went offline for three days. You had a bad reaction. Did they comfort you? Oh my god, are you still there? Did they give you orgasms to recover?"

I shake my head. "Sophie, I ran. I ran like they were going to come after me with steak knives. Then I drove home and hid in bed."

"Oh, Dani, you were alone? Why didn't you call?"

"Gee, Sophie, let me think ... maybe it was the innate trauma response of running and hiding?"

Sophie's tone softens, and I instantly feel bad for snapping at her. "No, you're right, I'm sorry. I just worried so much about you, and instead of physically checking in, I sat on my hands. And now I'm trying to blame you. It's not your fault, babe."

"Thanks," I all but whisper.

"Do you want me to swing by with some cookies?"

I hum. "No, I think I need a bit more time to process. Knowing that you've offered, though, it's a big help. I really appreciate it."

"I am *always* in your corner, babe."

"Same. Now go do something you can't afford before we both start to have feelings."

Sophie cackles in my ear. "Don't threaten me with a good time! Okay, love you, babe."

Smiling, I hang up the phone, a small spot of warmth in my chest after talking with her. She may have jumped down my throat, but I snapped back at her, and in the end we both know it's just heightened emotion. I've said it a million times, but I have no idea how I survived without her before we met. The warmth in my chest brings an ease to me, and I take advantage of the relaxed feeling to watch the television for a few more moments.

I know I'll need to take a look at the text messages from the guys, but for the moment, I'm enjoying watching amateur chefs trying not to burn the expensive food they're trying to cook. When the new batch of chefs come in, I decide it's time to see what messages were sent my way while I hid. I have a sneaking suspicion that it's going to be a little painful to read, so I take a deep breath before unlocking my phone. All three of the guys messaged in our group chat, apologizing for whatever set me off, and asking to talk. After a few messages there, they started texting me individually instead. Emmett offered to taxidermy whatever it was that spooked me. Colin has apologized repeatedly, before saying that he understands if I never want to see him again.

Tears sting the back of my eyes at that. He doesn't even know what triggered me, and he's already offered to remove himself if that would help. If we hadn't already built a small bond, his message would have sealed the deal for me. It shows me again that he's considerate and really does want the best for everyone involved. However, I don't think removing himself is the right action here. Finally, I turn to Jonah's messages. There are one or two apologies, a couple of begs for me to call him, a reassurance that he doesn't want to push me, then one more text begging me to at least tell him that I'm alive and functioning. I take pity on the poor man.

> Me: I'm alive, and kind of functioning

> Jonah: omg I'm so glad you texted me, we've been worried sick.

I'm not sure if I'm pleased or mildly weirded out at how quickly he texted back. He's either staring at his phone, or I just have really good timing. Maybe it's a mix of both.

> Me: Sorry, didn't mean to make you worry.

> Jonah: Please don't apologize, we clearly did something to scare you, and we want to help if we can.

> Me: It's not anything you guys did … I think it was just an oddly timed panic attack.

Hopefully he believes that and can let things rest. I don't want to cause more problems for them. They've been unbelievably nice and considerate, they don't need more of my shit stirring things up.

> Jonah: Those are not fun, I'm sorry you had that.

> Jonah: Um, I hope this isn't pushy, but would you be willing to meet? I mean, just you and I, no pressure though. I would just really love to talk to you one more time.

There's a sting on my lower lip, and I startle, realizing I've been biting it with increasing pressure as we text. Oops. Thankfully, it's not quite bleeding, but the sharp pain did pull me out of any spiral I may have fallen into. So, meet up with no pressure? I think hard for a moment, trying to decide if that's something I can manage.

> Me: I'm not saying yes, but where would you want to meet?

> Jonah: There's a park not too far from the gallery, we could meet there if that's more comfortable than at the gallery or one of our houses.

Yeah, go to their house again? Not happening. I don't need panic attack: round two. Do I want to see them again? I'm not sure about Colin and Emmett. I've grown to care about them in our interactions, but I don't think I can handle Colin's scent or face Emmett's disappointment when I walk away. Cowardly? Maybe. I just don't think I can do it, though. Jonah's a safer option, and I feel like I owe him anyway, since he gave me my first official solo exhibit. It can't hurt to hear him out, right?

"Right," I answer myself. "It'll be fine, I can do this."

Unfortunately, only silence greets my words, and I realize I don't even have a "Gertie" of my own to talk to. Crazy artist? Check. Officially talking to myself.

Me: Sure, can you meet in, like, three hours or so?

The time on my phone tells me I just had lunch, so a mid-late afternoon meet up is the right time of day. Close enough to dinner to use that for an excuse, or I could use the fading daylight, too. Even though we're firmly in spring, the days still don't stay light for a long time.

Jonah: That sounds perfect. I'll send you the name of the park. We'll find each other.

I release a deep breath and let my phone flop down into my lap. Three hours to get my mind in the right place and do something with my hair. I can do this. I can. I'm a big girl, and I've said goodbye before. Maybe this time I won't burn anything down when I do. Smirking to myself, I get ready, putting my hair into a dutch braid and making sure my clothes don't have any overly large stains or holes. Starving artist look and all that.

Mid afternoon finds me parking my truck downtown, wanting a spot close enough to escape to, but not so close that it's clear I'm skittish. I don't want kid gloves, but I want an easy escape route if I need it. When I reach the park entrance, I see a few trails that lead off to my right, a green expanse of grass for all kinds of outdoor games, and a few scattered benches around. There's a playground, too, but I'm grateful to see Jonah is on a bench closer to the trails.

His dirty blond hair is tousled from the wind, and I can see a few strands get picked up as a breeze passes through, his large frame fitting on the bench but clearly not a comfortable situation. His jawline isn't sharp, but there's no question of how handsome he is, a subtle beauty that men who are truly secure in who they are have. When I get close enough and his brown eyes look up and lock with mine, I realize I'm a total goner.

This is going to make things interesting.

Chapter 18

Jonah

Jonah

Danika, as always, takes my breath away when my eyes land on her. Her inky hair is tied into two braids, her blue eyes see right through me, and the fact that she doesn't dress up for me makes my heart melt. Lots of women I've interacted with in my past dressed up for every single occasion, and it got old pretty fast. I don't want perfect beauty, I want someone real. Butterflies run rampant in my stomach, the surging adrenaline making my hands shake, and it takes every bit of willpower I have not to race over and pull her in my arms. I realize that I'm standing and have already taken a few steps in her direction. I think I may have made her uncomfortable.

She pauses for a moment, like a wild animal trying to decide if there's a trap ahead. I take a deep breath as subtly as I can and try to relax my posture. If I look tense, she might not come any closer and that would put a damper on the goal of this outing. I need her to see us as a safe place, a pack that will take care of her and love her no matter what. Clearly we're not there yet with the "L" word, but she captivates me enough that it's not far away. *And if somehow I were lucky enough to be her match?* I push that thought from my head. I can't handle that much hope right now. She's too skittish for that level of hope.

"Hey, beautiful," I greet her.

Her cheeks turn a delicate shade of pink. "Hi."

Words fail me as I continue to stare at her, completely entranced by her as she seems to see everything around her, including straight into me. She's so perceptive, but also incredibly wary. I want to know what lurks behind her hesitation and walls; although that could lead to violence against whoever was involved.

"Um ..." she says, and I realize I've gone silent and have been staring at her with my mouth hanging open a little.

Oops.

"Hi, sorry. Um, I got distracted. I like staring at you. I mean, you're really beautiful, sorry, didn't mean to creep you out there."

She smiles and ducks her head to hide her amusement. I've already seen it, though, and warmth fills me, a joy at knowing I'm the one who put that smile there. I couldn't tell you why she snares my attention like this, but everything feels better when she's around, like a warm, cozy fire on a cold winter day.

"Let's sit, if you're comfortable?" I offer.

"Sure, okay," she says, taking a spot near me on the bench I just rose from.

Not as many people linger about the trail entrance, so it's one of the more private areas, but still open enough that she hopefully won't feel crowded. Once we're seated, I hear a small giggle escape from her. A smile pulls at my mouth before I can help it, and my eyes stay on her, hoping to see the smile that accompanies the giggle.

"What's up?" I ask.

"I'm so sorry, it's awful of me." She giggles more.

"Aw, you can tell me! I'm sure it's not awful."

She meets my eyes, then peruses down to my feet and back up to my face.

"You look so uncomfortable on this bench, like you're sitting on a

134

plastic kids' bench." Her voice is filled with mirth, and a chuckle escapes me.

"It feels like it, too." I laugh along with her.

Danika looks at me, openly curious as the amusement fades, and tilts her head.

"You're not mad about me saying that?"

The question startles me. Who the hell would be mad about the obvious? Never mind, there are plenty of alphas in the world who have egos bigger than my balls. I have it on good authority from my guys that they're pretty big, too.

"Nah, I know I'm a big guy, it's comical for sure." I grin.

She huffs a laugh. "Not my experience, that's for sure."

"Well, I'm happy to be a better experience," I tell her, watching for her smile to appear, a bubbly feeling courses through me as she grants me the view I was hoping for.

"So, um, you wanted to meet?"

I clear my throat. "Yes. Um, I mentioned that we were all worried about you, and I want you to know we meant that. We all really like you, Danika, and I'm hoping if it's just the two of us, you can tell me what went wrong and how we can fix it?"

Her eyes leave mine and stare out into the distance in front of her. Her fingers twist together over and over again, her eyes searching as she thinks. My body responds to the nerves rolling off her, wanting to hold her close and keep her safe from whatever it is she's upset about. After what feels like several hours, she finally lets out a deep sigh.

"My past is not ... um, easy, I suppose is the best word for it," she tells me.

A rueful smile tugs at my lips as my mind goes to my own childhood trauma. We all have some, but I think that Danika might be able to relate to mine; it sounds just as serious. Wonder's face flashes through my mind, and my heart clenches, but I push the grief to the side while I focus on Danika. This is about her, not me. My mouth opens to respond, but Danika's eyes are still fixed in the distance and she continues her thoughts.

"The town I grew up in was small, and I was one of two omegas. Shortly after I presented, there was a gathering out at a bonfire. I wasn't supposed to go, but when I was sixteen, I thought I knew everything." She laughs ruefully.

"All teenagers do," I agree softly.

She scoffs, "Right."

Silence descends again, and I stretch my arm out behind her on the bench, ensuring my arm is fully on the bench and nowhere near her.

"Sorry, not trying to hit on you, just trying to get comfortable. Unless you *want* me to hit on you? I'd be happy to oblige," I explain with a small smile.

She shakes her head, laughing without any pleasure to it. "You're fine. In fact, I actually don't mind at all and that almost feels worse. I don't like alphas as a general rule. But I like you. And Emmett. And Colin. I don't understand it. However, when I caught Colin's scent, I completely panicked. All the bad memories came swirling in and wouldn't leave. Deep down, I wanted to be comforted by you guys, but I would start to panic again when I remembered Colin's scent."

Well fuck, I wasn't expecting the issue to be a visceral scent reaction. Colin's going to blame himself even though nobody has a choice in what their scent is.

"Fuck," I say.

"Fuck," she replies.

"I'd give you a hug but you mentioned you're not a hugger," I offer.

"Aw shit. I, uh, I do like hugs, but I haven't had the best history with touch, and I'm pretty sure that I have Touch Sickness, if not Touch Loss," she confesses.

Dammit, this beautiful, wonderful woman has been through more than anyone should. There's alpha trauma, which tells me there's some sort of assault in her past, and to purposefully avoid touch is miserable for omegas. If she's truly in Touch Sickness phase, then she's plagued by fatigue and tingling/numb skin. Full blown Touch Loss? Most of that goes away, but she would never be able to feel a match, and I can't comprehend that level of devastation for someone.

"I'm so sorry you have to live with that. Do you know for sure which it is?" I ask.

"Probably Touch Loss, but every now and again I get a numb feeling in parts of my body, so maybe there's still hope. I doubt it, but maybe." She sighs. "Anyway, yeah, the campfire smell isn't something that I can handle, and touching is mostly off-limits. I'm too complicated to be bothered with."

Danika stands to leave, and in my shock I almost let her. Thankfully, my alpha instincts are sharper than I am, and I shoot to my feet, standing in front of her, but making sure she has plenty of room to go around me if she really wants to leave.

"Please don't go. It doesn't matter to any of us if you can't feel your match. We're happy if you are or if you're not. Plus, there has to be a way to figure out the scent issue. Please, give us a chance to make things work," I plead with her.

She lets out a shaky breath, her eyes going a bit glassy.

"Why? Why am I so special to you? Why am I worth the effort?" Her voice wobbles, but she's determined not to cry.

"Your soul speaks to all of us. When we saw the paintings, we just *knew* you. You are filled with hope but don't want to tell anyone, and you see good and bad in everything. You guard yourself fiercely, and we've never seen anyone so beautiful. Plus, you're hot." I grin at the last comment, showing it's a joke.

A laugh bursts out of her, short but sweet, before she sobers, blinking rapidly as she tries to keep her tears in. One leaks out, and without thinking, I reach up to wipe it away. My world shifts in that moment, and it almost feels like a sudden stop on a rollercoaster. Tingles break out all through my body, concentrating the most at my fingertips where I touched her skin.

Air has never tasted sweeter to me, and I want to cocoon myself around Danika, pulling her into me and protecting her however I can. Nobody exists in this moment between us, and my fingers hover in the air as our eyes stare unflinchingly into each other. Did she feel it, too? The shift in her center of gravity? Does she revolve around me as I do her? Letting her go would be the worst pain I can think of, but caging her and making her miserable is unfathomable. Slowly, as if moving through molasses, her hand floats to where I touched her skin, as if she's trying to keep my touch there.

"Dani," I breathe, the nickname not registering as I say it.

"Jonah. Wh-What was that? I felt ... I don't know. Something, but it was so quick, like a tickle on my skin."

"Will it freak you out if I say we're a match?" I ask her, keeping my voice low.

Her eyes bounce around my face, looking for any sign of insincerity or a prank. A smile tugs at my lips when I realize she lingers there before snapping her eyes up.

"I ... I don't know. Yes? Maybe? I don't know how I feel about the possibility of a match," she whispers.

The next interaction is going to be critical, I can tell. We're standing close and she seems to be accepting, but I can sense the underlying tension thrumming through her. My tongue darts out, licking my lips as I muster up the words I want to say to her.

"Danika, I want you, all of you, however you'll have me. We are a match, and I'm praying that you won't run from this. If you need space, though, I'll give it to you, so will Emmett and Colin. Please don't shut us out, though." My voice rasps at the end as my emotions break through.

She swallows hard and takes a small step closer, watching my reaction carefully. I bend slightly, but we're close enough that she doesn't have to reach far even if I hadn't bent close. She meets my lips, and I clench my hands at my side so I don't sweep her up and ruin her boundaries. I refuse to set the pace with her unless she asks me to, no matter how much I want to pin her down and fuck her until she forgets her own name.

A gasp escapes her as she feels my lips on hers, and I understand completely how overwhelming the feeling is. The kiss is soft, gentle, and we spend a moment sharing these soft kisses with no rush and no push for more. I pull back when she does, and the peaceful bliss on her face is everything. Her next words put me on Cloud Nine.

"Okay, Match, let's talk."

Chapter 19

Danika

I'm pretty sure that Jonah pulled a fast one on me. The man is too sexy for his own good, and his innocent "you're amazing" talk turned me into a puddle. I'm on to his devious plans. Next time I see him, I'm gonna throw him down and kiss him. No, wait, I'm going to give him shit. Yes, that's the one. Today is a complete lounge day, and I make no apologies as I scurry around in threadbare leggings, an oversized hoodie, and the messiest bun that has ever existed. I attack the pile of bedding in my room again, frustrated.

"Where the fuck is it?" I grumble.

I hear a beep and nosedive in that direction. My hands wrap around a small, square object and I whoop in victory. Take that, phone. I found you! Turning the screen on, I scan the messages from Sophie.

> Sophie: Girl! You promised an update and you said you had no extra time. Are you going to text me at any time? I don't want to die of old age over here.

Me: 😊

I dial her number before she can reply.

"You cheeky bitch," she answers, laughing.

"What would you do without me?"

"I'd waste away before realizing I can fill the void with cookies."

I laugh. "Fair enough."

I stay on the call with Sophie as I get my laptop and snacks to set up on the couch.

"So I need more information on what happened at the park," she demands.

"Well, Jonah and I had a good talk, and I actually told him a little about why I freaked out." I sigh.

"I knew that part, which I'm *insanely* proud of you for, by the way. I want to know what else happened. You were incredibly vague in your texts," she demands.

"Ugh, *fine*. So ... I agreed to do a video chat with Colin—"

I get cut off by a high-pitched squeal and I sigh with a mix of amusement and irritation.

"Which is happening in about ten minutes," I finish.

"Oh shit! Okay, be quick with the other stuff so you can actually talk to your beta boy."

I laugh. "I'm not sure he's mine, but I'll go with it. Um, there is one big thing."

"*I knew it! Spill*," she shouts.

"Uh, well, Jonah touched my face. I had a weird leakage running down my face, and he just reached up and wiped it away," I confess.

There's silence on Sophie's end.

"Sophie?"

"And?" Her voice sounds a little choked up.

"He said we're a match," I confess.

"Danika, oh my god this is amazing!" She's definitely crying.

"Why are you crying? Should I not have told you? Shit, I didn't mean to rub in it your face or anything!"

"No, no, Dani. I'm just so damn happy for you. He is a *good* guy, and I know you guys will work through things. Did you feel ..."

Dammit, I was going to avoid telling her this part. I'm not sure what to make of it and I wanted to think through it first. Sophie would respect that if I insisted, but I also know that telling her sooner rather than later will be easier. I just need to say it.

"A little, yeah," I whisper. "It wasn't much, just a small tingle where his fingers touched and some goosebumps. It wasn't anything life altering, but it wasn't a normal feeling. He feels more important now, but no life changing moment."

"Danika, this is so amazing and I'm so *fucking* happy for you!" she squeals.

I glance at the clock and realize it's almost time to video with Colin.

"Hey, I gotta go, talk later?"

Sophie sighs. "Okay, fine, go enjoy your beta boy! Call me if you need me, okay? Don't self-sabotage."

"Yeah, yeah, love you," I say with a smile.

"Samesies."

I grasp the phone in my hand for a few more minutes before setting it to silence and placing it on the table next to my laptop. I check over my supplies again and realize I've forgotten my water, so once I've grabbed some, I settle into my throne of blankets.

Originally, I planned to settle on the couch, but then realized Colin would be looking up my nose from that angle. No, thank you. So I dragged a cushion to the floor and surrounded it with blankets to make it extra cozy. My omega is really showing her nesting instincts today. Part of me wonders if Jonah is part of that, but I don't have time to think through that right now, I need to focus on this conversation with Colin.

When my computer shows the request for a video call, I accept it and am rewarded with a face that makes me a little dumbstruck. His wild, curly hair is in a bun that's almost as messy as mine, his jawline square, and there's a hint of a dimple in his cheek. The part that draws me in the most is his soulful, brown eyes, looking at me as if he's always known who I am. My internal reaction is instant, and it's familiar, like when I make my art but have to show it, a jumble of nerves that I dread and love.

"Um, hi," I say, feeling my cheeks flush a bit.

His responding smile is pure sunshine, and I'm concerned I've started drooling.

"Hey there," he replies. "I'm glad you had time to do this call with me."

"Um, yeah, same." A smile tugs at my face.

Colin grins at me. "Am I going to render you speechless any time you see me? You're going to give me an ego."

A small giggle escapes me. "I'll try to keep that in mind. I don't want to make that ego too large."

"I have a feeling you are going to keep me on my toes."

I flush, heat flooding into my cheeks as I think of the next topic I want to tackle. He deserves an apology from me after I panicked, and I don't think we can create any kind of relationship with this hanging over my head.

"Before we start talking, I wanted to make sure that you know I'm sorry. I didn't mean to just leave you hanging. It was rude to leave without saying anything," I tell him, unable to meet his eyes as I apologize.

There's silence after my apology, and I'm not sure what to do next.

Colin

She's sorry? She doesn't have anything to be sorry for! Danika had a reaction, not necessarily something she could even control in the moment. I hope she doesn't always think she has to apologize for something like that. Resolve fills me as I determine to show her she doesn't need to apologize for being herself.

"Danika, sweetheart, can you look at me?" I ask gently.

She's looking down, and at my request, she slowly brings her eyes up, shining with guilt and tears.

"You have nothing to be sorry for. You had a reaction to something you weren't expecting and it scared you. If you had thrown something at me and it hurt, I may have expected apologies in the form of boo-boo kisses."

She giggles at me, which makes my chest puff up in pride. We had a rocky start for our in-person interactions, but it won't always be that way.

"Thanks, Colin. I'm just so embarrassed by my actions. I didn't think that my past still had such a strong pull on me."

"It's okay, there's nothing to be embarrassed of," I assure her.

She nods, and her teeth catch on that luscious bottom lip of hers. I want to take her lip and pull it free so I can bite it instead. My heart has been slowly falling for her, and I want to show her that any way I can. My tongue darts out, as if I can taste her here and now.

"Okay," she breathes, a smile tugging at her lips, but not fully emerging.

"Anything else you want to get out of the way? Embarrassing tattoos? Weird drunken confessions you said during a girls' night?" I tease lightly.

"You'll just have to wait and see what tattoos I have, if any. That's earned knowledge," she shoots back.

My heart falls a little more for her. I don't want to be a barrier for anyone joining our pack, but I love a little spunk thrown my way. It makes life more interesting.

"So, tell me a bit about yourself," she says, changing the subject away from herself.

"Well, I'm the oldest child in my family, I have a younger brother, and the baby of the family is my sister. It's the typical three child dynamic, all the pressure is on me, my brother feels like he's always a disappointment, and my sister grew up spoiled rotten." I grin.

Danika grins back. "Sounds pretty perfect."

"It was a great childhood, obviously not perfect, and when I was in the midst of it, it didn't feel great. Looking back now, though, my parents really encouraged us to be ourselves. I think it bit them in the ass a little."

"How so?"

"Well, I chose not to go into the family business and just take my inheritance."

She blinks and her jaw drops a little. "Excuse me, inheritance? Is your family full of billionaires?"

A nervous chuckle escapes me. "Uh, not like multi-billionaires. Does that make it better or worse?"

"I don't know, maybe it depends on how your family makes their money."

"Not mafia or drugs or anything," I assure her quickly.

Danika just grins at me, and I realize she was teasing.

"Oh, you got me good there! My family is mostly generational wealth, but also good investments. My parents originally wanted me to be part of their investment company, but it never made me happy or fulfilled. So, I walked away."

As I talk, that familiar feeling of shame and embarrassment wells up in me, but I try my best to ignore it. My parents have said they hold no hard feelings and nothing has changed dynamically in the family. My sister and my brother joined the company, and they're doing wonderfully.

"Gosh, that had to be difficult for you. Do you still talk to your parents? Did they disown you or some shit?" She almost sounds offended on my behalf.

I chuckle. "No. I mean, at first it was difficult. My parents didn't really understand why I wanted to walk away, and we had some ... shall we say 'spirited' conversations?"

"Oh boy," she comments, popping food into her mouth.

Can I just say that watching a girl you're into be completely herself is crazy sexy? Danika joined this call in a cocoon of blankets, her hair up in a messy ass bun that rivals mine, and is just casually chomping on snacks. I don't think she has any idea how alluring she is, but I want to make it my mission to show her. Assuming she can ever be in the same room as me. My feet are getting ahead of me ... I need to win her trust before anything else.

"Yeah, it wasn't pretty, but my siblings are both invested in the company's success now and they're doing wonderfully. Family gatherings aren't tense or anything ... well, unless Seamus and Siobhan start to bicker about which of them is performing better at work."

Danika grins. "Which one is it, really?"

"One of their co-workers who is aiming for a seat on the board of directors one day," I answer her with a grin.

She giggles, and I'm pretty sure it injects butterflies right into my stomach. I want her to giggle all the time, but now I'm afraid my stomach would take flight if I heard it that often.

"Any dark skeletons I need to be aware of? Bodies you've hid, graffiti you put all over town? A secret society that fell apart?" Danika gets more animated with each idea, and I chuckle.

"No, no dark skeletons, although you can always graffiti on my heart." The terrible line pops out of my mouth before I realize it's happening.

We both stare at each other, waiting for the other to relax. She cracks first and throws her head back in a shout of laughter that gets me laughing as well. The two of us are cracking up, and I don't remember the last time I laughed so hard. Danika has tears streaming down her cheeks, but the second we calm, our eyes lock again and the laughing resumes.

"I cannot believe you said that," she finally gets out.

I shrug with only a little embarrassment.

"Usually I'm not so cheesy, but sometimes nerves get the best of me," I confess.

Her smile is light and welcoming, and I feel something loosen in my chest.

"Sometimes cheesy is too fun to pass up," she tells me.

"So tell me about your favorite color," I prompt her.

I'm settled in now, ready to enjoy our conversation and get to know this gorgeous omega.

Chapter 20

Emmett

There are ants buzzing beneath my skin, making my fingers twitch and my feet move, a whirlwind of activity that I can't seem to stop. We need more wood ... some kindling, and some logs for burning. *Oh, I need to get the roasting sticks from the car, can't forget those.* I don't want to look like someone who can't even provide roasting sticks.

"We can't look like losers, Gertie," I tell her as I jog to where we parked.

I start rifling through our camping gear, searching for what I need. This afternoon needs to be perfect; we need to look like we have all our shit together. Look, I love my men, I do, but they're clearly not as in tune with providing things as I am. I finally find them folded up and let out a small shout of success.

"Take that, camping gear. You can't keep my sticks from me!" I stick my tongue out at the trunk of the car before taking the sticks to our small area.

My men are sitting and relaxing near the fire pit, a beer in hand for both of them. I shake my head and click my tongue at them in disappointment.

"Do you see this, Gertie? This is what I have to work with," I complain.

Gertie chooses not to engage in this situation. Sometimes she can be such a chicken. Clearing my throat, I set the sticks down near the rest of the s'mores supplies and give them both a glare. Jonah and Colin glance at each other, bewildered by my stare before looking back at me.

"Sorry?" Jonah asks.

"You should be! I'm over here gathering all our wood and all the supplies while you two sit and relax!" I may or may not stamp my foot like a child. I admit nothing.

Colin smiles at me. "Baby, we have all the wood from the park's wood stacks that we need, the fire is already going, and everything is set out. Come sit with me."

I pick the sticks back up and shake them in the air.

"You forgot *these!*" I tell him, still indignant.

"How can we make it up to you?" Colin asks, indulgently.

I sniff and put my noise in the air as if I'm a rich snob. "Snuggles are a good start."

"I wouldn't mind some snuggles," a sweet voice behind me chimes in.

A lesser man would jump in the air from surprise and let out a manly squeak in the process. Thankfully, I managed to keep the squeak in.

"Stargazer!" I say loudly.

Do I shout it? No, it's a loud noise, not a shout.

She giggles at my reaction, and just like that my ants turn into butterflies and soar through me in exhilaration.

"Hey, guys," she greets us, her hands playing with the strap on her purse.

"Please tell me you have s'mores supplies," a new voice says.

It's then that I realize her emotional-support Sophie is here, too. I won't lie, a part of me was hoping that Sophie wouldn't come so we could take all of Stargazer's attention, but I know better than most when an emotional support is needed. Gertie goes everywhere with me, except in the bedroom, she doesn't get to see that.

"Emotional-Support Sophie!" I exclaim in greeting.

She rolls her eyes in annoyance, but I can see a trace of amusement in there, too. There's no fooling me, she has fun with my antics. I'm lovable, what can I say?

"Hey, you two. Glad you could make it!" Jonah greets them warmly, standing so he can move closer to Danika.

His body posture is open, giving Danika the choice of physical contact or not. She looks hesitant and seems like she's going to keep her distance until Sophie shoulder checks her. Hard. Danika trips over her feet, but stays upright, glaring at Sophie.

"Sorry?" she says, unrepentant.

Danika shakes her head but has a smile on her face when she wraps her arms around Jonah. How is an innocent hug something that looks so sexy? The way her head rests perfectly on his shoulder, and his arms wrapped around her. They're a puzzle that has come together, matching up perfectly. There are two more spots that need filling, though, and I can't wait for her to be comfortable enough to do that with Colin and I. Sure I got to cuddle her through an emotional breakdown, but that was zero skin to skin and was about comfort, not a purposeful act of pleasure.

The area we're having the fire in isn't very large, it fits probably six or so, and when I make my way over to Colin during the hug, people can hear me more than I assumed.

"Is it bad I want to grab her ass?" I ask Colin.

Danika pulls her head back from the hug and looks at me, eyes wide with shock.

"Emmett!" she scolds, but I see the smile she's trying to hide.

"Yes?" I look at her, the picture of innocence.

Her eyes narrow playfully. "I'm keeping an eye on you."

"Please do." I waggle my eyebrows at her.

"Come sit," Jonah says with a chuckle to the girls.

Everyone's laughing at the exchange, and it makes the atmosphere relaxed and cozy.

I take a seat in one of the saucer chairs, while Colin and Jonah settle in our three-person camping sofa. Sophie and Danika take the two-person camping couch. We do have a spare single chair since we weren't sure where she would want to sit. Danika, I mean, not Sophie. We don't dislike Sophie, but our focus here is Danika.

While they settle in some, I can tell Danika is taking measured breaths. Inhale for three, hold it for three, and exhale for five. The scent of the bonfire is affecting her, even if she doesn't want to admit or show it. I make sure to keep an eye on her as we go through the time we have together, I'd hate to have her spiral. Jonah offers them drinks, and while Danika opens hers, I see Sophie lean over and say something in her ear. Danika closes her eyes and nods, her expression smooths out a bit, and I can see her absorbing whatever Sophie said and holding it close.

"Soooo, do we talk about the elephant, or ..." I draw out, trying to tackle some of the hard stuff first so everyone can relax.

Jonah looks up at Danika, shrugging lightly. She nods back at him, and when his mouth opens to speak, Sophie cuts in.

"*Danika,* would you like to speak about it? Nobody will push you, but it may be a *good idea* to say it all out loud," Sophie says softly but insistently.

Despite the look she shoots at Sophie, Danika sits up straighter and begins to talk.

"Well, I think everyone is aware, but in the spirit of transparency and all that healthy relationship bullshit, I've got two things to add. Jonah and I are confirmed matches, and I'm happy about it but also scared as fuck. If he's my match, it's likely that you guys, Emmett and Colin, are also a match. Typically, the scent of bonfire makes me flashback to some bad stuff, and I don't know if I can handle smelling it all the time." She gets all that said in probably under ten seconds.

"That's some fast talk there, darlin'," I tell her with a smile.

She chuckles a little and her face flushes just a bit. "Sorry, I just wanted it out."

"It's fine," Colin assures her. "This whole thing is new and uncertain. You're allowed to express that however you need."

Danika shoots him a soft look, and while I want all her looks aimed at me, it makes my heart go all gooey that she's giving it to my pack-mates. This is going to work, I feel it in my bones, and Gertie agrees.

"How are you feeling right now with all of us here?" I ask.

Her poor bottom lip is tortured some more before Danika decides on her answer.

"Terrified, but okay? The smoke smell is a bit triggering, but I'm constantly reminding myself that I'm not trapped, you guys aren't my past, and none of you are pushing me for anything. It's reassuring," she answers.

"Well, we're not pushing *you* for anything, but I'm definitely going to push a marshmallow onto this roastin' stick," I tease her as I stand.

"See? I told you I'm not normally the one with bad lines," Colin comments with a smirk.

Danika giggles, and all of us relax just a bit more. Laughing means she's comfortable enough to be amused and that has to be a good thing. I offer to make her one, and she lets me, which makes my alpha puff his chest out like the neanderthal he is. I get the same thrill when I can serve either of my men, too. Being able to provide for the ones I love is an inherent need as an alpha.

We move into a comfortable atmosphere of chatting and laughing, and I know all three of us are watching Danika slowly relax. Sophie glances between us and Danika, a knowing smirk on her face, before she goes back to her book. I haven't seen her turn the page yet so I'm guessing she brought it to avoid conversation, not read. It's the perfect emotional-support move; she can drop it quickly and be unobtrusive in the meantime. Conversation continues to flow freely, and I notice that the sky is moving closer to twilight. Danika was insistent she did not want to be near the fire at night.

Clearing my throat, I look up at Danika and we lock eyes.

"I have a question for you," I tell her, the ants back beneath my skin.

"What's up?"

"It doesn't have to be today, but I wondered if I could touch you soon," I sort of ask her.

"Ummm ..." She looks a little concerned and seems speechless.

Sighing, Jonah rubs his face with one hand.

"Emmett, ask a different way, man. That was super creepy," he tells me.

Was it? I think through what I said, but I just wanted to touch her skin. *Why is that—* Ohhh. Oh, I get it now. Yeah, that is awkward. My eyes fly to Danika's in panic.

"I mean, just like hands or something! I'm not trying to be creepy. I wouldn't be creepy with you. I hope you know that. Well, unless you *want* me to be creepy with you? It's an odd kink but I'm not gonna yuck your yum, baby," I tell her.

I don't know why Jonah, Colin, and Sophie are all giggling like this is the funniest thing ever. I meant it! I'm in for whatever kinks she wants. Thankfully, Danika is a kinder person than the other people here.

"It's fine, Emmett, and I don't think I mind. If Jonah is a match, you likely will be, too, right? I don't see you being upset about it either way." She smiles.

I smirk at her. "I'm yours, match or no."

Soon the sky is dusky enough that Danika calls it; she doesn't want to be outside in the dark with the campfire smell. I can't say I blame her. I mean, I don't know exactly what her trauma is, but when you have it, you have it. I'm not going to judge what triggers her. She and Sophie help with getting some of the chairs put away, and when I look over fifty feet to where we're parked, it's just our car and one other. Good, they must be that other car, then. Unless Gertie figured out how to drive and tricked me. She's sneaky like that.

"Emmett?" Danika calls once all the supplies are ready for transport.

"Yeah?"

She bites her lip before straightening with resolve. "Would you walk me to my car? Well, Sophie's car?"

"I would be delighted." I grin at her.

We walk next to each other, comfortable in the small silence that accompanies us. It's familiar, even though we've really only been on one date. That time in the taxidermy museum was absolutely perfect, and this moment is one more that's going in the memory bank. Her hair is illuminated by the low sun, and I'm captivated by the hints of blue that seem to shine from it. Skin glowing, I can almost see each individual lash as she closes her eyes to take a deep breath.

When we reach the car, she turns to me, and I instinctively turn so we are facing each other. Silently, she raises one hand and touches my cheek. If I thought she was my world before, she is now my entire universe. A zapping feeling encompasses my entire body, and my alpha is rising up inside, recognizing our match and doing the equivalent of "I told you so!" to me.

The smile that Danika graces me with is heaven on earth. Tears make her eyes shine bright in this lighting, and my hand slowly raises to cover hers as she touches my cheek. A laugh bubbles up from her, and I'm sure my answering smile is just as big as hers.

My match. My Omega.

Chapter 21

Danika

Swirling my brush into my next color, I can't help but smile as I think through last weekend again. When Jonah touched me, it was a pleasant surprise to feel a small tingle in my cheek. However, when I touched Emmett's face, I truly felt a tiny zap, almost like a quick bolt of static electricity. I don't know if it's because I initiated the touch, but I had expected a similar small tingle. My world shifted when I touched his smooth, dark skin, and I'm pretty sure my knees almost buckled for a moment. That would have been a bit embarrassing, so I'm glad it didn't happen.

As my painting slowly comes to life, I wonder what it would be like if I were to actually act on the fact that I have two matches. Sophie squealed the entire way home after our fire at the park, and I couldn't wipe the smile off my own face. The feeling of having two matches is absolutely incredible, but the idea of acting on it is terrifying. Actually letting someone in my life so completely is almost unthinkable.

I don't really think the guys would do anything to hurt me, but what if I'm not up to their standards? What happens when I slip back and get lost in my thoughts of other men who took what they wanted? This is the kind of shit that keeps me from dating anyone or getting serious with anyone. Burdening them with my baggage seems like too much to ask, but I know deep in my bones that it wouldn't be that way. I wish my rational mind would catch up with my emotional side.

This is one of the reasons I stayed away from relationships since moving to the city. Too much thinking and too much complication. There really hasn't been any complications, if I'm honest, but I know they're coming. They always do.

Thoroughly distracted and out of my flow, I sigh and decide to be done for today. Trying to paint right now isn't getting me anywhere. My phone rings while I'm doing some light clean up, and I look to see it is Jonah. A smile tugs at my mouth, and I answer the call.

"Hey," I greet him.

"Hey, you. How are you?" he asks, his deep voice washing over me.

"Pretty good. Just did a little painting, so making some progress here."

"You must have a sixth sense ... I was calling to sweet talk you, then sweet talk you into doing another gallery showing," he says, teasing.

I laugh as I move to my living room, knowing he is completely serious even though he's teasing.

"I don't know, it could be a lot of work. I'd have to be around this really hot guy for hours, it sounds like a hardship to me," I tease back.

His chuckle seeps into my senses, and I find myself wanting to hear more of it instead of shying away. Stupid men and their stupid sexiness.

"Well, maybe I'll have to show up and save you from this other hot guy. Wouldn't want this whole thing to be a hardship," he shoots back.

It's my turn to chuckle, and the ease between us is as natural as breathing.

"I'm glad you'll be there to save me. When are you thinking of having the showing?" I ask.

He hums. "I want to do a special exhibition in a few weeks, so I'm hoping you could be the headliner for it, with a few smaller artists showing one or two pieces."

"Me? Headlining the exhibition?" I blink.

"Baby, your solo exhibition was one of my most successful events since opening Colorful World. We have frequent calls asking if you'll show again."

"Really?" I ask, grinning with joy that people are enjoying my work. People, not just a single person.

"Really, I swear. So now I have to keep my customers happy, and thankfully I have a direct line to the artist."

I can't help but laugh, joy bubbling out of me. "Okay, yeah, I'll do the showing. Is it for anything specific or just a general showing event?"

Jonah gets a little quiet, and I can hear the difference in his voice when he speaks again.

"It's the anniversary of my sister's death."

I plop myself down on the couch in surprise. That was not on my life bingo card: learn about someone's family member dying too young.

"Wow, um, will you tell me about her?"

He clears his throat. "Yeah, she was great. We lost her when she was ten, it was a complete freak accident. She was so full of color and life, I always wondered how she managed to pack so much vibrancy into such a small body."

"She sounds awesome just from that description." I smile.

"She really was. Her name was Wonder, and I absolutely sang that song to her just to bother her. I would always change the words to see what she would do, like a pushy big brother should."

"There's a song called 'Wonder'?"

"Well, it was Wonderwall, but I never hesitated to use it."

We chuckle at that, and hearing him reminisce is strangely comforting despite the fact that I have no idea who this girl was. She must have been really special in life ... well, I guess even in death she's special.

"My big brother was one of my closest friends growing up, but high school has a way of changing things," I admit.

"I wish I could have seen her take high school by storm. I'm sure she would have her fair share of problems, but Wonder was kind to everyone, even kids who picked on her. She actually loved to paint and got teased for constantly having paint on her body somewhere. Her love of art is a big reason why I wanted to open a gallery. I can make a mean stick figure, but that's about it."

My smile is wide. "I'm sure it's not *that* bad!"

"Well, if you ever want an ego boost, just ask to see me draw and you'll feel great about yourself!"

He sets off my giggles again before continuing.

"Anyway, I named the gallery Colorful World in her honor, and I like to do some kind of special event on her death anniversary to remember her by."

"I think that's beautiful. I'd be happy to participate in it, I'm just not sure what to show. When is it?"

We talk through more detail on when the event is and what kind of vibe he's going for. The event is a celebration of life and death, twisted with some hope, bringing that childish joy to everything that we easily miss as adults.

I think through the paintings I have ready to go, and I believe there are two that may fit. I'm still working on one that shows a woman blooming, and I could definitely finish that in time. I wonder if I could get one more completed before the event. I'm sure I could fill in with some of my older pieces, but the idea to create new has a hold of me. My mind immediately thinks of Emmett when I consider childish joy and hope. He's such a positive person, and I think capturing him on canvas would be an enjoyable challenge.

The event is about two months out, so I could do it in time, I think. Might need to push myself a little, but maybe that's a good thing for me right now. I'm pushing personal boundaries, so why not stretch myself creatively, too? Speaking of personal boundaries ...

"So, I was thinking about our fire evening today," I tell Jonah.

"Yeah?"

"Uh, I, um, well, maybe you guys would, if you want to, no pressure, uh, maybe you guys could come overforafireatmyplace?"

Well, that was the most awkward thing I've said in a long time. Tongue tied then way too fast. Jonah is quiet on the other side, and I close my eyes in embarrassment even though I'm alone. One more second of silence and I'm about to give in and take it back, but Jonah saves me from myself.

"We'd love to, Dani," he says, and I can hear the smile in his words.

A high-pitched giggle escapes me, exposing my nerves. Jonah gives a small huff of amusement.

"If you're comfortable with that, I know all three of us absolutely want to see you again. Will it be too much for you, though?"

I feel a little swoon of my heart as his thoughtfulness shows itself.

"It's okay with me. The fire pit is a little ways from the house, and we won't actually be in the house, so plenty of space."

"Should we make it a dinner date? We could bring hotdogs to roast and s'mores for desserts," Jonah offers.

"That sounds great! I'm definitely a fan of hot dogs. So classic."

"I like to add some tacos in with my hot dogs," Jonah says, his voice going a bit sultry.

"Like a hot dog taco? That sounds like it would taste funny. Tacos should be juicy," I say, my brows drawing together at the idea of a hot dog sitting in a tortilla.

"Good point. A juicy taco is delicious, too, just different delicious," he continues in that voice.

What the hell is he talking about? This conversation is getting confusing. It's just food. It shouldn't be causing this odd feeling as I hear him. It's not a bad feeling, but I can't quite label it; I just know I want to understand what he's talking about, but if he never tells me then I'm just happy listening to his low voice.

"Well, I know I'm going to enjoy eating the hot dogs you guys bring," I tell him, "but tacos would be way to messy around a fire."

He clicks his tongue. "I don't know, your taco would be pretty delicious."

"M-My taco?"

Oh shit, is he saying what I think he's saying?

"Your taco. It would be my new favorite meal," he confirms.

"Oh."

I'm quiet for a moment while I try to think of how to respond.

"Sorry, did I make it weird?" Jonah asks when the silence goes too long.

I shake my head, trying to remove the clutter of thoughts that are built up now.

"No! Sorry, I was just busy thinking about if you like the hot dogs you're bringing or just general hot dogs," I ask, hoping I sound sexy, but knowing it's probably just awkward.

He chuckles. "I've always liked hot dogs *and* tacos, but the hot dogs and taco I have now are the only ones I want."

Heat rolls through me as I imagine Jonah's mouth bobbing between Emmett's legs. *Fuck.*

"Do all three of you agree on that?" My voice is definitely breathy now.

"Absolutely we do."

"Oh. All at the same time?" I can't help but ask, my panties getting wet as I continue the conversation.

"Sometimes, but sometimes I like to give them special attention. They deserve to be savored once in a while."

"Will you ... will you tell me?" I all but whisper, my clit pulsing with my heartbeat until all I can think of is getting relief while Jonah talks.

"Mmmm ... dirty girl. First thing you gotta do is prepare it. Take time to show affection with kisses and bites everywhere. Savoring the feeling of them in your hands."

My fingers crawl down my pants, searching out that little bundle of nerves. I almost detonate at the first swipe. This isn't going to take long.

"Then when it's ready, it needs a long lick, and sometimes it's nice to give it some condiments, so there could be spit thrown on there, too," I hear him moan as he talks, and I'm right there with him.

My breath hitches as I swirl around my clit, alternating between soft strokes and hard circles.

"Jonah, please tell me you're touching yourself," I boldly ask.

The question may be bold but my voice is soft and shaky. My mind can't bring up any memory of being this turned on outside of my heat.

"Oh fuck, baby, I am. I can't stop thinking about how you would taste, how soft you would be surrounding my dick. Are you imagining that? How good I'd feel inside of you?" He drops all pretense now, and it creates more fire that burns through my veins.

"Yes. Oh god, I haven't been this turned on in so long, Jonah. Please help me come," I whine.

"My pleasure. Tease your hole for a second, then plunge two fingers inside and tell me how it feels, then swirl those fingers around your clit, fast and hard. Don't make me wait to hear you, you deserve every drop of pleasure you get." His breathing is harder now.

I follow his instructions, letting him hear how fast my breath is, the little whimpers that escape me, and I can feel my body winding up, about to snap like a rubber band.

"Jonah," I whine.

"Do it, baby. Come for me," he pants through the phone.

His words help me to give myself permission and the rubber band snaps, sending pulses through my body while tingles spread to my head and toes. My pussy is clenching around nothing, making an obscene wet noise as I come harder than I knew I could. On the other end of the phone, Jonah is groaning in pleasure as my name escapes through his lips.

"Fuck, Danika, oh ... oh fuck!"

I can tell when he hits his release, only seconds after mine finishes, and I can't help the lazy smile that appears on my face. That was definitely a fun way to end our conversation. I'd be up for a repeat.

Chapter 22

Danika

My nerves are taking over, and as I make another trip to where I'm creating our fire, I find myself jittering. If my hands are shaking, then there's a driving urge to nitpick every single detail of how things are set up. The only things I need to set up are the chairs, fire ring, and a small table. It's not exactly hard. There's something urging me to do it just right though, and I can't seem to shake that nudge within me to keep fussing over everything.

Should I grab blankets? It's a little chilly but honestly not bad. I'll grab one, that should be plenty. Did I grab drinks? No, the guys said they're bringing everything. Oh! I should go grab the peanut butter cups for s'mores. Don't knock it until you try it. Adding that peanut butter in does something life altering to the taste of marshmallow and graham cracker. The kindling is sitting near one of the chairs, and I've promised myself to try and light the fire tonight. If one of the guys needs to help, I'll relent, but I want to do it on my own.

After a fast walk back to my house, I nab the candy for s'mores and start back toward the fire. A few steps forward, I hear a car pull up and butterflies take off in my stomach, alerting me to something new in my space. Someone other than Sophie. Shit, am I ready for this? It suddenly feels like a terrible idea to let them be here, but what's done is done. I'm not going to kick them out. I move so I'm in view of the driveway and internally scold myself for being a nervous Nelly. I'm a badass, I can do this.

I made it through the last fire and nothing happened, so I have hope for this one, too. Well, I wouldn't mind a little flirting and a kiss or two, but I remind myself that these guys are different and they've shown me that. Not once have they pushed me in a bad way. They've only ever asked things out of concern and to know me better. When Emmett steps out of the car, I feel a wash of peace roll over me. Seeing him brings a calm that I hadn't noticed before. His eyes immediately find mine, and I can see Gertie in his shirt pocket as always. We smile at each other, and he gives me a wink before moving to the trunk.

Jonah steps out next, looking like dessert, and part of me would rather eat him than s'mores tonight. His confidence draws me in every time—not a cocky self-importance, but a quiet assurance that he knows who he is and what he's doing. If he doubts himself, I've never seen him show it. He's wearing a long-sleeved, Henley style shirt, and I just want to unbutton that top one and let some more skin peek out. His blond hair shines in the late afternoon sunlight, drawing my attention like a moth drawn to flame.

Colin escapes the vehicle last, and I note that his movements are extremely cautious. A smirk finds its way to Jonah's mouth as he passes Colin, shaking his head. Apparently, he doesn't think Colin needs to exercise this much caution. I think it's kind of sweet. His curly hair is wild and free today, bouncing around his shoulders like it has a mind of its own. Every time I see him, I realize I've forgotten how damn hot he is. I want to fan myself and check for drool. There isn't the same confidence that Jonah has, but he's as genuine as the other two in his reactions and desire to keep me feeling safe and considered. When our eyes connect, we both light up with a smile, which sets off those damn butterflies again, but in a good way this time. I'm not sure if I really want to scent him without an actual fire yet, so I decide to call out to them.

"Head straight back and a little left from the house, I've got us set up closer to the shore of a small lake." I gesture so Colin can see, then turn and walk away when he nods back at me.

He holds his hand in the air with a thumbs-up, making me huff a small laugh. I was expecting a verbal response, but Colin doesn't seem to fit anything that I think he will. It's fun, if I'm being honest. It's a nice unpredictability instead of a dangerous one. I set my s'mores candy upgrade down and grab some supplies for the fire.

After putting two logs in the ring, I add two more on top, so it looks like a pseudo log cabin, before adding kindling and tinder in the middle. I fuss for a moment before deciding it's good enough and turn to grab my candle lighter from the table behind me.

"Lookin' good."

The voice surprises me, and I gracefully choose to sit on the ground and make a noise of joy when I hear it. That's my story and I'm sticking to it. Standing a few feet downwind from me, Colin has a smile on his face that he's trying to mask but is clearly failing miserably.

"Before you say anything, I chose to sit on the ground," I insist.

Colin gives a mock-serious frown. "Of course you did. Nothing about the sudden movement or small scream indicated accident."

My eyes narrow at him, but he's unrepentant in his amusement, and honestly, I love it. Emmett and Jonah choose that moment to arrive and come all the way to where the chairs are, leaving Colin standing apart from us. A flicker of loneliness crosses his face, but just barely. Determination rises in me. I never want to see him on the outside of the group, so I am *going* to get past this scent thing, no matter what. If I have to wear nose plugs around him, then that's what I'll do.

The fire is calling me, so I turn back to focus on my task of getting this tinder lit. Emmett and Jonah are both giving me looks of extreme uncertainty. I can tell they want to intervene, and I'm tempted to mess with them, but I don't think that will go over well. That's something old me would have enjoyed, which means it's probably a bad idea. Either way, I'm able to light the small tinder bundle in my palm before I carefully settle it in the center of my log structure.

I'm pretty sure the fire gods are shining down on me because the rest of the tinder takes and the kindling picks it up with no problem. In less than two minutes, we have steady flames burning the edges of the logs from the inside. Making a point to inhale the scent of the fire and logs, my eyes rotate between Emmett, Jonah, and Colin. Rewiring my brain isn't going to be easy, but maybe if I keep them in sight while I'm focusing on the scent it will help.

Emmett reaches down and takes my hand before pulling me back up to standing, then he promptly puts his arms around me in a big hug. I inhale his comforting worn leather scent, and try to take in the campfire's scent at the same time. Associating the bad with something new is a way to try and process this, at least that's what the internet said. His hum of pleasure runs through me, calming any nerves that wouldn't settle by my own efforts.

"Good job on the fire, Stargazer," he tells me, pulling back to look at me.

"Thanks!" I turn my head to find Colin and see he's still standing apart from us. "Get over here!"

He grins ruefully and walks over to stand next to Jonah, who wraps an arm around him.

"Let's sit, guys. The fire's stable, so it's time to chill out," I tell them.

I grab the one camping chair I own and watch as Colin and Jonah set up the ones they brought. Emmett ends up in a solo chair next to me, while Colin and Jonah share a double chair with Colin closer to me. My hands shake a little in reaction to the addition of his campfire scent. It's a smell already in the air, but it seems thicker to me now. Air doesn't seem to do anything for me, and I'm worried I can't get enough oxygen.

"Where did you learn to build a fire like that?" Colin asks.

My eyes snap to his.

"The Internet, but I'm good at starting fires, just ask my old town," I say, my reply indicating that my brain is likely offline.

The guys pause at that, and my first thought is to play it out as a joke, but I choose to leave it as is. They need to know the kind of crazy I can be.

"Why is that so hot?" Jonah asks.

"Beats me, but I agree," I hear Emmett say.

A laugh escapes me, my head thrown back. The levity I was worried about was brought forward, but I didn't have to pretend anything and it feels freeing. An underlying need to explain myself has been rooted in me for years now, but it doesn't feel necessary. The instinctive need to placate someone else in the conversation lifts and my smile widens.

"How are you doing with me sitting here?" Colin asks gently.

"Honestly, I was worried at first, but I'm glad you're right here. It's giving me a chance to associate the scent with you and not my shitty past," I admit.

"I'm glad," he replies.

"So, who's ready to put a wiener in their mouth?" Emmett asks.

I burst out laughing at the unexpected innuendo, but Jonah and Colin must be used to this because they just let out small chuckles.

"Show me how you roast a weiner, baby? I need some meat in my mouth," I quip back, lifting my eyebrows at him.

Emmett giggles, delighted with the banter I provided him. He stands and gathers the hot dogs and sets them up on a second table that I completely missed seeing. How in the world did they get that set up without me noticing? Are they secret table ninjas? When I ask Colin about it, he chuckles.

"Not ninjas, unfortunately. You were just really distracted. We knew you had at least one table but figured another never hurts. Would you like a drink?" Colin replies.

I give him a nod, and he stands to move to the cooler, grabbing me a beer. It's not my first choice, but a nice beer with these guys feels right. Of course, while Colin is up, Jonah slides over to take his spot, grabbing my hand in the process. The cheesy goof then brings my hand to his mouth and kisses the back of it.

"Hey, beautiful," he says softly.

"Hey yourself."

"I'm glad that this is ending up to be okay with you. I know you and Colin have hit it off virtually, but this scent association has to be difficult."

I shrug at him before taking the beer Colin offers me with a smile. "It's definitely more work than I anticipated, but it's worth it. You all make me happy, and you're my matches, I don't want to walk away from that," I say honestly.

"Well, we don't know if we're *all* matches," Colin teases.

Emmett chuckles from the other side of the fire ring. "Big talk, man. Better put your money where your mouth is."

Colin grins at me. "Wanna find out?"

I bite my lip gently before nodding. "Yeah, let's do this."

We stand and face each other, close enough that Jonah gets a close-up show. We look into each others' eyes for a moment, and I expect him to touch my face or grab my hand, but this smooth guy does neither.

He leans in, and our lips connect.

Chapter 23

Jonah

Colin is a smooth son of a bitch, and I couldn't be prouder of him. We all expected him to touch her with his fingers, same as the rest of us. My jaw drops, and I'm sure Emmett's as well, as I watch their lips meet. Panic shoots through me once the shock wears off. Will she be okay with this? Will it set off her PTSD, or will she lean into it? My alpha wants to tear them apart and smother her to ensure she stays with us.

Slamming him back mentally, I wait to see what happens next. Watching her and Colin kiss is incredibly hot, and my own body starts to respond to the image. A glance at Emmett shows that he's not unaffected, his pants showing a bigger bulge than usual.

Danika lets out a shaky sigh when they part, and her hand comes up to touch her lips in awe. She and Colin keep their gazes locked together, and tears shimmer in her eyes. I'm halfway to standing before she lets out a small laugh and brings Colin back to her for another kiss. His hands move to her waist, pulling her hips flush against him.

"Dani, do you want *his* wiener instead of the ones I'm making? I can put this away!" Emmett teases from the fire.

They break apart suddenly, and Colin turns to frown at Emmett.

"Way to cock block over there!" he says loudly.

Emmett holds a hand to his chest as if wounded. "Could you please not be vulgar around Gertie? She's very sensitive! If I wasn't holding these delicious roasting wieners, I'd be covering her ears!"

Dani giggles at them before launching into a full belly laugh. My eyes are glued to her, watching her weave her spell over us effortlessly. As she continues to laugh, a snort flies out of her, and for a moment she looks horrified, but then starts laughing again. Colin and Emmett have fully joined in, but I can't help myself from sitting outside of the laughter, watching the moment to try and permanently ink it in my mind.

We settle into the process of roasting up hot dogs and eating dinner, of course various jokes and friendly barbs included. It's wonderful to watch Danika slowly relax into our environment and get comfortable. There's something in my soul that settles, knowing that we were able to get her to this point, that she trusts us. It's everything to me and my alpha. After we're appropriately full, Danika jumps up and squeals with excitement.

"Guys, are you ready for s'mores?! I have a special ingredient that makes them like twenty times better than normal," she tells us.

"How do you make the perfect campfire dessert better? I don't think it's possible." Emmett smirks at her.

I give Danika a wink. "Something tells me you're about to be proven very wrong, my dear Emmett."

Slowly and with much dramatic flair, Danika reaches into a nearby bag and slowly brings out an orange package with round chocolate cups pictured.

"Why have just chocolate in your s'more, when you can have peanut butter *and* chocolate on it?" She flashes all of us what can only be described as a devious smile.

"Alright, gorgeous, show us what you got," Emmett says.

Danika spears two marshmallows on a roasting stick, grabs graham crackers, and places the chocolate on two of the crackers.

Then she roasts with painstaking perfection while Emmett and I lobby innuendos back and forth. A few catch her ear and make her giggle, but overall, she's laser focused on her task. Once they're roasted to a beautiful golden hue, she slides them on to the graham cracker and chocolate, triumphantly holding them for us to see.

"Who wants to try first?" she asks.

Emmett's hand, of course, shoots straight into the air, but I move faster and nab one from her.

"As Pack Lead, it's my duty to ensure the quality of this product," I announce solemnly.

"Pack Lead? What the hell is that?" Emmett asks, bewildered.

Colin chuckles. "It's a title he made up so he could justify stealing your dessert."

Emmett's eyes lock with mine, and with a seriousness I didn't know he was capable of, he says, "You wound me, sir."

"Want me to kiss it and make it better?" Colin grins.

Emmett returns the grin. "Promises, promises."

Danika's frozen, watching this play out between us, so I decide to dive right in. My teeth crunch through the cracker and meet smooth sugar as I bite. The typical flavor combination floods my mouth, and the marshmallow was the perfect temperature. Hot enough to melt the outer bit of chocolate, cool enough to eat. When the peanut butter flavor kicks in with the chocolate, it brings a savory element I was not expecting, and I'm pretty sure I get an endorphin high from the taste.

A low moan of delicious pleasure rumbles out of me, and I look at Danika to see if she's eating hers. She's paused with her treat halfway to her mouth, which is hanging slightly open as she stares. I have no problems with her taking as long of a look as she would like. I drag my tongue along my lower lip and watch as she traces the path with her eyes.

"Did I miss a spot?" I challenge her.

Her eyes snap to mine, and she takes a shuddering breath. I'm not going to push her but I'm hoping she will do whatever wild idea is flashing in her eyes. That mischievous spark is back, and I want nothing more than to see her act on it and do something uninhibited.

"Your alpha looks like he needs to be cleaned up," Colin says lowly, temptingly.

Danika nods. "He does."

"What are you gonna do about it, Omega?" Emmett teases.

She swallows thickly and leans forward, one hand gently pulling my face closer to hers. Tentatively, she uses her tongue to clean the smears of marshmallow from the corners of my lips. The feel of her soft but firm lick pulls a sharp exhale from me, my cock stirring to life at the sensation. It wants the same treatment as my face is getting. After the fourth lick, I can't take it anymore and gently grasp her chin in my fingers.

I turn her face up so I can see her eyes. She searches mine in turn, then tilts her head slightly up and closes her eyes. If that's not a sign, I don't know what is. So I take the invitation and bring my lips to hers in a firm but gentle kiss. She responds beautifully, body softening and melting into me. Our mouths dance and tease each other, tongues flicking against each other gently. A pleased rumble builds in my chest, and I release it, unable to keep my pleasure and contentment silent.

"Please tell me this is dessert now," I hear Colin say from nearby.

Danika whimpers at Colin's words, telling us that she is definitely on board with Colin's idea. The two of them surround us, ensuring that Danika can easily escape if she changes her mind. Colin brushes her hair off her neck and lands soft, open-mouth kisses to her soft skin. Emmett's hands reverently explore her body, experimenting with squeezes and tugs in specific spots to find her reactions. I pull back from her lips, smiling as she tries to chase my mouth with hers.

"Are you okay with this, Omega? I need words," I tell her, my voice thick.

"Yes. Please touch me ... Alpha," she all but whispers the last word, causing Emmett and I to groan with pleasure at the word.

There's a deep, primal satisfaction in being identified by your omega as her alpha. I would never expect a stranger to use my designation, but now that I've heard my omega do it, that's the only way I want her to address me. My cock hardens, and I bring her hips to me, pressing against her briefly.

"Can you tell how much I want you?" I ask her.

She nods her head but still seems uncertain. Apparently, she needs more confirmation that we're hers and we don't want her for just her body. It is a big bonus, though, I can't lie about that.

"Danika," I grip her chin so she's looking directly at me, "we will stop any time you ask us to. The three of us? We want *you*, not just physical pleasure. We will go at any damn pace you choose. Even if it means stopping right now and leaving."

Her eyes widen, as if I've said something profound enough to change history. She searches my eyes, then looks at the others. The three of us wait, bodies frozen, waiting to see what she wants us to do.

"I want you, too," she confesses softly.

"Thank fuck," Emmett says.

"How do you want us?" Colin asks.

Danika bites her lip like she's a kid in a candy shop with unlimited money. Her eyes dart around, and when she figures out what she wants, her eyes light up.

"Emmett, will you show me how Colin likes to be touched?"

Emmett salutes her and moves to her other side where Colin's standing. She turns her eyes to me next.

"Jonah, you need to find out what you started … and finish it."

If all my blood wasn't already in my cock, it is now. I'm so hard it's painful, but this isn't about me. This is about showing Danika how much we want her. When I hesitate, unsure of where to start, she takes my hand and brings it to the waistband of her pants with a sassy smirk. Her sass is only somewhat surprising, but I'm not going to look a gift horse in the mouth. I love her sass, and if she's finally saying what she wants, I'm not about to protest.

"Whatever you say, Omega," I tell her honestly, and get to work.

My fingers slide beneath the fabric and inch down toward where her panties are soaked with slick. My breath leaves my lungs, and I'm not sure if I'll ever breathe the same again.

"Goddammit, you're soaked," I rumble, rubbing my fingers on her clit, the fabric of her panties still between our skin.

Emmett maneuvers between Colin and I, dropping to his knees and opening Colin's pants with smooth, familiar movements. The only betrayal of his excitement is the tremor of breath that escapes him every so often. Danika watches with heavy eyes as he pulls down Colin's pants, letting his thick cock free from its confinement. My fingers continue their ministrations, and I bring my lips to her open neck, licking and nibbling at her skin. Her hands fly up to clutch at my shoulders to steady herself.

"That's right, baby, hold on to me," I whisper in her ear.

Her body shudders and her breath hitches as I bypass her panties and touch her hot, slick-soaked skin. Feeling her skin directly on my fingertips is a high I never knew existed. I've never felt anything as luxurious as her soft skin, the slick heat welcoming me like it's where I've always belonged. I explore for a moment before finding her clit, circling that bud of nerves softly. A soft whine escapes her, and I can't help but glance over at my guys. Emmett is almost choking on Colin's length, while Colin holds his head in place gently.

Emmett doesn't mind being used, but I can tell he's holding back so Danika doesn't get overwhelmed. Normally he encourages Colin to fuck his mouth as hard as possible. We both watch as I start a rhythm of stroking and pumping, my single finger growing to two as I continue to slowly work her higher and higher.

"Oh, fuck, Emmett, this damn mouth is going to kill me. Just like that, I'm so fucking close," Colin says quickly, borderline babbling.

"Jonah!" Danika gasps, voice high pitched but soft.

I hum in pleasure and increase my pressure on her clit. Her body winds higher and higher, her muscles tensing as her orgasm creeps ever closer.

"Did you know that anyone could see you out here? They could walk right by and see Emmett and Colin, but I promise I won't let them see you," I growl softly. "Nobody gets to see you fall apart except for us."

As soon as the last word leaves my mouth, she shatters. Her pussy pulses around my fingers as I continue to pump them, prolonging her orgasm as much as I can. In the midst of her orgasm, I hear Colin's release into Emmett's mouth and the greedy gulps as Emmett drinks him down. We all pause, breathing heavily and basking in the post-orgasmic glow of Colin and Danika.

Slowly, I pull my hand from Danika's pants and lock my eyes on hers as I bring my fingers to my mouth and suck on the nectar I pulled from her body. She tastes like a decadent mint dessert, sugary sweet with that hint if mint freshness.

"Best dessert ever," I tell her.

Emmett sounds his agreement, causing Danika and Colin to look at each other before she giggles and we all join in. I think our scent exposure plan is going well.

Chapter 24

Colin

After our campfire night with Danika, Jonah insisted we needed some guy time. At first, I rolled my eyes a bit, but when Emmett lit up like a damn Christmas tree, I caved. He did suck my soul out via my dick the other day, I owe him one for that. However, when Jonah insisted on doing all the preparation along with Emmett, I immediately started feeling antsy.

I'm not sure I trust those two to remember everything we're going to need for this date. I was allowed to know that we're going for a mild hike before a small picnic. Deep down, I do trust them, they're not idiots. I'm just so used to being in charge of this kind of thing that it feels uncomfortable to not handle it all myself. The guys take care of the gallery, and I take care of them. Maybe it's been too long since the roles have been reversed; this might actually be good for us. Who am I kidding? Of course it will be. Especially if we go for a happy ending.

I've got my hiking shoes on, my water pack in hand, and I'm just waiting for my men to stop bickering like old ladies and get to the door. I can hear them debating which food item goes in which backpack and I can't help but smile and shake my head at them. Alphas. So fussy.

"The food will be delicious no matter how it's packed," I call out to them.

Emmett pokes his head out from the kitchen. "How dare you, sir? This is an art!"

Laughter bubbles up at Emmett's playful response and I hold my hands out, palms facing him. He smirks before disappearing back into the kitchen to finish the task he and Jonah are working on. Moments later, the two of them all but saunter out to where I'm waiting, looking entirely too sexy. I move my water pack so my hand holds it over my shoulder, with my other hand in my pocket.

"You two come here often?" I ask, making a show of leering at them.

They both chuckle, and Jonah stands in front of me, leaning on the wall with his forearm over my head. Our eyes meet, and his lips tip into a small smile.

"Baby, I'll be anywhere you want me to be," he replies huskily.

My cock hardens at his sultry voice, but thankfully only a little. Having him this close sends my imagination running wild and I want to kneel for him and take his dick in my mouth. I can almost feel it hitting the back of my throat, making tears stream down my face for him. He'd growl as I let him fuck my mouth and it vibrates through my body. Wait, why is my body vibrating? Jerking myself back to the present, I realize Jonah is actually growling softly.

"Beta, you better stop looking at me like that if you want an actual date today."

I'm stuck in his orbit, but I desperately want this date, so my only path forward is snapping us out of this. I lean forward quickly, nipping his nose with my teeth, then scrambling out from under him. Emmett's roaring with laughter as I attempt to use him as a human shield. Jonah accepts defeat easily—he just points two fingers at his eyes, then points them at me.

After a quick drive, we pull into the dirt parking lot of the hiking trail Jonah chose. We each grab our packs and start down one of the trails. My alphas insisted on carrying the food packs, so all I have to worry about is the water on my back. It's a beautiful day today, my eyes take in our surroundings greedily. Fluffy white clouds sail through the air, covering the sun every now again, like a game of peek-a-boo. Small puffs of dust rise from our footsteps, and I can hear the slight crunch of rocks as we step though the dirt path.

"It's so beautiful out here," Emmett comments.

Jonah huffs a short laugh. "As long as the bugs stay away."

"I could be your bug." Emmett turns to give him big puppy eyes.

"You already are, love." Jonah smiles softly.

My hand drifts to my back pocket and I pull out my cellphone to snap a quick picture of them. Their smiles in the shot are soft for each other, eyes teasing, love evident between them. I'm so damn lucky to be with these two ... hopefully Danika, too, at some point. I can imagine her walking along with us and giggling over our ridiculous antics.

My legs are feeling the burn from walking, and now we're trying to hike up a hill. Burning muscles distract me from watching Emmett and Jonah as I focus on one foot at a time. Martial arts and hiking use very different muscles, and I'm remembering that lesson right now. Emmett and Jonah are both ahead of me, Emmett because he ran up the hill "for fun" and they turn around to see me trudging along.

"You gonna make it?" Jonah asks.

"I thought this was a date, not a murder attempt!" I snark back with a smile.

Emmett cups his hands around his mouth. "Do you need me to carry you? Gertie says she's okay with that!"

"Maybe I do! You should get over here and put your money where your mouth is!" I laugh.

Emmett's head tilts so his left ear is closer to his shirt pocket. "Oh, Gertie says never mind, she doesn't want you to ruin her hairdo today."

"Gertie! I thought we were friends again!"

"She says hair before hunks," he reports back.

I'm a few feet away by now, my feet aching from the hike, and I look him straight in the eye.

"What does that even mean?"

Emmett scoffs, "Obviously she cares more about her hair than having a hunk on my shoulder."

"Oh, of course. I'm so sorry I didn't get it, Gertie." I laugh quietly.

Jonah walks up behind me, surprising me with his hands lightly on my hips from behind. His breath tickles along my neck and causes some of my loose strands to move around. His chin is gentle on my shoulder, and my head leans against his instinctively.

"Just look at the view," he murmurs.

There's a clearing nearby for us to rest in, but beyond that it's all green trees. This trail must have a valley, since I can see a sea of different shades of green dotting the small rolling hills. We're not up so high that we should be able to see this, so it must be a valley of some kind. We stand there for a moment, soaking in nature and watching the leaves rustle as the gentle breeze goes by.

"When are we eating?" Emmett calls from the clearing.

He's smiling at us, a blanket spread out beneath him and his phone on the blanket next to him. There's a small tube next to him that used to house chips, but now holds Gertie so she doesn't get dirty on the ground. Jonah's answering smile is big enough that I can feel his expression change where our cheeks touch.

"We better feed him before he turns into a monster," Jonah tells me quietly.

He presses a light kiss to my neck, and I smile at him in response as we walk to Emmett and take seats so we're in a circle. Emmett and Jonah pull out all the food, and I'm torn between laughing and crying at the spread. They've brought a smorgasbord of snack food. There are ten small bags of chips, eight varieties of snack cakes, three different flavors of pre-popped corn, a few ghost pepper beef jerky sticks, and a foot-long baguette.

My eyes take in the different colors and packaging, and my brain finally catches up with the fact that the only decent food in this spread is too spicy for me to even smell, let alone eat. When I glance up at my alphas, though, they look so proud of themselves. Then I catch the playful expression that appears on Jonah's face for a moment and narrow my eyes at them.

"You assholes did this on purpose, didn't you?" I ask, tearing into a snack cake.

"Purposefully pack nothing healthy for this hike? We would *never*," Emmett replies.

Letting out a bark of laughter, I figure, Fuck it. *I'll find something healthy later.* Emmett and Jonah laugh along with me, and we dig into the junk food spread. Emmett grabs one of the ghost pepper jerky sticks, and both Jonah and I yell for him to stop. The last thing we need is for him to eat something too spicy and be miserable the rest of the hike back.

"I'm just looking," he says innocently.

"Yeah, and Jonah's going to buy us that kitten you asked about," I scoff.

Emmett turns serious and looks to Jonah. "If I eat this jerky stick, will you promise to buy us a kitten?"

"Absolutely not!" Jonah's face is incredulous.

Emmett tears the package open and takes a large bite. He looks pretty satisfied with himself.

"I think I'd like a Maine Coon, those cats are cool," he muses.

"I said no to the cat," Jonah points out.

Emmett shrugs. "You said absolutely, so it's a yes for me."

I can't help the laughter that overtakes me, and once I lose it, Jonah and Emmett aren't far behind. We laugh for a few minutes before dying down, then look at each other and take off again. Jonah has tears running down his face.

"My abs, I can't ... my abs!" I gasp.

We eventually settle, and Emmett finishes his jerky without batting an eye. I'm just gonna let that one go, and file it under 'new information' in my head. Now that the laughter is gone, we settle into a comfortable silence for a few minutes, crunching and humming over the snacks.

"Check in. How are you two doing? We've got a busy gallery right now, we're courting Danika, and we haven't had much time just the three of us," Jonah says.

Emmett hums, but gestures for me to go first. I narrow my eyes at him in mock offense, and he just smirks at me. So damn sexy.

"I'm doing okay. Hearing that I was the reason for her freakout at first kind of killed my self esteem for a bit, but knowing I'm her match? That means everything. She fits with us perfectly, just like she's meant to. I just want to make sure we have more dates with the three of us. I've missed this," I confess.

"Same. Feels like I don't get to see you two at the same time often," Jonah agrees.

Emmett nods. "I think we're all on the same page there. My stargazer literally knocked me off my feet when we met, and she's obviously perfect for you two as well. I've been feeling a bit useless lately, but I'm not sure why."

"How can we help?" I ask.

"I'm not sure," he confesses.

I scoot closer to him and land a kiss on his cheek before settling in fully inches away from him. He smiles softly at me, and even though we don't have a bond yet, I can almost feel the love pouring out of him.

"If you think of a way, will you please tell us?"

Emmett looks at me. "Yeah, I'll make sure you guys know if I think of something. Or maybe just when the feeling pops up."

Jonah clears his throat once or twice before speaking. "Sorry, I'm not emotional, I swear."

We all chuckle at that.

"I definitely think it's time to re-visit hiring someone in the next year. The gallery is getting more popular, and it would be nice to get away but leave the gallery open. I don't think I lean enough on you guys for that, and I'll try to work on it," he says gruffly.

"Jonah pile!" Emmett exclaims as he tackles Jonah.

I don't understand how he did that so fluidly from sitting, but I'm not going to ask questions when there's a cuddle pile happening. Quickly moving my feet, I lay myself on Jonah from the other direction so it's even. Emmett and I snuggle in for a few moments before we hear Jonah's voice, muffled by something.

"I'd like to breathe now."

Emmett and I oblige his request and move off of him, but stay at his sides. We lay like that for a while, just the three of us, watching the clouds pass by and finding shapes in them. Each cloud morphs at least a little bit when it floats by, and I can't help but compare it to us. We've changed shapes over the years, but we always come together again.

They're pack, and it's exactly where I want to be.

Chapter 25

Danika

My brush slides over the canvas, making a small sound as the fibers deposit their paint to the new surface. It's almost like scratching, and my brain melts at the noise. So satisfying.

"Wait, hang on, so you're telling me they *fingerbanged you in public?*" Sophie all but shouts.

I shoot her a quick look before going back to my painting.

"It's okay to be jealous." I smirk.

"You son of a ..." she starts, making me snicker.

I sigh as my eyes inspect the painting, working to decide what areas need more highlighting.

"I mean, it just kind of happened. Colin kissed me, and then Jonah wanted in, then things just escalated." I shrug.

"Are you okay?" Sophie asks gently.

Putting down my brush, I turn on my stool to face her fully. She's sitting in one of my plush extra chairs I keep for when she visits on a painting day. Not all painting days are good ones for her to come over for, but when it's finishing touches, I don't mind. It helps pass the time on those tedious little details I obsess over.

"Honestly? I think so. I'm not sure why, especially since it was all so fast, but I feel okay about it."

"They didn't pressure you?" she presses.

I smile gently. "No, they reassured me that they'd stop the moment I said to, and I believe them. I felt ... precious when Colin kissed me. Everything faded away, and all I could focus on was the three of them. Sounds really cheesy when I say it out loud."

She chuckles. "Legit. Maybe we should go find some forest animals to come sing with you."

"I said cheesy not a movie princess." I laugh.

"What was it like? Feeling Colin's match with you?"

I sigh gently, remembering the feeling that swept over me.

"It felt like a puzzle piece falling into place. I could feel it on my lips, Soph, the tingle everyone describes. I couldn't feel it all through my body, it was almost like static electricity, but the shock was pleasant rather than hurtful. I could have stood there and kissed him for hours. I think it helped with the scent, too. I didn't even register it as unpleasant when I walked them to their car. It was just *him*, nothing else," I tell her.

Sophie puts her fingertips over her mouth, her eyes watering slightly.

"My baby girl is growing up!" she says dramatically.

"You are ridiculous!" I sass.

Cackling, she drops the act and looks at me with glassy eyes, real this time.

"I hope you are fucking proud of yourself, Danika, because you have come a long way. I'm fucking proud of you, and I hope you know that."

A knot forms in my throat at her words. Deep down I never actually expected to be proud of myself, let alone have someone else be proud of me. To have my best friend really see me and the progress I've made is touching and validating. It feels like I can actually be the spunky, sassy girl I used to be. I really liked her. Blinking away the stinging in my eyes, I turn to gather my paint supplies.

"I think it's cookie time," I tell Sophie as I clean my brushes.

"Wait, *cookie* or *nookie?* Because I'm only down for one of those with you."

My hand flies to my chest in mock offense. "You wouldn't cookie with me?"

She cackles and leaves the art studio, my feet following her closely. We make it to the kitchen where she grabs the cookie container, and we perch on the two stools I have. As we each begin to stuff our faces, I inspect the cookie in my hand while the delicious combination of sugar and dark chocolate chunks swirls in my mouth.

"Why don oo make ova flavrs?"

Sophie blinks at me. "Chew, swallow, *then* talk, heathen."

I flash her a grin before finishing my bite.

"Why don't you make other flavors? We always have this one," I ask.

"You complain any time I bring a new flavor to try!"

I scoff, "We have a tradition, you bring me the dark chocolate chip ones."

"*That's* the reason." She looks pointedly at me.

All I can do is giggle at the expression on her face. She smiles back and rolls her eyes good-naturedly.

"I'll make you a deal," I tell her.

"Oh? This should be interesting."

"If it's a showing day, then these are required. But I promise to be open to new flavors if you want to bring them on hang out days. Deal?"

"Okay, deal."

She nudges her shoulder against mine, and all I can do is smile. A tickle starts up in the back of my throat, and I growl a bit to try and scratch it. Standing, I try a glass of cold water next.

"You okay? You got all growly on me just now," Sophie asks.

"Got this weird tickle in my throat." I clear my throat again.

"Aw, I hate when that happens," she sympathizes.

"It'll be fine. Now, tell me about your love life."

Spoiler alert: my scratchy throat didn't go away and now I'm sick. Full on, sore throat, coughing, congestion sick, and I'm pretty sure I want to die. A constant pulse of pain courses through my head after I blow my nose or have a big coughing fit. My lungs are trying to escape my body, and at this point I would let them if it made the coughing and sore throat stop. Who needs lungs anyway? My omega is pushing me to call the guys and ask them to come baby me, but I don't want to burden them with a cold. Especially since I know I'm dramatic when I'm sick.

Maybe I should try to do some cold water again for my throat. My legs swing over the couch where I've been lounging for a couple days now and make my way to standing. Everything feels fuzzy, my head full of cotton, making any movement feel like I'm in slow motion. Eventually I make it back to the couch, and when I lay down, it's the best feeling I've ever had; the struggle of moving gone, my limbs able to just flop and exist. A sense of relief flows through me once I'm under my blankets and have my water close.

I don't remember the movie on the TV when my phone startles me awake. Must have had auto-play on, I'm sure I was watching something else just a minute ago. My phone tells me that it's several hours later than I thought and Jonah is calling. I hit the "accept" button and put it on speakerphone.

"Hey," I croak out.

"Hey, did I wake you? I tried calling a couple times and now I feel bad," Jonah says.

"No ... well, yes but I didn't hear the other calls," I tell him before a coughing fit kicks in.

"Oh, baby, that sounds miserable. Do you want us to come by and check on you?"

Of course I want them here to comfort me, but I don't want them to be exposed to whatever cold this is. I also look like shit and I'm not sure if I'm ready to be quite that real with them. Even if the idea of them here brings me more comfort than resting after walking.

"You don't have to, it's okay," I say reluctantly, not wanting them to feel obligated.

I can almost feel the stern look I'm getting from Jonah. "We're coming over to check on you. I can hear it in your froggy voice that you need someone to come over and pamper you a bit."

"Froggy throat?" I try to sound offended, but a smile tugs at my mouth.

"With the way you're croaking out those words, we might need to speak full frog soon. Ribbit."

His word makes me laugh, but that laugh quickly turns into a coughing fit.

"We'll be there soon, okay?"

"I'd like that," I finally admit.

We hang up the phone, and I drink some water down to try and sooth my throat. I'm not sure it does much, but at least I'm staying hydrated. Gotta find the silver lining while I can. I switch the movie to an old romcom and relax into the couch and my pillow again.

The door sounds with someone knocking, and I startle awake, triggering a headache to take up residence. My hand moves to my head, trying to stop the blooming headache and spinning feeling. I peek at the door handle, and flop back down when I see it's unlocked.

"Come in," I call out weakly.

Thankfully my weak call is still loud enough that my three guys (*my* three guys?) open the door and step in. They immediately lock on to where I'm laying, and I raise my hand in a small wave with a tiny smile. Colin holds up a large, clear container that's full of soup.

"I brought you some of my favorite soup. It's a potato cheese, goes down smoothly and is filling," he says.

I clear my throat. "Sounds perfect, can you put it in the fridge for now? I'll have some later."

"You got it." He smiles.

Jonah comes over and strokes my hair back from my forehead, his hand firm and soothing. The gentle strokes help me to relax even more and, much to my surprise, a purr starts up in my chest. My eyes fly to his, and I place a hand on my chest.

"I don't think I've purred for anyone before," I confess.

Jonah smiles, the way only a smug alpha can. "I'm glad I get to be the first to hear it."

"Silly alpha."

"Adorable omega."

His hand continues to move as I glance around a bit. "I don't see Emmett."

He must have sonic hearing because he comes around the corner the moment I say his name. He's got a broom and some cleaning supplies in hand.

"You rang?" he asks in a low, sonorous voice.

I smile. "Yes, Igor. I wasn't sure where you were."

Emmett turns his nose up and corrects me, "It's EYE-gor."

While I've never watched that movie, I know exactly what he's referencing and laughter spills from me as he grins, pleased to have made me laugh. Until it throws me into a new coughing fit. Emmett's face turns panicked, and I wave him off with a hand before reaching for my water. Jonah's got it almost to my mouth already, and I shoot him a look of thanks. The cold water slides down my throat, soothing the sting and stopping my cough. Jonah takes it back and gently sets it on the table.

"Thanks," rasp at him.

Emmett sets down the cleaning supplies and takes the broom and dustpan with him to the kitchen. Colin walks out of the kitchen and taps his ass when they cross paths. Emmett giggles and continues on his way. Smiling, Colin makes his way to the couch and sits down, my feet in his lap.

"Hey, sweetheart," he says warmly.

My answering smile comes easily, and when he starts to rub my feet, I completely melt. My omega is reveling in the gentle care of these three men. Emmett is doing some basic cleaning, my worries lifting about the state of the house. My other guys were giving me all the comfort I could ask for, and not once has it felt forced or as if I'll need to pay them back later. Is this what having an actual match is like? Being taken care of, no questions asked?

Sure, these three have made my heart happy and given me joy, plus one outstanding orgasm, but I never expected this. I've worried that they would be like my previous experience with men, the minute things stopped being perfect, I stopped mattering. Or, maybe I never mattered from the start. I'm not sure if I *want* to get used to this in case it all comes crashing down, but my omega insists we enjoy ourselves for now. I'm not about to go against my instincts like that.

I grab Jonah's hand as he attempts another stroke against my hair, and I make sure our eyes meet.

"Thank you, all of you, for being here."

Jonah smiles as if I'm the only reason he's living. "Anything for you."

Chapter 26

Danika

It's been a few days since the guys came and pampered the shit out of me, and two things suddenly strike me. I didn't freak out at Colin's scent (to be fair, I was pretty congested), and I want them to do it next time I'm sick. Sophie is my best friend, but I've never felt as cared for and precious as I did when the guys showed up. Sophie makes me feel cared for, but this is more. Different in a way that my mind can't quite determine.

My cold feels miles better this morning, so I set myself the tasks of a long, hot shower, wash a load of laundry, and eat the soup Colin brought. I wanted to try it when they dropped it off, but I knew that swallowing something with any kind of chunks in it wasn't going to feel good on my throat. So I stuck to broths for a few days. Now, I'm showered, my laundry is going, and I'm going to tear up some potato soup. It's been a while since I've had anything like homemade soup, and I plan to savor it. I can almost feel the soft potatoes as I pull the container from the fridge. I can even see little bacon bits and herbs hanging out in the mix.

As though it can sense food, my stomach lets out a loud grumble, and I swear I can feel it move in my body. A wave of muscles trying to find any food that could be in there. My hand absently pats my stomach.

"I know, it's coming," I say to it.

When my serving is ready to go, I set it in the microwave and go to switch my laundry. It chimes just as I walk in, and I give myself a mental pat on the back for such great timing. Once my clothes are transferred and the dryer is running, I walk back to the kitchen.

I stop on the threshold of the kitchen, and my chest goes tight. It's hard to breathe. My heart and my stomach are battling for position in my throat, and I'm not sure if I'm going to vomit or pass out. Maybe I'm wrong. I take another deep inhale, feeling my nostrils flare while I try to take in the scent that's stopped me. No, I'm not wrong, it's the same scent. A smoked gouda scent. My mind immediately remembers what it smells like sour.

Out. It needs out. I can't have it in here. My limbs all but vibrate as urgency crashes over me, my mind scattered in a million directions, but able to focus on the one directive. Get. It. Out. Now. Fingers shaking, I grab the main container of soup, open my front door, and chuck it away from my house. My feet dash back to the kitchen where I grab the steaming bowl of offensive smell from the microwave and give it the same treatment. Out. It can't be here. Not allowed. The scent still lingers.

Slamming the door shut, I inhale again, seeking to see if my home is no longer tainted by it. Unfortunately, I can still smell it. I think it's permeated everything, and my panic increases almost to fear, a cold feeling taking up residence in the back of my head and spreading down my spine. For a moment I'm frozen, my body refusing to move as the sour cheese smell sinks into my bones. Dirty, I'm too dirty, everything is ruined. House needs saving.

Knowing my house needs saving has unlocked my muscles long enough for me to get my cleaning supplies out. Can't wear gloves, need it gone from my hands. This will help. My first target is the microwave. Plate comes out, chemicals sprayed inside, scrub. Scrub harder, not clean yet. Smell still there. Maybe door needs cleaning.

Scrub door on microwave before scrubbing inside again. It can't be here, the smell can't be here. *He* can't be here! Can't, not allowed.

Sense and awareness leave me as I scrub every damn inch of the kitchen. Behind the faucet, under the fridge, all dishes, the oven, the stove, the floor. A toothbrush is employed for the tiny cracks where the floor meets the lower cabinets. It needs to be clean, smell needs to be gone. My body takes over fully as my mind circles on *his* scent, how I once craved it before the fire. My family dismissing me, friends mocking me, the town judging me. When *he* came to taunt me, trying to tell me it was all my fault. No, I wasn't at fault, I didn't want that.

My awareness filters in and out, and I register that I'm scrubbing the living room floor now, single-mindedly trying to get the scent out. A coherent thought floats through my mind, *Maybe it is gone and I'm just remembering the smell …*

But my mind pushes past it and locks back down, re-focused on cleaning. Scrubbing out the bad. The bad has to go, it has to go, it *has* to.

When I feel a hand on my shoulder, I scream and stumble back, a whine rising out of me, calling for my alphas, my beta. They should be here, why aren't they here? I thought they would protect me. A lost feeling descends, and I know I'm alone. Nobody wants to save me, nobody can save me. There's a voice and I try to find it, it's familiar. An okay voice. A voice I like.

"It's me, Danika. It's okay."

No, it's not okay. It's never gonna be okay again.

"Omega, look at me," a sharp command comes, not quite a bark.

I have to listen to this voice, I can feel it in my bones. It's not the one with the cheese smell. Eyes blinking, I look up to see a face, gentle and worried, staring directly into me, chocolate eyes, blond hair. It's a face I know, why don't I know his name? I should know his name! How could I forget it? What is it? My ears register the high-pitched noise coming from me, and belatedly I realize I haven't stopped whining. How long have I been whining?

The face doesn't break eye contact, but his hand brings mine to his chest, where I can feel his breath going in and out. A gentle motion of his chest growing with inhale, then shrinking with exhale. The breathing starts to go slower, taking longer to expand and longer to contract.

"Breathe with me," he says.

As if we're linked, I follow his command and his pace. I can feel the fear fading, the cold feeling slowly ebbing away, the panic slowly receding along with it. More deep breaths, in and out, slow and steady. Awareness sinks into me again, and my eyes widen as I take in the face in front of me.

"Jonah," I whisper.

He smiles and nods gently before I throw myself at him and sob. His arms hold me tight as he sits back, pulling me on his lap, my legs on either side of his. Our bodies are flush. I bury my face into his neck so he's all I can scent, and he rocks me gently as the weight of my panic attack falls on me. The soup, the memories, the trauma, the fear, the loneliness. Deep down, that feeling of being alone took over and not only was the scent alarming, I was the only one here to experience it. Alone, like always.

Except this amazing alpha is holding me tight, whispering how wonderful I am, how much he cares about me, all kind of sweet words settling into my bones as I continue to cry. I still haven't regained any sense of time, but at some point my breathing evens out, and the sobbing stops. Sniffles set in, but they're not bad, and my body feels wrung out. When I pull my head back from his neck and shoulder, his shirt is completely soaked.

"Fuck, I'm so sorry!" My face flames with embarrassment.

A chuckle escapes from his handsome face. "I'm happy to wear your tears whenever you need me to. I'm just glad you're back."

"I'm so sorry."

"No, don't apologize. Something set you off, and I'm just glad I could be here to get you out of whatever spiral you were in. Truly," he insists.

His eyes hold nothing but sincerity as I examine them, and I slowly nod my acceptance. There's no reason why Jonah would lie to me, so I choose to accept his words. I rest my forehead against his, and we exist together for a moment. Nobody needs us right now, we can just *be*. My breathing evens out fully and I sit upright. Now that I'm calm, the entire situation plays again in my mind and I'm positive that my face is bright red. Or I have some non-existent magical power that turns my face to fire. I mentally smile at myself, realizing that's exactly something Emmett would say.

"I'm really fucking embarrassed," I confess.

Jonah nods, but doesn't push.

"This is kind of what happened after I met Colin the first time. I had a scent trigger me and I completely blocked out the external world. I don't know how long I've been doing ... whatever this is."

My eyes take in the room, seeing all the freshly cleaned spots and the chemicals lined up neatly next to us. The kitchen grabs my attention from across the room, and the little bit I can see is spotless. My brain slowly pieces together that I deep cleaned while in my own heat. Just at that realization, my hands start to hurt.

"My hands." My throat tightens with emotion, tears threatening my eyes.

It *hurts*, oh god it really hurts! When I look down, I see they're completely red and some of the skin is starting to peel away. There are red blotches on my knuckles that look like raw skin. I don't think I'm bleeding but it fucking *hurts*. Jonah looks and hisses out a breath.

"Shit, that looks bad, baby. Hang on," he says, pulling his cell-phone from his pocket. "Yeah, come in, it's not great."

I'm super confused about whatever that conversation was, but the aching, stinging, and burning in my hands immediately grabs my attention. My curiosity and confusion are pushed aside so my pain can be noticed.

"Fuck!" a new voice sounds.

I look up, and it's Emmett, staring at my hands with watery eyes like he's about to cry. I'm not sure why he's crying, I'm the one with painful hands.

"I'm not gonna ask if you're okay, I'm not quite *that* dumb, but I'm so sorry you hurt, Stargazer."

I shoot him a small smile before a grimace takes over and a whine escapes. The pain is getting stronger.

"Car's ready!" Colin's standing in the doorway looking anxious, feet shuffling as if he can't stand still.

"Let's go," Emmett says as he swoops in to pluck me from Jonah's lap.

"Alpha," I whine, not sure if I'm glad to be with Emmett or if I want Jonah.

As we walk toward the door, Jonah leans down to give me a kiss on my forehead. cdThe small comfort soothes my omega. We arrive at the car, and Colin's in the driver's seat, ready to go. My omega changes her mind again and wants Colin, but I don't want to hurt Emmett's feelings. He just got to pick me up.

"You want Colin, sweetheart?" Jonah asks.

When I look over, surprised, Emmett chuckles. "You were whining his name, Star. I'm sure our beta would be happy to hold you."

I nod vigorously, and Colin abandons his seat as if someone lit his ass on fire. Well, I suppose I did a little when I asked for him. His body slides into the seat next to me, carefully wrapping one arm around my shoulders, and gently holding my wrists in the other. I bury my nose into his neck and breathe deep, his scent soothing me as we go.

How funny is that? The scent that once triggered me is now bringing me peace.

Chapter 27

Jonah

The image of Danika on her hands and knees, scrubbing the floor and muttering to herself is something I won't soon forget. We told her earlier this week that we would come by to check on her, but she didn't respond to any texts today. I worried she was still really sick, so we just showed up at her place. Emmett and Colin noticed the soup and its container on the lawn, a bowl not far away.

"What the hell?" Emmett said.

When I parked, we piled out quickly, and I told the others to wait outside. We had no idea what was happening, and as head alpha it's my job to handle these things. Once I finally laid eyes on her, she was on her hands and knees, hair sticking up from her messy bun, movements jerky and frantic. I called out and stepped closer, but she didn't seem to realize I was there.

"Out. Get him out. Clean. He can't be here. Clean. Out," she muttered over and over again like a mantra.

I'd finally gotten her attention, and that's when my heart stopped. Her face had tear tracks down her cheeks, eyes wide and frantic like she expected to be attacked at any moment. She had no idea who I was, and the amount of confusion and terror on her face blew me away. When she eventually came back to herself, she crumbled. I called the guys in to help, and now we're sitting in the Emergency Room, waiting for her to be called back.

"You guys are coming, too, right?" she whispers to us.

"Absolutely. If you want us there, we'll be there. No questions asked," Colin promises.

Emmett leans in closer to speak quietly in my ear.

"Do we know what caused her breakdown yet?"

I shake my head. "No, I'm not sure how to ask her either."

"We'll figure it out, don't worry." He places a hand on my knee, and I repeat the gesture.

Danika is still letting out small gasps and cries of pain, while Colin whispers whatever assuring words he can come up with. He places a kiss on her temple, and she turns into him, seeking more comfort. My heart is full as I watch him comfort her, despite the awful situation we're in.

"Danika?" a no-nonsense woman appears and asks.

Colin helps her stand, and the three of us are her entourage as she walks toward the woman who called her name. When she's close, the woman looks down at her hands and tsks.

"Oh my, let's get you to a room. Come on, sweetheart." She moves to guide Danika away from us, but Danika isn't having it.

She jerks back from the woman and turns farther into Colin. Emmett releases a small growl, and while I'm tempted to do the same, I need to set an example. So I turn a stern look on Emmett, who apologizes and looks a little embarrassed. The woman just smirks and tilts her head so we can follow.

We walk down the hallway, the glass doors and walls in each patient room draped closed for privacy. The woman stops at a room and ushers us all in. She goes through the standard questions to make sure Danika is the right patient, and once she's got confirmation, we finally get an introduction. The nurse who guided us here is named Julie, and while she still exudes a no-nonsense vibe, she seems to have an extremely gentle bedside manner.

She gently asks Danika to let her see one hand, and as she reaches for the closer wrist, Colin makes sure she has a good grasp before he lets go. Julie turns Danika's hand over and visually examines the skin, taking care not to touch it. It doesn't look quite as bad now that we're at the hospital, but maybe that's just my own wishful thinking.

"Would you like a pillow to rest your hands on? If your beta is tired, at least."

Colin smiles. "I'm not tired, baby girl, but it's up to you. Whatever is most comfortable, you won't hurt my feelings."

Danika looks at her hands, then back up at Julie.

"Can I have the pillow and his hands?"

Julie's face softens instantly. "Of course you can. I'll be right back."

We're quiet while the nurse is gone, but I take the opportunity to sit in an extra chair. Colin has one, obviously, next to the bed, so I grab one that's closer to the door.

"I'm sor—" Danika starts.

We cut her off with three growls, and her eyes go wide.

"Don't apologize, you have nothing to be sorry for," I tell her, a growl still in my voice.

Her eyes tear up again, and my heart freezes. *Fuck, did I upset her?*

"But I ruined your soup container," she says.

"You're worried about the *soup container?*" Colin asks.

She nods, eyes downcast as if she can't bear to look at us. Emmett walks closer and sits gingerly on the bed near her feet.

"Hey, can you look at me?" he asks.

Danika's eyes slowly move until she's looking up at him through her lashes. Her lips quiver ever so slightly, and I can see her trying to hold some tears back.

"I need you to know something, and this is important, okay?"

She nods, keeping their eyes connected.

"I fucking *hated* that soup container," he tells her, completely serious.

She sputters and then starts laughing. Small chuckles roll out of her before she moves into a full belly laugh, Emmett grinning along with her and Colin shaking his head in mock exasperation. Colin's smiling, so it ruins any idea of him actually being upset. I find myself chuckling quietly as I watch them.

"It's okay ... truly, Dani. Emmett really does hate that dish, so I've been keeping it and saying I love it just to irritate him," Colin adds in.

They banter for a few moments, Danika watching with a warm smile on her face the entire time. It strikes me, not for the first time, that she's absolutely perfect for us. Even if we weren't a match, she just fits. She doesn't treat any of us different than the others, except for the scent issue, which is gone now, and she lets us be however we need to be. She accepts us as we are.

My teeth ache with an overwhelming urge to bite all three of them and make us an official pack, but I know I can't right now. I fight down my alpha, burying the instinct as much as I can so I don't fuck it all up on a thought. When the door slides open, Emmett hops up from the bed and moves so Julie has plenty of space.

She puts the pillow down on Danika's lap and shows her where to rest her forearms so the pillow won't touch her hands. Colin keeps a hold on her wrists, moving closer to the bed to give her all the support he can.

"Okay, if you're comfortable, then great. If you want your beta to snuggle in and hold your hands that's fine, too. Just be extremely careful. I wouldn't want them to get bumped and cause more pain. I'm going to go put some notes in, and the doctor should be in shortly to see you."

Julie turns to leave, but Colin stops her with a question, "How did you know I'm a beta?"

She turns and smirks at us. "Been doing this for more than a few years, gentlemen. It's rare that I can't tell a designation when meeting someone."

Julie walks out of the room, sliding the door closed so we're encompassed in our own little world once again. Danika giggles softly.

"I like her."

"Me too." I grin at her.

Since I've already talked, I take the opportunity to continue to talk.

"I was wondering ... Danika, I know we haven't had much time as a group yet, but, well, if you'd like us to be there for your heat, then we're there. Hell, I'd bond you right away but I'm sure that's too fast."

She pauses for a moment, thinking it through without any input from Emmett or Colin. We're all on the same wavelength that this needs to be something *she* wants.

"I think I'd like that. My heat is pretty close to the special showing at the gallery though. What if it overlaps? I don't want to make you choose me or the event in honor of your sister," she says.

Possession rolls over me, and I see red at the thought of her with anyone else. She's ours, nobody else gets to touch her, nobody else gets to see her like that. My body surges up from my chair and I start pacing. It takes every effort of willpower for me to control my breathing so I don't sound like a bull about to rampage. I keep my eyes focused on my feet, one step at a time, getting it under control. The last thing we need right now is me going into a possessive rut. A few more deep breaths, then I'm ready to talk. When I turn back, all three are staring at me.

"You can't—" I start, then clear my throat to try and remove the growl still there. "*I* can't handle the idea of you with anyone else. You're ours, our match. You will always come first in our lives."

Emmett stands and moves over to where I am, wrapping his arms around me tightly. I grasp him back, my eyes closing, wishing I could pull Danika and Colin into this moment.

"I feel the same," Emmett whispers.

His words give me a sense of calm, knowing that I'm not the only possessive asshole in this group. We release each other, and Emmett claps me on the shoulder before we both move closer to Danika and

Colin. In an attempt to de-escalate any anxiety I caused, I kneel on the floor by her bed before looking up at her. What I see about blows me away, and I realize that she wants us, too. She doesn't want anyone else.

"I'm sorry I lost it there for a moment. If you would rather not have us for your heat, I'd ask for you to be sedated, but I also know it's your choice. I promise, I swear to protect your choice and support whatever it is that you want for your heat."

Softly, so softly, she says, "I can't imagine spending it with anyone else, Jonah. As much as it scares me, you guys are it for me. You're mine, and I'm yours."

Smiling, Colin kisses her on the temple. Just barely I hear him whisper, "Good girl, proud of you."

Danika's cheeks stain pink, and she looks at Colin as though he hung the moon and like she's ready to devour him. Fuck, she is so damn sexy. Before my thoughts get away from me, the doctor comes into the room and introduces himself. He asks Danika some questions about what chemicals she was in contact with. She gives him the list, and he listens as he inspects her hands. When he asks about any home treatment, we all admit that we didn't do any kind of treatment, we came straight here.

"Okay, the first thing that you should have done is rinsed her hands with cold water for twenty minutes. Let's get your hands under some water," the doctor says.

He gently guides Danika to a sink in the room and helps her to figure out a good way to hold her hands in the stream, but she winces the second the water touches her skin. He's more professional than I probably would be if I heard my patient didn't do basic burn care at home. We should have known to run cold water on her hands; we'll have to do better if she ever gets hurt again. If I have anything to say about it, she'll never be harmed again. However, I know that's not how it works.

Danika is absolutely amazing. She complies with all the directions given to her, and eventually we're released from the Emergency

Room. Her hands are wrapped with gauze, and we have a prescription for an antibiotic ointment for her to use when we need to change her bandages. Emmett helps her in the car this time, and I choose to drive. Colin turns to look back at Emmett and Danika, a soft smile on his face.

"You doing okay, baby?"

Danika grins and slurs, "Yuuuup. Sooooo good."

"They really gave her the good stuff." Emmett chuckles.

Colin turns on the radio to softer music, and by the time we hit the highway, she's totally out. The three of us have an unspoken agreement that Danika is coming to our place for at least the night. Hopefully we can convince her to stay longer in the morning. While we didn't plan to spend time with her in close quarters, we're not about to pass the opportunity by. Especially when she'll need help with most tasks her hands can't do right now.

I hope she's ready to be thoroughly loved.

Chapter 28

Danika

I slowly come to awareness, my mind noting that this is the most comfortable I've ever been. I must have gotten out the weighted and heated blankets. The slight pressure on my body is soothing, and the heat is just right. Letting out a little sigh of satisfaction, I wiggle to bury myself under the blankets more. However, there's a body behind me. I freeze, panic trying to take over in my mind. Instincts are screaming at me to run. My omega, though? She's in heaven. She has no worries, and when my "run" response kicks in, she ignores it and brings up the feeling of being safe and cozy.

My nostrils flare as I take in the scents around me. If my omega side isn't worried, then I'm assuming I'm with my guys. Sure enough, Emmett's warm scent of worn leather and wood sinks into my awareness, comforting me without trying. Needing to see for myself, I turn my head to look at him, but he squeezes me in place, humming his dissent.

"Five more minutes," he groans sleepily into my hair.

A giggle escapes me as his arm wraps around me from behind, pulling me closer. In the process, my hand drags along the sheets, and I hiss in pain and surprise. What the hell? When I hold my hands up,

I see they're mostly wrapped in gauze, and the spots not wrapped are an angry red. I shoot up in bed.

"What the hell?"

Emmett's eyes fly open and he looks around, scanning the room for danger before seeing where my eyes are fixed. Gently, he puts an arm around my lower back and holds me as close as he can in this position.

"Hey, did you bump your hand? Sorry if I did something," he preemptively apologizes.

"Why are you sorry?" I ask, baffled.

Emmett rubs the back of his neck. "Because I might have hurt you."

I move to put my hand on his cheek, then remember the gauze bandages. Fuck, this is already annoying.

"You didn't hurt me, I promise. I would, however, like to know why you're in my bed and my hands look damaged."

Emmett looks at me in alarm, and the creeping sensation that I've forgotten something big slithers down my spine. The uneasiness in my veins gives me a light head. I take a second to look around before panicking, and realize we are *not* in my room. I don't even think this is Emmett's room. There's very little in the way of decorations, and this bed is massive. How am I supposed to get out of it without help? I don't want to hurt my hands more than they already hurt.

Thankfully Emmett takes pity on me.

"Let me help you out of this monstrosity of a bed and we'll get you some answers," he promises.

I allow him to guide me across the bed, which means I let him pick me up and move me. When we get to the edge of the bed, I sit with my legs bent and feet touching the floor. Looking down, I see that my legs are bare and I'm in an extremely oversized T-shirt, which boldly states "Betas do it better."

"Why am I in Colin's shirt?" I ask.

Emmett just gives me a look and I sigh, resigning myself to waiting.

"I know this is embarrassing, but if you need to pee, I can wipe for you," Emmett offers, sincerity leaking from every pore on his body.

Hard pass. I'm wiping my own damn ass. Or whatever.

"No, I can do that much," I tell him and move when he directs me to the ensuite.

So fancy. *Ensuite.* I'd giggle and spin around with giddiness if I wasn't already feeling wary. As I finish my business, I'm glad that none of them can feel my pain. It fucking hurts. I grimace and breathe, trying not to cry out; I really don't want Emmett to come busting in here while I'm sitting on the toilet.

"Emmett?" I call out once standing.

"Yeah?" He must be right by the door.

"Can you open the door please?"

He swings the door open gently, watching to make sure he doesn't accidentally hit me. As I stand by the sink, I look at him helplessly.

"How do I wash my hands with all this shit?"

Emmett grimaces. "I'm not sure we can without all the gauze getting wet. We probably need to change the bandages anyway, so let's go find the others. We can remove the gauze, wash your hands, then reapply."

I nod my acceptance, and we exit the bedroom, heading for the kitchen. This house feels *huge* ... like my whole house could fit in that room we just left. I giggle at the idea of trying to cram it in there, and Emmett turns to give me a curious look. We head down some stairs as I wave him off, and I can hear two male voices now. Walking into the kitchen, I see Colin and Jonah working together to get breakfast ready. Jonah appears to be moral support.

They both immediately turn when I step foot on the tile, and I can't help but smile at them.

"Good morning," I greet them.

Jonah stands and pulls me into a gentle hug, being careful of my hands and rocking us back and forth for a moment.

"Morning," he replies with a kiss on my forehead.

Peering up at him, I reach up with my body to give him an actual kiss. He may be taller than me, but I'm close enough that I don't have to yank him down to my level. He responds without hesitation, kissing me back before guiding me to a stool at their large kitchen island.

"You guys do know how bougie this house is, right?" I ask.

Colin gives a long-suffering sigh. "Yeah, we know."

"Is there a story there?"

Colin begins to plate the food, giving himself a moment before responding.

"Have I ever told you about my family's financial situation?" he asks.

"Ummm, yeah, you mentioned your family has money."

"Right. So, you know my family has a shit ton of money. Like, generational level money. As a result, my parents have no concept of a 'normal' gift and got me this house as a present."

"If I was drinking anything I would have spit it out just now," I deadpan.

"It's true. The three of us were starting our relationship, and I think that's why the house was gifted? What did your dad say?" Jonah asks.

Colin draws himself up and lowers his voice slightly. "No son of mine is going to live in squalor. Take the house."

I bite my lip; my house is absolutely what his dad would consider "squalor." Maybe I'm not good enough for living in a place like this. It's so ... big. Do they look down on me without realizing it? Am I a pity case to them? Poor omega match living in her tiny house.

"Stop it," Colin says, plonking a plate in front of me.

It's an adult size children's plate with comic characters on it. My face splits into a grin before I look back at Colin.

"I don't care where you live or how you live. I honestly tried really hard to get my parents to not buy the house. In the end, we took it ... not because we need fancy things, but because we think it's a house we can grow our pack in. Maybe consider kids down the road. If not, we'll sell it and move on." He shrugs.

"Really?" I ask.

"Really. Now eat your breakfast, I slaved away for hours," he demands.

On my plate is scrambled eggs with cheese and a side of toast. How the hell am I supposed to eat eggs right now? I can't use a fork. I could maybe grab the toast if I'm really careful. Determination sets in, and I reach down to grab a piece. Apparently, that was the incorrect path to take as all three of them make noises of alarm.

"What?"

"Let us, please?" Jonah asks.

I huff, "Only if you promise to tell me why my hands are like this."

Jonah picks me up despite my protest and seats me directly on his lap, sitting sideways across his legs. He grabs a fork and picks out a bite of food before feeding it to me. I feel ridiculous sitting here, but when I see his eyes light up in satisfaction, I resign myself to the situation. How could I not when he looks fulfilled like that?

"Baby, you don't remember about your hands?" Colin asks.

"No. The last thing I remember is going to grab soup since I was feeling better, then waking up this morning," I tell him.

Colin's face falls a little and I'm worried I've upset him. Before I can ask if that's true, Emmett chimes in.

"You broke my least favorite container in this entire house, so really, you did me a big favor!"

His words are familiar, and I stare at him while images of us in a small hospital room float into my head. Was that real? Confusion stirs, and I can feel my chest getting tighter as I become more frustrated.

"Was I in the hospital?" I ask, trying to get more information before exploding.

"Yeah, sweetheart, we took you to the emergency room," Jonah rumbles before feeding me another bite.

"Do you remember doing any cleaning yesterday?" Emmett asks gently.

Cleaning? Oh, fuck. The memory slams back into my head; the soup scent, throwing the containers out, spiraling in my mind and doing my psycho cleaning routine. I was so upset I didn't put gloves on this time.

The guys are going to think I'm crazy. As that thought comes in, I begin worrying about if they'll stay. My heart breaks a little at the idea, and it hurts so much that I let out a sniffle or two, my sight going hazy from the tears building.

"Hey, hey, it's okay," Jonah says, putting the fork down and pulling me closer as gently as possible.

My head lands on his shoulder and my body slowly releases the tension that built up. First with my insecurities, then with the memory, it crept up so slowly that I hadn't registered how tight my body was. My emotions take over once my body calms and I let it out. This time it's normal crying, unlike yesterday when I sobbed so hard that half his shirt was wet.

"I'm so sorry. I know you guys said not to apologize, but I have to. I need you to know I'd never purposely do something like that to hurt myself. And, I know you all said you're in, but if this is too much for you—"

"Don't," Colin says firmly.

My eyes meet his across the island.

"Don't minimize yourself. You are not too much. You are exactly what we need, no matter what. Understand? I will take the apologies if it helps you, but not one of us will let you believe that you're too much."

Smiling, I nod my head. "I'll try."

"We'll be here to remind you," Emmett chimes in.

After breakfast, the guys change my bandages, and then we all sit on the ridiculously large, soft couch in their living room. Silence settles over us like a comforting blanket, and we all choose just to exist for a moment. I think that is turning out to be one of my favorite things we do—taking time to just sit and exist together.

"I know the answer is no, but are you guys planning to let me go home?" I ask, teasing.

"No!" they all say in perfect synchronization before laughing.

"It's up to you, but we'd really like you to stay with us for a few days until you can use your hands again," Jonah says.

"I agree on one condition," I say, knowing perfectly well that while I love my home, I want this chance to be with my guys more. And I really can't do a lot for myself right now.

"What's that?" Emmett asks.

"Can we go get some of my clothes? At least new underwear?"

The guys explode into laughter, all their faces turning red, in what I assume is embarrassment. Emmett rubs the back of his neck, his classic tell, and Colin avoids my eyes. When I pin Jonah with a look, he grins unrepentantly. He has no shame.

"I will *gladly* go through your underwear drawer for you," he purrs.

My chuckles join in with theirs. I'm helpless against them, even their bad jokes and innuendos.

Chapter 29

Emmett

It's been a week now, and I'm starting to think of ways that I can convince Danika to stay for life. We've given her the omega suite built into this house without specifying that's what room she has. There's no way she hasn't identified the room that way, but we didn't name it to avoid her feeling pressured. She was insanely resistant to help at first, but has slowly opened to it. In addition to getting her as comfortable as possible, we made sure to find her boundaries at the start, which included wiping herself after the toilet, and we've slowly worked to lower boundaries so we can help with everything. When she told us about not wiping her, I ran out and bought her a bidet.

It may or may not be my favorite toilet now.

"What the hell, Emmett?" Danika yells from the door to her bathroom.

I look up from my spot on the toilet. "What?"

"There are so many bathrooms in this house, go use one of those!"

"But this one has the bidet." I pout at her.

She closes her eyes and takes a deep breath, holding it for a moment before slowly letting it out.

"Emmett. Go. Buy. Another. One."

"Okay." I widen my eyes and pout. "Can I finish this poo first?"

Danika throws her hands up in exasperation.

"Oh my god!" She turns to leave, but I can see the amusement on her face, so I know she's not really mad.

However, she has a point. I really should go buy some more bidets. When I finish, I go downstairs to find Jonah and beg for more bidets in the house. Instead, what I find is Danika trying to rearrange decorations in the living room with hands that aren't quite ready to be used. Colin is standing off to the side watching with blatant amusement as she tries to work without her hands.

"This is more amusing than it should be," Colin says.

I hum in agreement as she growls in frustration at the lamp that isn't moving where she wants it to go. Amusement bubbles up in me as well, but I tilt my ear toward Gertie and hum. She does have a point; I would want help, too. I move to go give her a hand, literally, but Colin grabs my shoulder.

"I wouldn't do that, but if you insist, make sure you guard yourself," he warns me.

I turn and frown at him, but nod in understanding. My feet are gentle as I approach, and it feels a little bit like I'm stalking a wild animal. Angling my body so she should be able to see me, I step close.

"You need a hand with that?" I ask.

Danika freezes for a moment before her head slowly turns to look at me.

"I am not invalid. I can move some damn trinkets, Emmett. You need to move! You're crowding the area, it needs to breathe."

I hold my hands up and step away. "Okay, I'm here if you need anything."

She growls at me, and it takes every muscle in my body not to giggle at her because she's so damn cute. We might need Jonah in here to help out. Oh! I can ask him to buy more bidets, too. Two birds. One Emmett. Ensuring my steps are light and swift, I make it to Colin to let him know my plan. He nods and resumes his vigil over Danika.

After hunting around the house for a bit, I find Jonah in his home office, doing whatever it is he does on the computer. He looks up with a small smile.

"Hey, you," he greets me.

I saunter over and sit my ass on the edge of his desk, facing away from the door. My eyes move down to look at him.

"We need more bidets," I say.

Jonah raises an eyebrow.

"What?" I ask.

"You came in here to tell me we need more bidets?"

"Yes."

"Why do we need more bidets? Better question, why didn't you just buy another one?" he asks. "You bought the one we have."

Oh, he's hitting me with the hard questions. This is why he's our head alpha, he's a thinker.

"First of all, I don't think there's such a thing as 'too many' bidets, so that negates your first question. Second of all, I didn't think I could buy more. Third of all, Danika said I need to stop using her toilet." I count off the reasons on my fingers.

Jonah blinks at me. "That's a lot to unpack but why would you think you can't buy one on your own?"

I blink back at him, not sure how to explain my thought process. He waves me off before I can figure out my words.

"I don't want to know. Go buy a bidet for every toilet if you want. Also, you do need to stop using Danika's toilet, your poos are nasty. I don't understand how or why they smell so bad."

I nod in agreement. "I agree, it's an anomaly of life we may never get the answer to."

Jonah smiles and shakes his head, but then my other reason for appearing pops to mind.

"Oh! Danika's trying to move shit in the living room and won't let us help her," I tattle.

"She's doing *what?*" Jonah stands and immediately heads out of the room.

I skip behind him, not because I want to see her get in trouble, but because I want to see her growl at Jonah like she did to Colin and I. We reach the living room, and he stands there, watching in disbelief as she picks up a blanket with her elbows pinched together, then moves it to a new spot. I take up my position next to Colin and watch the show, wishing I had some popcorn. Jonah finally approaches, but he doesn't try to sneak; he makes plenty of noise so she knows he's coming.

She glances up for a moment before resuming her task of trying to spread the blanket out with her elbows. Honestly, I'm a little impressed. She's not giving up on this. When Jonah gets close, Danika looses a small growl at him. I have to hold in my sound of adoration at the cute little noise. He doesn't seem deterred by her growl, and moves another step or two closer.

"I can do it just fine!" she snaps before Jonah can say anything.

He holds up his hands in surrender. "I know you can, you're my amazing omega who can do anything she puts her mind to."

I'm almost bouncing in my shoes, waiting to see her send him away, which honestly Gertie disapproves of, but I can't help it. I love to watch things like this play out, especially when it seems like the roles are getting flipped on their head.

To my surprise, she melts.

"Amazing?" she says softly, blinking up at him.

"Of course! You're an amazing omega, and a beautiful person." He starts up a purr for her.

Oh, he's playing dirty, and I love it.

"Do you see this?" I whisper almost silently to Colin.

He shushes me and keeps his eyes on the other two.

"Will you allow me to help? I'd love to let my omega tell me what to do," Jonah says smoothly.

Danika preens before nodding and directing him where the blanket should go. The spot, the angle, the fold, it all has to be specific to her desire. She proceeds to then make him move the lamp she struggled with earlier, photos, knick-knacks, tiny sculptures, and even the rug. When it's how she wants it, she sighs and sinks into the couch. That seems to snap her out of whatever that was.

"Oh my goodness, I am so sorry!" she squeaks when she looks at everything rearranged.

Jonah shushes her and sits with her, wrapping an arm around her back.

"Your omega side needed to nest, it's perfectly fine. It looks wonderful, we never would have thought to make it look this nice," he assures her.

While I can see the praise go to her head, she's no longer running on pure instincts.

"I don't know about that, but thank you for letting me do it. I'm not sure what came over me."

Colin and I join the two of them on the couch and sit back with a sigh. Danika looks at us, and I can see embarrassment flood her face.

"I'm so sorry I snapped at you guys!" she says, her face red.

Colin puts a hand on her knee. "Hey, it's okay. I'm glad Jonah was able to help you. Sometimes pack means letting others step up to help. Please don't feel bad."

She nods and leans her head into him, resting it on his shoulder. The two of them sigh in contentment, and a burst of perfume floods the room, almost making us dizzy with her scent. Colin nuzzles his nose against the top her head.

"Baby, are you going into heat?" he asks gently.

Danika whines softly, "I don't want to be."

"I'm not sure it's something you can control, sweetheart," Jonah adds.

Danika pouts instead of answering.

"Did you decide if you want to have your heat with us or alone?" I ask tentatively.

Danika sits straight up, as if the thought hadn't occurred to her before. She looks over all three of us before staring into the distance, her thoughts almost spilling out of her head with how hard she's working through her options.

"I want to have it with you three … but I want something else, too," she confesses.

"Anything you want, baby, you only have to ask," Jonah promises.

"Um … this is fast, but … I want us to bond. All of us. If you help me."

We all go still for a moment, and I can smell Danika's scent getting more bitter as nerves start to take over. I can't have that, not with this big of a moment.

"I will. I'm in. I mean, how could I not be? I love all three of you like crazy. Of course I'm in. I'm just worried you're going to bite in and regret being stuck with us," I tell her, baring my big fear to her.

She looks at me in surprise, her eyes wide and staring.

"You love me?" she asks in disbelief.

"How could I not?" I reply.

She grins, but then her features morph into confusion.

"Why in the world would I regret being bound to the three men who are my matches and have helped me in ways I'm still striving to understand?" she asks, genuinely confused. "Men who I'm falling for every day."

I grin at her. "Well, when you put it that way …"

She smiles back, and by now, Jonah and Colin have pulled their heads from their asses.

"If you're sure it's what you want, it's what we'll do," they both promise.

Standing, I hold out my arm in a formal gesture and use my most posh, terrible accent.

"Madame, if you please, I shall escort you to your nest. You may use or ignore it as you see fit."

Danika giggles and stands, looping her arm around mine, her forearm atop mine and her hand floating in the air.

"Lead the way, my good gentleman," she says, but no accent.

Oh well, not everyone can pull out the talent like I can. Colin and Jonah trail us, and it feels a bit like they're security, ensuring the safety of our journey to Danika's current suite. When we walk in those doors, she removes her arm from mine and waves forward, the gesture giving me permission to lead the way. I walk to an unobtrusive door in the back of her room, and grandly open it, but don't step inside. One lesson I will always remember is to never enter an omega's nest without permission.

Danika steps in and sighs in delight. There's a small room that she steps into, outfitted with a small kitchenette and counters, then beyond that is an opening straight into the rounded room. The nest has a tall enough ceiling that we can stand, but the ceiling is low enough to feel cozy and safe. She walks the perimeter of the room, looking at the walls and evaluating how it looks. All we have in there right now is a gargantuan circle mattress made specifically for omega heats.

She turns and grins at us. "I can't wait to use this room."

After pulling out my wallet, I hold it up in the air. "Let's go shopping."

Chapter 30

Danika

C olin barely makes it into the backseat of the vehicle before Emmett's racing us off to the nearest store. It's an adorable, locally owned shop with access to a wide variety of items. It's not quite mom and pop, but they manage to find that vibe anyway. When I walk in, I can't smell much of anything, even myself. They must have some industrial strength air filters to make it so scentless. Good on them.

We wasted no time in getting to a nesting store, my omega almost salivating at the idea of getting that gorgeous room filled with soft, plush pillows and blankets. I'm already picturing swaths of soothing blue fabric draping along the walls with fairly lights strung around the perimeter. They'll be wrapped loosely in gauzy gray fabric to give them an ethereal glow. I might add some richer blues or purples to contrast the light blue fabric draping.

My omega is chomping at the bit to go through all the fabrics to find what we love, but I'm second guessing myself now that I can see all the wonderful items in this store. Should I really let them pay for any of it? Do I really need a nest? I could probably be just fine bringing them home to my not-a-nest. It's worked well enough in the past.

Thinking back to the last few heats I've had in there, my omega shakes her head at me, reminding me that we spent that last one hopped up on muscle relaxers and minor sedation. I could eat and use the bathroom, but it was slow moving and took effort. Maybe it didn't hurt, but it wasn't fun either. Even with the medication, I felt tense, absolutely convinced that someone was going to find me and take advantage.

So, maybe it didn't work well enough in the past. Maybe it just let me survive. Now that I have the option to have my own *actual* nest, it feels overwhelming. I take a step back and find a solid body behind me and an arm wrapping around my waist to keep me steady. Even without scents, I know the feel of this body. Colin.

"You okay?" he asks softly.

I nod my head, but then shake it. I am, but I'm not, and I don't know how to articulate what the problem is. Putting the feeling into actual words seems too hard, and I'm not sure if I can do it.

"Too overwhelming?" he guesses.

I nod my head.

"Emmett," he calls my scattered alpha back, "we need to take this in small pieces. I have a suspicion this is our omega's first time building her own nest."

Emmett's eyes snap to mine, wide with surprise, awe, and excitement.

"We get to help you build your first one? I'm so fucking honored, Stargazer."

Of course that's his reaction. My beautiful Emmett, who sees the opportunity in everything. He could have turned away in disgust or frustration, or confusion, but he embraces the chance to make this experience wonderful.

"I love you," I tell him, realizing how much I mean it after hearing him say it earlier.

"I love you, too," he replies, landing a soft kiss on my lips.

"One stop at a time. Let's start with wall fabric," Colin says, grabbing a cart.

Emmett snatches a second one and we start moving. When the first fabric catches my eye, I stop to admire it and see if I can imagine it in my nest. *My* nest! Emmett and Colin are a step ahead of me, but close enough that I can hear them.

"I'm sorry, I didn't mean to make it weird for you," Emmett says.

Colin shushes him. "You love her, and she loves you. She'll love Jonah and me, too, in her time. Don't worry, baby, you didn't make anything weird."

I don't think I have a heart anymore. I think I have a pile of goo that somehow twitches enough to keep my blood pumping. These men are so fucking tender that I have a hard time believing they're not just figments of my imagination. Focusing back on the fabric, I decide it is something I would like.

"Can we get this one to drape on the walls?" I ask them.

Colin and Emmett turn back and grin when they see I'm holding up some fabric. They agree enthusiastically, and we add the bolt of fabric to our cart. Shopping goes by quicker than I assumed it would, and it's actually fun. Emmett and Colin offer suggestions excitedly, and happily throw back any items I'm not interested in. The two of them created a game out of the experience called "yeet or keep." Anything labeled "yeet" gets thrown back into the container it came from. Giggles erupt from me when Emmett decides to declare the choice loudly, not caring who might hear.

That part of me hid long ago, the part that doesn't pay attention to societal norms. It would have loudly joined Emmett in his declarations, enjoying every moment of the experience. Warmth infuses my bones as I watch him exist carefree in the moment, willing to do anything that makes shopping easier for me to bear. My healing hands are sore, and our carts are piled high when we reach the checkouts; full of pillows, blankets, curtains, fairy lights, and even some stuffies. My favorite one is the marshmallow with a smile.

Trying to be sneaky, I step in front of the guys so I can pay while they pile our spoils on the counter for purchase. Unfortunately for me, they're on to me, and Emmett slides his card to the cashier as she grabs the next item. She looks up at him with an eyebrow raised and he just grins.

"Trying to make sure my omega here doesn't pay for her own stuff," he explains.

The cashier smiles and holds his card to run before looking at me. "You're so lucky to have someone so generous to be with."

Flushing with pleasure at her compliment, I smile at my guys. "Thanks, they're pretty great," I tell her.

The guys stuff all the goodies into the back seat and truck of the car and enforce the need for me to sit up front. I only relent because I know that when I start to nest for real, it's going to be a lot of effort, and I won't want them helping. I do need that fabric up, though, so I'll have them hang that and then kick them out. My omega is satisfied with that, and eager to get started on making our very own nest.

This relationship is moving quickly, but I'm not scared. I thought I would be, but there's just this deep feeling of home and belonging, anchoring me to these men when I might otherwise feel adrift. We reach home, and I scurry upstairs while Colin and Emmett grab bags to bring upstairs.

"Jonah?" I call out.

I want to make sure he's not trying something sneaky in my nest. A sudden stab of possessiveness comes over me, and the idea of him being in that space before it's ready spikes my anxiety. I will want him in there when it's ready and not one second before.

Silence meets my voice. I frown slightly and call his name again as I walk toward my room, but there's no response. Maybe he's locked in his office; I'll check that once the nest is how I want it.

Colin and Emmett come into my suite and drop the bags outside of the nest before turning to grab more.

"Wait! I need one of you to help me get the blue fabric and fairy lights up." I stop them.

"Why don't you do it? Your scent probably won't linger as much as mine," Emmett says to Colin.

Both of their scents are potent to me, but Emmett has a point. Beta scents rarely last as long in the air as alpha scents. Something to do with pheromones I think. I grab Colin's hand and pull him into the nest with me. Before he reaches the circular part of the room, I stop him with a stern look.

"This is the *only* time you're allowed in here until it's complete, do you understand?"

Colin looks at me, and I can see that he understands the weight of this moment, that it's a pivotal point for me in accepting the nest and accepting them as pack. He nods solemnly.

"I promise I will not step foot in this room again without your express permission."

My omega eyes him for a moment, ensuring he means it. I believe it, but my omega instincts are a little more wary. This nest has to be perfect before they can see it, but once she sees his sincerity, I relax marginally.

"Okay, grab the fabric and fairy lights, then meet me back here in the doorway."

Colin gives a cheeky salute and steps back into the suite, digging through the bags until he returns victorious with the fairy lights and swaths of fabric. Once I've led him inside, I demonstrate where I want the fabric and the fairy lights. Colin starts with the fabric, installing subtle hooks for the fabric to cling to, while I make sure I have enough sheer fabric to wrap around the light strings.

Joy overflows in my heart as I see my vision for the room coming together. Silky blue fabric drapes smoothly around the room, encasing it without shrinking the space. I hand him the fairy lights, and as he installs the strands, I follow with my fabric, gently wrapping the lights so they give a bit of an ethereal glow. Smiling wide, I'm almost in tears as my joy overflows.

"It's more than I ever let myself dream it could be," I tell Colin when we finish.

"It's perfect," he tells me, placing his hand on my lower back.

The jarring realization that he's in here hits me, making my omega prickle. He finished his job, now he needs to get the fuck out. The nest isn't ready!

"Get out!" I turn and push him toward the door. "Out, out, out!"

Colin goes willingly, and I'm pretty sure I hear him laugh but I ignore it, wanting to get started on making this space cozy as fuck. When we emerge back into the main suite, I pull all the bags into the nest's entry area and close the door without a word. It's time to get to work. First, I put the sheets on the bed.

Part of me wants to dump it all out, and the other part is asking for precise placement, so I compromise with myself. I dump out all the blankets, and then rearrange those to cover where I want them. After that, I do the same with the pillows, but those get strategic placement. Each part of the nest needs to have a minimum of two pillows, and the variety goes from a small decorative pillow to a perfectly positioned bolster for when I can't hold myself up to take a knot anymore. There's a throbbing pain happening in my hands, but it's background noise to my instincts right now.

My skin itches, desire to touch all of those beautiful fabrics is riding me hard, telling me to just dive in and snuggle, but it's not right. There's something off, and it takes a few rearrangements of the pillows to figure it out. It doesn't smell right. I need their scents to make it right. I need them *now*.

I slam the door to the nest open, causing Colin and Emmett to hop off the bed and stand straight up. I'm pretty sure they were making out based on their red cheeks, but I don't have time to worry about that. *Wait, where's Jonah?*

"Where's Jonah?" I ask.

"He went to get more of your clothes," Colin explains.

Huffing in exasperation, I pin them both with my glare.

"Get him here *now* and give me your shirts."

Their brows furrow in confusion, but neither of them questions me. It takes seconds, but the moment I have their shirts in my hands, things start to settle. My skin isn't quite so itchy, a cooler, soothing feeling eases my sharp edges, but it's not right still. Realizing he's missing agitates me and my sharp edges come right back out. I let out a whine and look back at them, full of frustration and need.

"I need Jonah!" I demand before slamming the door to my nest closed.

If they won't bring me Jonah, they don't get to come in.

Chapter 31

Jonah

The drive to Danika's place is peaceful, a quiet car to myself, decent traffic, and the chance to bring my omega her belongings. Something to help her feel more at ease as she moves in with us. I'm looking forward to pampering her as much as she'll let us. I don't know if she'll want to use the gallery all the time, but I might ask her to let us have one display with her art year-round. Rotating it whenever she sees fit. If she doesn't want to, I'll never pressure her, but my body feels buoyant at the idea of her providing us beauty to show the world.

The three of us aren't sharing *her* with the world, but if she's willing to showcase her beauty, we're honored to have her do it with us. After her showing, the gallery has picked up momentum, and we're booked out several months for art exhibits. We used to contract for longer exhibits, but now that we have more inquiries, we're allowing shorter ones, too. It gives us more variety and gives newer artists a chance to get their feet wet in the world of exhibitions.

Our current short-term exhibition is all line art, and it's fascinating to me how one black line can be transformed in so many ways to evoke so many emotions. I wonder if Wonder would have enjoyed these. She always saw so much more than I gave her credit for, and the hole she created when she left aches a little more. I wish I could see who she would have grown up to be. I'm not sure if I would have been as driven to create my gallery, but maybe the trade off would have been worth it.

I suppose I'll never know, which makes me think of my big sister. I should call her at some point; it's been a while since we talked. We're not terribly close, but we've always been there for each other. Maybe it's time for more regular check ins.

Pulling into Danika's driveway, I note that it's empty still. Her door is closed, and windows all look good. A sigh of relief courses through my body. There's no reason someone would break into her little house, but it's back into the woods a bit, so it would be easy for someone to get away with a robbery. Hopefully my alpha will stop worrying about that kind of thing once she lives in our house. He can be so over the top sometimes.

Letting myself in, I gaze around her house, absorbing everything that makes Danika who she is. I could spend hours in here looking around, but that feels a little creepier than I want to be, so I make a point to keep the visit short. First things first, clothes. I brought a couple of suitcases, but I want to find her bags and luggage if I can, that way her things still smell the way she remembers. I do find a couple of suitcases, so I pull those out and start filling each with clothing. My eyes snag on some of her sexier items, because I know she didn't pick them to specifically look sexy. I know her well enough to see that she just liked them, and my dick hardens slightly as I think of how she'll look wearing them.

"Down, boy," I mutter to myself.

After tossing a couple of blankets and pillows in, I get the cases zipped up and decide to look around. Breach of privacy? A little. Can I resist? Absolutely not. Danika consumes my thoughts so heavily that I can't resist the opportunity to look at her home without anyone judging me for looking. I've seen the living room before, so I wander into her studio and stop frozen in the doorway. The room is alive with traces of her, a place full of calm and endless possibilities. Light pouring in through the large windows highlights the room perfectly, and the image of Danika painting in here floods my mind.

I can see the slight frown between her brows as she focuses, her eyes lasered in on the canvas, coaxing her image to life. Her history of passion is lined up in neat rows, each canvas sitting in its own specific place, waiting for the world to see it. My fingers itch to move each one so I can see what she's created and experience what she sees, but I know better. It would be a bigger invasion of privacy than I'm already doing, one that may not be something I could recover from.

Resigned to behaving myself, I leave her studio and grab the suitcases before heading to the door. Her kitchen catches my eye, and I take a step in without thinking, my mind fixated on how clean it is. How she looked frantically cleaning the living room, knowing now that she scrubbed this room first, kicking off her chemical burns. On the counter, there's a container sitting out of place, and I peek through the clear plastic sides to see cookies. They immediately go into my stash of things to bring back with me.

I'm closing my door in the car when I see my phone ringing. It routes through my car Bluetooth, and I can hear some frantic movement in the background.

"Hello?"

"Jonah! Glad you picked up, you need to get home *now!*" Emmett says frantically.

A spike of fear jolts through me, and the world sharpens around me, my mind singularly focused on getting to my pack.

"What's happening?" I snap into the phone.

"Danika's hardcore nesting and she wants everyone's scent. She's locked herself into her nest."

"She what?" I race out of Danika's driveway and ignore road rules as I rush home.

"Yeah, we tried to bring her some of your dirty laundry, but she told us that if you weren't here to get away from her."

"Just ... just stay in the room with her, try to soothe her if she comes out."

Emmett scoffs on the other end, "Duh."

"Yeah, yeah, be there in five," I smirk.

I arrive in six minutes flat, after speeding the entire way. My bounty of goods is forgotten in the car as I race into the house. I had an expectation of noise and yelling, but it's strangely quiet. It's an odd sensation, rushing somewhere in a panic, knowing something isn't right, but hearing no distress at all. Uneasiness settles in, making my stomach turn and all my senses go on high alert. My ears strain for the slightest noise, and my eyes search for anything out of place. Nose leading me upstairs, I can detect the small hints of emotion and scent woven together, a complex bouquet of desire, anxiety, worry, and excitement.

When I push open the door to the omega suite, Colin and Emmett turn to me from their perch on the bed, relief flooding their faces.

"Thank god," Colin mumbles.

I stride toward the door and knock gently.

"I *said* I want *Jonah!*" I hear her demanding voice clearly through the door.

She must be sitting in the entry area of the nest, and I know she'll pick up my scent if I stay quiet, but there's no way I'll be able to stay quiet when she needs me. Ever.

"It's me, baby girl. Open up," I say smoothly through the door.

She swings the door open and wastes no time climbing me like a tree. With zero hesitation, I wrap one arm around her thighs and pick her up, nuzzling my nose into her neck while she does the same. A purr starts up in my chest, and I let it rumble to life as I feel her muscles slowly melt while she's in my arms.

"There's my girl," I rumble into her neck.

"Alpha," she whines quietly into me.

I hold her for another moment before she pushes away and

squirms until I let her down. When she's standing in front of me, her hands tug at my shirt, pulling it up.

"Off."

A smile comes to my face at her demand. "Yes, ma'am."

Once the shirt is off, she snatches it, inhales deeply, then slams the door in my face. It takes a moment for my brain to catch up to the fact that I'm now looking at a door instead of my omega. What the hell? I turn to the guys, completely confused.

"What the hell just happened?" I ask.

"Nesting, man. Nesting just happened," Emmett says, flopping back on the bed to stare at the ceiling.

Still dazed, I move to sit next to Colin. He claps a hand on my shoulder and squeezes gently.

"She'll let us in when she's ready," he assures me.

A heavy sigh escapes me, but now that the immediate threat is over, I remember all her stuff in my car. I stand up and groan, not wanting to leave the room right now, even though I saw she's fine.

"Where are you going?" Emmett asks.

"Need to get her stuff from the car," I answer.

"I got it!" Emmett pops up and scurries out of the room faster than a cheetah.

Colin meets my questioning stare. "He's been really antsy."

"Makes sense." I nod before resuming my spot on the bed.

"Do you think we're ready for this?" he asks.

"I'm honestly not positive. It's going to be a whirlwind for sure, but if we focus on what Danika wants, I think we'll be okay. We just need to remember that she comes first."

Colin smirks. "Literally."

Chuckling, I push his shoulder lightly, earning a full grin from him. We sit in companionable silence, holding hands and sharing the unspoken fear that maybe we're not good enough. Along with the unspoken fear is that underlying hope and devotion, the knowledge that we'll do anything for Danika, and she'd do anything for us. As long as we remember that, we'll be okay. We have to be.

Emmett makes it back to the suite with the suitcases, his breathing picked up but not heavy.

"Feel better?" I ask.

He nods. "A little, yeah. I hate not being able to *do* something."

"I know, baby. Come here," I coax him close and bring him to face level—me on the bed, and him on his knees.

"You are wonderful," I tell him before my lips gently land on his.

He leans into the kiss, and I can feel his restless energy. It's clear he was restless and in need of a task. Well, now he can kiss me for a task so I can soothe my inner alpha and care for my pack. Colin moves behind me on the bed, lips going to my ear.

"Alpha, you care for us so much, let me care for you," he whispers.

Colin proceeds to pepper my neck and shoulders with kisses and love bites, our exposed skin touching and rubbing, creating a heat that none of us want to ignore. A loop of pleasure begins with the three of us, but I can feel the strain trying to keep the situation from spiraling. We don't need to start a sex party out here while our omega is making her nest for us.

The door to the nest swings open dramatically, and Danika stands there, proud and excited. Her eyes catch on the three of us, and her sweet scent floods the air. All three of us groan at her scent and turn so she's completely in our focus. Her breathing picks up, scent getting impossibly sweeter, almost all sugar now with just a hint of mint to keep it from being overwhelming. Her pupils are dilated as she runs those eyes over our bodies.

"I think I'm ready," she rasps.

The three of us stand and look at her, gazes hungry and ready to devour this amazing omega we've been gifted. There's no stopping the rumble in my voice.

"Well, let's not keep you waiting."

Chapter 32

Danika

My skin is on fire as I invite my pack into my nest. With my inhibitions lowered, it's easier to address them for what they are: my pack. I'm still nervous, hesitant that this will be a good thing in the long run, but I know I can't keep living hidden away. I have matches right here in front of me, and if we can't make this work? Nothing will work. I'm placing all my bets on these men, and I'm praying it works out. The burning feeling in my body snaps me out of my internal thoughts and I lick my lips, my eyes roaming up and down each of the men standing before me. I'm blocking the entrance to the circular nest, while they're in the entry room, door to the suite closed and eyes burning into me.

It's silence for a few seconds, all four of us drinking the moment in, reveling in the mix of sexual tension and absolute certainty that this is inevitable. All my thoughts have bled out, my worries gone as I take them in. They've made no move to come closer, so I raise my eyebrows at them before slowly tugging my shirt off. A trio of groans ring in my ears as I toss my shirt behind me in the nest. They're still as statues, so I inch back into the nest, just barely past the doorway.

The three of them lurch forward before Jonah stops them. He

clears his throat, but it does no good. His voice is still gravely with desire, and my body shivers in pleasure at hearing his next words.

"May we enter your nest, Omega?"

As much as I want to tease them and drag this out, I'm in too much need to delay any longer. Instead of words, I grab his hand and yank him toward me. Jonah almost trips, but then catches himself and takes control of the movement, pushing forward and laying me down on the large mattress. I'm still in my leggings and underwear, so Jonah works to peel my leggings off before looking at the other two and using his head to indicate they should come help.

They hesitate for only a moment before entering my nest. Jonah had said "we" so my omega isn't bothered at all, but we *want* them in here with us. It feels right. The three of them communicate wordlessly and work to slide my bra off my body while worshiping it with kisses and nips. Need drives me higher and higher, bliss flooding my body as they continue their ministrations, and I feel weightless.

As Jonah's tongue slides up my thigh, closer and closer to my clit, the first cramp hits. I'm dragged from my blissed out feeling into pain. My stomach feels as though someone is trying to scoop out my insides. My hands fly to my stomach, and a pained whimper falls from my lips. Colin freezes, fingers pausing in their task of tugging at my nipples.

"Do you need a knot, pretty girl? Are you hurting?" he asks.

I nod my head frantically and whimper, "Yes."

"You heard her, Jonah. Better get a knot in her unless you want our omega in pain," he teases.

Jonah growls, and when I look, his eyes are almost completely black. He must be entering a rut. It's something I should probably be worried about, but the intensity of his gaze just makes my pussy gush with more slick. He crawls up my body, somehow already naked, and I can feel his hard length dragging across the skin of my legs as he moves. When I look at the other two, I realize I must have been blissed out longer than I thought since they're both naked as well. My tongue darts out as I let my gaze roam over them in hunger.

Colin and Emmett respond with renewed vigor in their suckling, kissing, and nipping. Their lips meet mine in brief but heated kisses, tongues and mouths sucking at my nipples, my neck, anywhere they can reach. Jonah brings a hand to my neck, bracing me but not squeezing, and tilts my head so my eyes meet his. Colin and Emmett turn their affections to each other, somehow understanding Jonah's signal to back off.

The tip of his cock nudges at my entrance, testing, prodding, but not entering. Not yet. His lips meet mine, and he controls the kiss, full of heat, passion, desire. My mind turns floaty as he stakes his claim with his mouth. When we part, it's only for him to growl, "Omega," before sliding himself home. His knot inflates just the smallest amount, but it's a new sensation for me. Wanting his knot and being aroused changes my entire experience with knots. This time it feels *amazing*, and I want more of it.

"Alpha," I whine, keening as he thrusts into me again.

His pace speeds up, his hips snapping faster and faster, unrelenting in the pleasure coursing through my body.

"Omega," he growls against my lips, and I tilt my head instinctively, baring my neck to him.

His teeth drag gently across the skin of my throat, and my pussy clenches down on his dick. Loud groans escape the two of us, his knot swollen and ready to take its place in my body.

"Please!" I beg.

"*Mine,*" he growls before sinking his teeth into me, breaking the skin and marking me.

The pure pleasure sets off my orgasm, and I scream at the intensity; wave after wave rolling across my body while I milk him. His teeth finally release me, tongue now attending the bite with gentle licks meant to help the skin heal. This man is a machine. Not once has his pace faltered as he gave his bite, and now he uses that momentum to slowly stuff my body with his knot. One, two, three thrusts and he's in, settling deep inside of me as he continues to rut shallowly.

Taking the opportunity, I strike at the juncture of his neck and shoulder, burying my teeth deep into him, the tang of blood telling me that I don't need to bite any harder. Before I can withdraw my teeth, our bond snaps into place. Ecstasy overwhelms me as his emotions invade my senses, his pleasure amplifying my own as he comes inside of me.

"*Fuck!*" he yells before stilling in one last shallow thrust.

Jonah collapses on his elbows, body hovering over me while his face bends down to find his bite and lick it lazily. His body is close enough that I can do the same, helping his skin to heal as much as he's helping mine. He repositions us on our sides, face to face while we wait for his knot to go down. I can feel some vibrations in my chest before realizing that I'm purring for him. We both relax into the sound with soft hums of contentment.

I wake with my stomach cramping again, painful enough to cause tears in my eyes. A whimper of pain escapes me as I move my hand around, trying to find one of my guys. My brain doesn't register that I fell asleep, but right now I don't care about that. Logic gets shoved aside as I frantically search for my other alpha. I *need* his knot. Now. Right now. But I want my beta, too. A high-pitched whine of frustration and pain generates from my throat before I feel a hand grasp mine.

"Shhhh, Omega, we'll take care of you," a deep voice says.

My eyes crack open enough to see the delicious dark skin of my other alpha, and I turn to wrap both arms around him, working to rub my pussy on his cock. He flips onto his back, bringing me with him, and places his hands on my hips. Encouraging the motions, his hands rock me back and forth, making sure I'm grinding down hard enough to get the friction my body needs.

"Colin," I hear him grunt below me.

A second set of hands appear from behind me, grasping my breasts with tender care before pinching and tugging my nipples harshly. The difference in sensations has me moaning in pleasure, arching my back so they're easier to access.

"Have I told you lately that I fuckin' love your boobs?" Colin asks from behind me.

My beta. This is exactly what I needed, my alpha and beta taking care of me at the same time. Eager for more connection, I try to push my ass against him at the same time I grind down on my alpha while still pushing my breasts out for attention. Needless to say, it doesn't work and I lose my momentum. Growling in frustration, I try again to get as much contact as I can but end up with the same result.

"Hold on, sweetheart, let Emmett in," my beta says.

He helps lift my hips so I can drop down on my alpha's cock. The stretch is amazing and the sigh of relief that I let out is loud in the quiet moment of connection. Moaning in pleasure, my alpha uses his grip on my hips to start bouncing me up and down, making sure to grind my clit on his pelvic bone each time he slams me down. A hand snakes around my body, sliding between my alpha and me, teasing my clit as I'm fucked on my alpha's cock. The additional friction drives me higher and higher until I can't take the pleasure anymore.

"You want to come?" My beta's lips touch my ear as he commands, "Come all over your alpha's cock, baby girl."

My body shatters, my pussy clenching around my alpha's cock, tingles racing up and down my legs as waves of pleasure wash over my body. Slick gushes out of me, completely soaking my alpha's hips.

"Just like that, what a good girl gushing everywhere. Fuck, you're so damn gorgeous, are you ready for me?"

Looking down, I see my alpha's eyes look over my shoulder, then his head nods slightly. He moves one hand to my head, pulling me down so our noses are touching.

"Let your beta in, Stargazer. We're gonna fill you up until you're absolutely stuffed with us and our cum. You gonna be a good girl and let him in?" he asks, whispering, making the moment intimate.

"Yes, Alpha," I breathe.

He stops moving me, and when I try to take over, my hips are held in place so I can't move. Then I feel a second blunt tip pushing in next to my alpha's cock. I moan, wanting to be stuffed, but also a little afraid, so I try to move my hips. I'm tugged back and held firmer while my beta slowly enters me. When I let out a whimper, he stops.

"Do you need to stop?" my beta asks.

"No!" I snap at him.

He chuckles before resuming his progress into my tight channel. Slowly, he pushes and pulls, ensuring that he's completely covered in my slick before finally seating himself fully inside of me.

"Oh god!" I cry.

This wakes up my head alpha, and he looks over at the three of us before he growls. He sits, eyes fixed on where we're joined, then crawls over to get a closer look. The two dicks in me start to move, alternating who thrusts so there's constant movement in my body, my men giving and receiving their own pleasure as we move in sync. The front of me is still plastered against my alpha as I'm used and it's everything I could ask for. My head alpha reaches over to move my hair off my shoulder, opposite of his own bite.

"Fuck, baby girl, I can't hold it, I'm gonna ..." my beta groans as he comes.

The hot splash of his cum inside of me triggers a moan of pleasure from my alpha and me, before pulling out and sinking his teeth in the back of my neck. The pierced skin stings at first before the pleasure sets in. Without thought, I grab his arm and bite down, my teeth sinking deep, snapping our connection into place. His unwavering love and steadiness fill me, and the sting of tears hits my eyes. There's a surety in him that I've never felt before, and I feel safe down to my core.

My alpha will not be ignored, though, and begins to thrust up into me as he pulls me down. Our bodies slam together, my pleasure ramping up again, tingles concentrating around my entrance, alerting me to the cliff I'm about to shoot over. He tightens his hold before slamming into me so hard his knot pops in then expands large enough that it almost feels like I still have two cocks in me. My orgasm hits hard and fast, my vision blacking out for a moment before I feel that familiar pinch of teeth staking their claim on me.

He laps at the fresh wound, working to soothe and seal it before he pulls his head back, baring his throat to me. My heart stutters at his surrender to me, and I lunge for his neck, not wanting to waste another moment. Sinking my teeth into his skin, that familiar bond snap pulses through me and playfulness wells up, bringing a lightness to the world.

I collapse fully onto my alpha, reveling in the different bonds coursing through me. I'm safe and content for the first time in years.

Chapter 33

Emmett

F our days after Danika's heat starts, and my dick is ready to fall off. Worth it.

Danika was insatiable in the best way, and after we all completed our mate bonds with her, we pack bonded each other and spent the rest of our time enjoying each others' bodies. My grin is permanently on my face now; I'm not sure that it will be physically possible to remove it. I don't mind the least; everyone can see how happy I am to have a fully bonded pack and an omega match. We're all sticky and sweaty, but none of us wants to be alone, so we all pile into the over-sized shower in Danika's suite. It's a tight fit, but we're able to get clean without being distracted. All four of us want comfort right now, not sex.

Once we're clean, we migrate to the couch and snuggle in a big pile. Jonah starts to ask about what everyone has planned now that Danika's heat is over, but I boo him whenever he tries to talk.

He tries four times before turning to me and snapping, "What the hell, man?"

"Too soon after heat. Adult tomorrow, not today," I tell him.

Danika raises her hand. "Omega seconds that."

"Proposed and seconded, the movement shall pass!" I declare in my best low-pitched, serious voice.

"You are *both* nuisances," he insists.

I can feel his amusement through our bond, though, so it's pretty obvious that he's not serious. I've never thought that he was in these moments, but it's nice to have the bond confirming it. A wave of love flows through me, and I lock eyes with my alpha, our gazes soft. My own love is pushed from me to him in response, triggering a small smile on his face. We spend the rest of the day snuggling, kissing, and lounging in absolute peace and love.

The next day, I wake to the sight and feel of Danika in my arms. Our bodies curve together perfectly, and I get lost staring at her. I manage to tear my gaze away long enough to check the time. It's just past nine, so I'm guessing Colin is at the gym and Jonah's left for the gallery. Time alone with my omega? Yes, please.

She sighs and turns in my arms, opening her eyes slowly to look at me. A smile spreads across her face, and a zing of happiness that comes down our bond hits me, causing my own smile in return. I don't think feeling her emotions will ever get old.

"Morning," I say softly.

"G'morning," she rasps back, voice still sleepy.

"It's just us this morning."

She hums. "What should we do?"

"I vote breakfast, and then I was thinking that you need space in this house."

"More than this gigantic suite?"

"Well, we could probably fit your art stuff in here, but it's gonna get messy."

Her eyes go wide. "You want me to have my art studio here?"

I gently run my fingers through her hair, the silky strands slipping through my fingers.

"If you'd like that. We can keep your current one, too, but I want you to have options. Me and my alpha want to take care of you, and I hope that by having a second studio, you can create whenever the inspiration strikes."

A slow grin spreads over her face and her eyes go glassy. Down the bond I can feel her disbelief, joy, and gratitude flowing freely. I send back my own awe and adoration for her, and the two of us lay silently, basking in the multitude of feelings and smiling at each other. Eventually, we move and get ready for the day in our own rooms. One of these days I'll have to commandeer one of her drawers so I don't have to leave her room to get dressed.

Once I'm clean and dressed, I reach up and take Gertie off her shelf. She slots nicely into her pocket, and I feel more like myself again. As much as I love Danika and the guys, something about having Gertie in my pocket settles me. I feel ready for the day.

As I make my way to the kitchen to get breakfast, I can smell food already cooking. When I look in the room, I see Danika standing by the stove, stirring eggs in a pan. She looks up at me, smiling before she turns back to her task at hand.

"Can you make some toast?" she asks.

"As you wish," I quip.

She giggles. "You're so cheesy."

We're still smiling and giggling as I grab out the bread to pop in the toaster. It's like being in high school again with my crush, except on a soul deep level. When we're done eating, we share dish duty before starting our hunt for an art room. There's nothing in the basement that would work for her, so I decide we should start on the upper level. One of our spare rooms has to have enough light. The house is giant, so we have three or four rooms that could work, but when we walk through them, Danika looks less than impressed.

"I just don't know." She hums as we look at the last room. "None of these feel quite right."

I tap a finger to my lips, thinking about where else could possibly work. I'll start building her a studio if I have to. She wraps her arms around me, holding me close to her.

"I'm grateful that you tried, nobody's wanted to give me something so personal in a long time. Well, except Sophie."

I nod sagely. "Sophie doesn't count, she's your emotional-support friend."

She giggles, and we leave the room, hands intertwined. When we get back to the main floor, Danika pauses, her eyes drawn to the light that streams into the kitchen from large windows. The kitchen and dining room are in the same overall space, no walls to separate them. It's a large area, but we spend the majority of our time at the island eating instead of using the table. Wait, eating space … that's it!

"I've got it!" I say excitedly and pull her to the far side of the kitchen, where a lone door sits, waiting to be used. "I completely forgot about this space because none of us ever use it. We always eat at the island or table, but this might just be what we're looking for."

Danika looks at me curiously, waiting for me to show her what I'm talking about. My hand wraps around the doorknob and I twist it open. Light spills into the kitchen as Danika walks through, eyes wide as she takes in the space. It's not as big as I'd like it to be, but it's not much smaller than her current studio. The room is a breakfast nook that was built into the house. There are three giant windows on one side with two skylights letting in additional light. She grins and walks around the room.

"I think we found it," she says.

"Let's go get you some supplies so we can transform the space."

She takes my hand and pulls me to the car, as excited as I am to go get her studio put together.

Our arms are overloaded with supplies, and it takes careful maneuvering to get everything stored in the small SUV we're using. We get it, but we have to load up the back seat as well with the smaller items. Pushing her hair out of her face, Danika sighs.

"Man, I wish I had my truck. Can you take me to get it soon?"

"Sure thing. I'm surprised we haven't done it sooner."

She holds up her hands. "Burned hands, remember? They're way better now, I wonder if bonding sped up the healing process?"

I grab her hands, looking them over with a hum. "That's gotta be it, these look almost healed. We should call your doctor to have them do a follow up. That's an insanely quick healing time."

We get the truck door closed, and Danika walks around the car before freezing in place. I follow her eyes and see a store called Paws and Claws with a cat tail designed into it. Her eyes snap to mine, and I can see the longing written there. She's so adorable.

Smirking, I put my hands on my hips. "Did you want to go look?"

She bounces in place, holding her hands under her chin. "Can we?"

"Let's go." I laugh, and we cross the street, fingers tangled together.

There are a few cats in the windows so people can see them as they pass by, and Danika stops to coo at them through the glass. Their mouths move in silent meows, and warmth fills me to see her interacting so happily with them.

"Did you want to go in and say hi?" I ask.

She turns to look up at me from her crouched position, and her cheeks flush with embarrassment.

"Oh. Right. Yeah, let's go in!"

I chuckle as I hold the door open for her, taking the opportunity to give her butt a quick pat as she goes by. The bond zings with happiness and a touch of arousal. She puts both hands on her ass and turns to look at me, her eyes playful.

"Excuse me, sir, we are in *public!*" She tries to sound scandalized.

I waggle my eyebrows at her. "And?"

She giggles and walks past the entry space into the main part of the store. Kittens and cats can be heard easily throughout the store. It's not a cacophony of birds in a zoo, but a steady hum of high pitched and adult pitched meows. We wander a bit between the different cats that are up for adoption. Some are in crates, but the sign above them says they're either waiting to be groomed or waiting on a quick vet check.

"So this is like an all-in-one kind of place," Danika mutters to herself.

"That sounds kind of nice. I wouldn't mind getting my yearly checkup while they trim my hair." I run a hand over my locs, pushing them back before they flip over to whatever formation they prefer.

My hair doesn't like to be tamed, so I typically have it up in some kind of tie and it flops wherever it pleases. Walking farther along, there's a small corral for the kittens, and I think Danika's ovaries explode based on the gasp she lets out. To be fair, if I had ovaries, they'd also burst. The small, little faces with too-big eyes look up and meow at us. A few are playing together, a few have shied away, and others still just ignore us. One little kitten, though, comes trotting right up to the cage-like wall that keeps them in the same area.

Danika crouches down, a huge smile on her face as she puts a couple of fingers near the gaps of the cage-wall, and the tiny, long-haired orange cat comes over, sniffs at her fingers, and meows. She beams in response and replicates the noise back to the tiny kitten. The kitten cocks her head, surprised at the noise that comes out of Danika. She grins when the cat does it again before rubbing its face against her fingers.

Gertie is also happy with the kitten, I can tell. Jonah and Colin never said we *couldn't* have a cat, just that they had no plans to get one a while back. Besides, Danika is bonding hardcore with that kitten, and who am I to break them apart? Danika looks up at me, her face pleading without words.

"I'll go find a cat bed," I say to her grin.

As I walk away, I can hear Danika's quiet, "Yesss!" of victory before she turns to tell the tiny kitten that its coming home with us.

Chapter 34

Jonah

All the artists are booked for next week's celebratory exhibit, and I've gotten the catering confirmed as well. We won't be serving anything substantial—after all, it is still an art gallery—but people need little finger foods to nibble on. The last thing I need to do is confirm pre-purchased ticket count, ensure our sales system has each artist in it so we can catalogue anything sold appropriately, and finalize where the work will hang. All things that I can handle from my home office. I have a basic floor plan of the gallery, so I can mark which painting is going on which wall. I'm hoping Danika will be willing to look it over and confirm if it looks good to her.

She may not run the gallery, but I'd like her artistic eye. Looking at the clock, I decide I've been away long enough today and decide to get home. I don't think Emmett and Danika had plans, so I'm looking forward to seeing them; Colin too if he's done at the gym. Sometimes he hangs around to help with fixing anything that's needed. He's toyed with leading some basic self defense classes in the future, but we've never pushed him on it. Thanks to our parents and the success of the gallery, we're just fine in the money department. He can take his time figuring it out.

Pulling my car into the driveway of our house, I note that our SUV is parked out of the garage with its trunk open. *That's odd.* After I park, I take a look and see a bunch of art supplies. I grin. We had talked about converting a space for Danika to use as an art studio, so Emmett must have found a spot she loves. May as well help out while I'm standing here. I lean in and grab an easel, sliding it gently out of the back space and walking toward the door with it. Once I'm in the house, I don't see anyone immediately and it occurs to me that I have no idea what room they picked.

"Emmett? Danika?" I call out.

I hear their voices but I'm too far away to figure out which direction they're coming from, so I call out again, and the response is closer so I assume they're coming to me. As I wait for them to appear, I hear a bell ringing. I bring one shoulder up to my ear and try to rub it.

Why is my head ringing like a bell? Do I have tinnitus? Is my hearing going? What the hell? The ringing gets louder before I feel a sharp pinch on my lower leg. I'm holding Danika's easel, so I can't just reach down and figure out what's pinching me, but I feel like something is crawling up my leg.

"*Emmett! Danika!*" I shout, terrified about whatever the hell is crawling up my leg.

Do we have rats? Oh my god, our house is infested! The weight gets closer, and I'm finally able to peer down to see a fluffy, orange fur ball scramble up my body to rest on my shoulder. Danika and Emmett skid into view as I realize that the fluff is a kitten. A tiny, adorable, evil kitten that is now purring and licking my ear. Ah, the ringing, it's her collar.

"Princess!" Danika gasps, before dissolving into giggles.

Emmett isn't far behind with his own laughter, and I give him my best glare.

"Who the hell is on my shoulder?" I ask him, no smile in sight.

"Just give it a second, we need to grab her," he says soothingly.

Danika walks closer crooning to the kitten, pulling tiny little noises from it on my shoulder. She manages to snag the kitten, but as her claws leave my shoulder, they snag on my shirt, scratching my skin.

"Are you okay?" she asks.

I sigh, not really angry. "Yeah, I'm fine."

When I look at her, I realize Danika was talking to the kitten. After rubbing the kitten's head, she peeks up at me and gives me a small, apologetic smile.

"Sorry," she says, cringing a little.

The sight of her apologetic face loosens the tension in my shoulders. As I feel the muscles in my body relax, I realize that perhaps I overreacted, but that damn kitten scared the shit out of me. My leg hurts, too. Feelings of guilt trickle down the bond, and I can't have that, she's got nothing to feeling guilty about.

"It's okay, sweetheart, no harm done. Want to show me your new art space? I've got this easel to set up in the room for you," I tell her softly.

"Yes! I hope it's okay that I took the room I did, Emmett said nobody uses it."

"I'm sure it's perfect."

Emmett reaches out to take the kitten from Danika. "I'll hold her highness while you show off your space."

The smile they share warms my chest, adding to the feeling of fulfillment that's been present and growing the longer we have Danika with us. I will never take her for granted, that's for sure. We walk through the kitchen, which confuses me for a moment before it clicks. Emmett really did pick the perfect spot. She opens the door on the far side of the room and spreads her arms in presentation.

"Ta-da!" she says proudly.

With a grin spread across my face, I step into the room and take in the supplies strewn about, noting that there's zero organization right now. This is the perfect space for her with all the light pouring in.

"You're right, this is perfect. I'd almost forgotten about this room.

It felt pretentious to have a room specifically for breakfast, so we never use it. Do we need to dust it at all?" I ask.

"No, Emmett and I did a quick sweep down before we left for supplies, so it's clean enough. We can just lean the easel against a wall. I don't want to set it up until I figure out the best spot and get my floor canvas down."

"Sounds good." I do as she instructed.

My arms open as I walk toward her and pull her close. She hums and happily returns the embrace, face angled toward my neck, taking in my scent.

"Have I told you how grateful I am that you gave us a chance?" I ask her.

"I think so, but you better tell me again just in case." She hums.

I lean down and leave a kisses on her face as I speak.

"I." Kiss. "Am." Kiss. "So." Kiss. "Grateful." Kiss. "For." Kiss. "You." Kiss.

She giggles and pulls my mouth down to hers, connecting us with a deep kiss. Our lips play for a moment before her tongue licks at me. I open, and our tongues playfully wrangle together, and the feelings of love and joy she sends my way make my knees weak. This woman who was once scared and standoffish now brings me to my knees with her love and passion. She's slowly escaping the shell she placed herself in, and I'm so lucky I get to witness it.

When we finally break for air, I hear voices talking in the distance. I land another peck on her lips, and we share one more smile, hers a bit mischievous.

"Sounds like Colin's home," I comment.

"Excellent," she says before breaking away from my arms and leading me out of the room.

We follow the sounds of arguing between our packmates. They don't sound angry, mostly confused on both sides. After walking through the kitchen to the entry hall, I can hear them in the bathroom. Our main floor bathroom isn't a full bath, but it is a large half bath. When Danika and I peek in, I can see a litter box next to the pedestal sink with Colin and Emmett debating about the placement.

"Why here, though? Can we put it in the basement or something?" Colin asks.

"What? And make her use the toilet away from us? That seems awfully mean," Emmett argues.

"I don't know if I want to pee in the same place the cat does!"

Emmett throws his hands in the air. "We all pee in here! Why not the cat?"

While the debate rages on, the kitten is batting at their shoelaces and capturing them with intent to disembowel. I gotta admit, the fluff ball is pretty adorable. My gaze stays on the kitten as I ask Danika what they named our new terror. She looks at me with a massive smile on her face.

"Princess Biscuits!"

I blink twice at her before I let my face crack into a smile, chuckling at the ridiculous name. It's perfectly fitting for Danika and Emmett to have chosen that.

"Since when did we decide to get a cat, anyway? I thought we said we weren't getting one!" Colin eventually explodes.

Danika's joyful face *falls*, and irritation rises up in me. Maybe I was the one who told Emmett we're not getting a cat, but how could Colin say that in front of Danika? Did he not notice her here? How is that possible with our bond? My irritation and anger at Colin must come through the bond, because he looks straight at me, surprised. Then his eyes take in Danika's face and any protests about the kitten fly out of the window.

"Oh, sweetheart, I didn't mean we don't want the cat!" Colin backtracks.

Spoiler alert: he's never wanted at cat. I'm watching that change in real time as he wrestles with his emotions and works to change his frown into something else. If that wasn't evidence of how far gone we are for her, I don't know what would be.

"I'm sorry! I begged Emmett when I saw her and I didn't think," she says softly.

"Fix it!" I hear Emmett hiss at Colin.

I roll my lips in to keep from laughing at the panic on their faces.

"No, you don't need to be sorry. I'm the one who's sorry," Colin says as he steps out of the bathroom to wrap his arms around her.

She lets him hold her for a moment, her sorrow written all over her face. Then, I'm not sure if I imagine it, but I swear I see a look of mischief come over her when she looks at Emmett.

Little trickster over there.

Danika's eyes fly up to me in surprise. She looks like she's been caught with her hand in the cookie jar.

"I'm not trying to be a trickster!" she protests.

Colin and Emmett give me the side eye.

"I never said you were!" I exclaim.

Her face turns confused. "But I heard you say it. You said 'little trickster over there' while Colin was hugging me."

Colin and Emmett both look bewildered, but Emmett chooses to be brave and speaks up.

"He didn't say anything, Stargazer ... at least, not out loud."

Her eyes widen, and she stares at me.

"Supercalifragilisticexpialidocious!"

I frown. "Mary Poppins?"

"It worked!" she exclaims, bouncing out of Colin's arms and into mine. Her laughter is loud, and with the volume and the movement, Princess Biscuits decides she's outta here. The little bell on the collar jingles softer and softer as she moves away.

Looking at the guys, they still look completely bewildered. So I try one more experiment.

"Group hug?"

Their eyes widen, mouths dropping open, before they bound over for a big hug.

"How is this possible?" Emmett asks.

"I'll do some research, see if there's some kind of explanation," Colin volunteers.

Danika gives each of us a kiss on the cheek. "This is going to be so much fun!"

Amusement bubbles up through me, and between our bond and my own amusement, I can't help but laugh. We all get a few chuckles in before I grab Danika's hand.

"I need your help, Dani. I need to finalize a few details about art placement for the gallery event next week."

"Of course! Anything for you guys." She beams.

We start walking, and my heart warms at how easily we've fallen into this routine as a full pack.

Chapter 35

Colin

"I've got coffee!" I hear Danika shout as I add one more hanger to this wall.

The gallery is still empty of art, most of it will be delivered later today, but I wanted to make sure we have all the hangers in place. The last thing we need during the event tomorrow is someone's art to fall and get damaged. We're doing really well with the gallery, both in reputation and income, but we don't want to deal with an angry artist *or* any accusations that we're careless.

"Have I told you lately that I love you?" I call back.

"Yes, but I demand to hear it again," she teases, closer now.

I turn from the wall and find her standing next to me now, so I snake an arm around her waist, careful of the two coffees in her hands, and pull her close gently. My lips descend on hers, and I show her my gratitude through my body, even if I can't take her here. *Fuck, I want to fuck her in this gallery with her art up.* My dick hardens at the thought, and I have to break from the kiss to try and cool off. Another time. We share one more quick kiss before I let her go and take the offered coffee.

"It's looking good," Danika says, stepping away from me to take in the set up.

I take her through each exhibit space, even though we've already planned it all out with her. I want her eyes on everything so I know I didn't add the wrong thing. The artist will always have a better eye than I do about how to hang work. We also inspect her art areas to ensure the pieces that need special lighting have it. This time we installed black lights along with the regular lights, so we can leverage that *and* use the UV wands to see all the dimensions she's painted in.

Danika can't find anything that needs changing, even in her own display space, so we set our coffees down on the reception desk and walk around back to get her art. We took her this last week to get her truck so she could load up stuff to keep at the house and stuff she wanted for his exhibit. So when we exit the back door, her beat up truck is waiting for us to unload her work, and Emmett is stepping out of the front seat.

My wonderful alpha is wearing some kind of body wrap with Princess Biscuit sticking her head out and looking around. One of his large hands is cupping the kitten's butt to support her, and I stare for a moment.

"Is that a *baby carrier?*" I ask.

Emmett's dark eyes meet mine. "No, that's ridiculous. It's a pet carrier."

Danika giggles next to me.

"I told him it was ridiculous, but he saw it at the store when we got P.B. and he wouldn't take 'no' for an answer," she explains.

My lips tug into a soft smile and I can't help but walk closer to him. Our mouths meet in a quick kiss, careful not to squish the kitten.

"*I love you,*" I tell him mentally.

"*I love you, too, my beta,*" he replies.

Danika and I move to get down to business and bring her art inside. Once all the pieces are in, we work together to get things hung in their designated spot. She ends up switching two of her pieces and hums in satisfaction at their new spots. This time, she doesn't have a special painting that's covered, but I know there's one in here that she made special for us.

Jonah's been in the back office while I work out here, and Danika scurries to the back so she can pull him out to see the piece. We stand around as she bounces excitedly on her toes, Princess Biscuits meowing as if she's cheering Danika on. Danika gestures to the painting next to her, and it's simple, but beautiful. A man and a woman stand next to each other, colors muted on the edges of the painting, but they become more vibrant as they meet in the middle.

The two figures are looking at each other with adoration written on their faces, and it's peaceful, calm. A steady sight of two people who are obviously affectionate with each other. Then she flips the black light and it changes abruptly. The woman's face is now covered in tears, with the man kneeling down, hands clasped as if begging her for something. Again, it's not extreme, just an abrupt change in scene. My emotions are pulled from safety and peace to uncertainty and concern. What caused the picture to change? Why is he begging? Can this be fixed? I don't want to think this is where the painting ends, but I know that artists end where they want to, not where viewers want them to.

"I was going to leave the painting like this, but then I had an idea. Close your eyes," she says softly.

I see her reaching for the UV wand and close my eyes as requested. When she gives permission to open them, I hear Jonah and Emmett's sharp inhale, and I know they match my own. She's turned the painting around again. Now there are two more men, holding the woman, her tears are gone and she looks at peace again. The man begging is standing, helping the other two to surround her. It's healing. She's painted the process of healing, and it hits me hard. My throat feels tight, my awe for her growing as I realize how acutely she brought the concept of healing to life with paint.

"Dani ..." I breathe.

"It's amazing," Emmett says.

"It's perfect," Jonah adds.

"It's us," she says simply.

Our eyes snap to hers as she turns off the black light and puts the wand back in place. She bites her lip softly before explaining what she means.

"I know that none of you wronged me, so the man in the beginning of the painting doesn't represent you guys specifically, it represents my trust in the world and myself. I thought things were good, but when I realized that my picture of the world was wrong, I didn't think I'd be able to get past it. Friends begged me, I begged myself, to get up and try again, to make my life fulfilled. But ... but it wasn't until you three came that it felt like I could. The support you guys give me. I can't put it into words. So I thought putting it into paint would do."

We all converge on her at once, kissing her hair, her face, her lips, touching her anywhere our hands can, still being careful of the kitten Emmett has tied to him. We spend a moment like that, the three of us here, together, showering each other and the woman we love with endless support and adoration. It confirms what I've thought since Jonah and Emmett first mentioned Danika. We're complete with her. We wouldn't be where we are today if she hadn't chosen to take that chance on us.

Eventually we have to part, Jonah's phone alarm dinging to remind us of other artists arriving soon, but we're all a bit glassy-eyed. The moment is beautiful, and it feels like I'm going to burst at the seams from joy and love. Eyes wiped, Jonah and Danika move to make sure the back doors are open for incoming artists, and Danika moves her truck out of the way so others can back straight up to the door if needed. Emmett and I walk around slowly, waiting for our orders. It occurs to me that I haven't seen Gertie, and I doubt that Emmett would want the kitten so close to Gertie.

"Hey, where's Gertie?" I ask.

Emmett looks a bit shy as he responds, "Well, I talked to her and neither of us wants Biscuits to accidentally claw her, so she decided to stay home today. She likes being surprised by the art anyway, so it's okay that she's not with me."

I grab him around the shoulders and pull him close to my side, placing a gentle kiss on his temple.

"It is okay, and I'm sure she'll love the art when she sees it."

The assurance lights up Emmett's side of the bond, leaving us both grinning at the moment. Having permission to be without Gertie isn't something I think Emmett needs, but *he* thinks he needs it, so I'm happy to provide for him. Maybe this kitten will be good for him when it comes to Gertie. If he doesn't feel the need to carry the hamster around all the time, I'd imagine that his self-confidence will only go higher. There's no problem with having Gertie close by, but watching him flourish without having to rely on Gertie would be a beautiful sight.

Before I can say anything more, Emmett and I are alerted through the bond that more artists are here. We straighten up and wait for the first one to round the corner. Between Danika helping with carrying and hanging the art, Jonah greeting artists and fielding questions, and Emmett and I's help, the job is easy. It only takes about ten minutes per artist with all the extra hands, and soon our gallery is full of color and light. Jonah smiles as he walks around, looking at all the colors and lack of colors that have been hung on our walls. One artist paints in an intentionally immature style, almost like a kindergartener, and an idea strikes me.

"Jonah? What would you think about connecting with some local schools to do special school exhibits?" I ask.

His eyebrows raise at the idea, and a smile curves his mouth. "I can't believe I never thought of that! That would be an amazing thing to do."

"We could call it Wonder's Night or something, a way to connect your sister to the art of the kids who will be here," Danika suggests.

We're silent for a moment, and she pushes on, "I mean, I know *tomorrow* is in her honor, but having a specific event for kids in her name would be neat, too, I think. You don't have to, obviously, it's just an idea."

Jonah turns to her with a massive smile on his face and picks her up, twirling her in a circle. She shrieks in protest at first but is giggling by the time Jonah's finished. He kisses her with a passion so fierce that I want to join in. I did say I want to fuck her in here with her art, right? May as well take advantage. I move behind her and place my hands on her hips, massaging the skin there, my hardening cock poking into her ass.

"Not here," she gasps.

"Why not?" Jonah pouts, nipping at her neck.

"Kitten. Other art," she manages to get out.

All three of us grown men pout like children. Danika throws her head back and laughs, light and free.

"You guys," she chides lovingly.

Then she walks off, leaving the three of us standing around with hard dicks and bewilderment. She makes it to the corner of the back before turning to look at us.

"Well?" she says into our minds.

We scramble to follow, turning off lights and wrapping up as she laughs in delight and continues to her truck. I can't wait to fuck her when we get home.

Chapter 36

Danika

I wake up, deliciously sore from last night. The guys definitely made good on their desire to wring pleasure from my body. I lost track of the orgasms and slept more deeply than I have in a while. Between the nerves of the gallery event tonight and the emotional exhaustion of showing them our painting, I needed the sleep. However, now that I'm awake, there's a delicious hard poke nudging at my ass. My eyes are still closed as I slowly press my ass against the erection behind me. The low groan sounds like Jonah, so I roll my hips, seeking some friction.

His arm wraps around me tighter, and he pulls one of my legs back so he can grind his length between my legs. "Did my greedy omega not get enough last night?"

A low gasp escapes me as his teeth nip at my ear. "You're fucking soaked for me."

"This is nice to wake up to," Colin's voice comes from in front of me.

My eyes open to see him staring at the position Jonah has me in, so I reach out to feel if he's as hard as I hope he is. He is; my amazing beta always delivers. I wrap my hand around him and stroke a few times experimentally. I spy a dark arm wrapped around him and an equally dark head moves into sight, licking and nibbling at Colin's open throat.

"What round are we on?" Emmett asks.

"It's a new day, I think we should reset the counter," Jonah rumbles behind me.

All I can do is whimper as the friction from his cock drives me higher. Jonah's moving at just the right pace to get my slick all over his cock, but can avoid slipping inside of me. It feels amazing and I'm almost drunk off the sensation, but I want to be filled. Colin takes some pity on me and reaches down with one hand, swiping at my slit freely since I never did get around to putting underwear on last night.

"Goddamn, you're wet, Omega. Is this for us?" Colin asks, fingers moving to enter me around Jonah's dick.

The feeling of his fingers rubbing in just the right spot floods my body, and it's not enough to scratch the itch, but it's soothing the need for now. He pumps in and out of me a few times, making that delicious "come hither" motion with his fingers, before Jonah gets impatient. He growls and grabs Colin's hand, sticking those thick fingers into his mouth and sucking. I almost come on the spot at the sight. Once he's satisfied that Colin's fingers are clean, he reaches down and helps his cock slide into my pussy.

Jonah thrusts in and out, slowly, torturing me and chuckling at my frustration when I try to make him move faster. Frustration builds up, but that only drives me higher as I'm denied. Apparently, I'm a sucker for orgasm denial. Who knew?

As the slow thrusts continue to drive me crazy, I hear the click of a bottle opening and look to see movement under the sheets. Based on the concentration on Emmett's face and Colin's quick breathing, I can see Jonah isn't the only alpha with the need to fuck this morning. My hand reaches down to stroke Colin again, but I feel a light swat against my hand.

"Mine," Emmett growls.

I smile at my territorial alpha. "Yes, Alpha."

He gasps in pleasure at my words and sinks the rest of the way into Colin.

"Fuuuuuuuck," Colin whimpers.

The alphas must be using their mental link because as Jonah speeds up, so does Emmett. The two of them work perfectly in sync as they thrust in and out of Colin and me. Colin leans forward and grabs my head so we can pull together and kiss, wanting to feel connected all together. My pussy starts to tingle, as I'm driven higher between Jonah's firm thrusts, the sound of Emmett's grunts as he works Colin, and the sensual dance of mine and Colin's tongues.

In sync, Emmett and Jonah reach their spare hands around to stroke Colin's dick and swirl around my clit. Colin and I are breathing too fast to continue kissing, and I throw my head back against Jonah's shoulder.

"Are you gonna come for me again?" Jonah asks, a growl reverberating through him. "Show me how much you like alpha cock. Come for me, Omega. Give me what's *mine!*"

The dirty talk gets me and I shatter, my mouth open and silent as thunderous waves of pleasure cascade over me. Tingles rush up and down my legs, overwhelming me with how good it feels, my pussy clamping down on Jonah, trying to milk him for every drop.

"Fuck yes take it all!" I hear Emmett growl as Colin comes, spraying my low belly with his release.

My voice returns, and I cry out as Jonah finishes pounding into me and pushes hard in place, letting his cum spray all over my inner walls. His low, "Fuuuuuuuuuuck," reverberates against my chest, and I move one arm above my head to grasp his and hold him close.

We sit in the quiet after our releases, and Emmett groans in annoyance.

"What's wrong?" I ask.

"I just changed these sheets last night, now I gotta do it again!" he whines.

Laughter bursts out of me, his words unexpected and so appropriate. Who wants to change sheets twice in less than twenty-four hours? The guys catch on to the laughter, and we're stuck in the laughter loop for a good ten minutes before we can stop long enough to get up and out of bed, readying ourselves for the day. It's event night so we're not doing much at home, we want to conserve energy. Especially after the wakeup we all just had. These men will be the death of me, but I'm loving every minute.

I have Sophie on video call as I put the finishing touches on my makeup and hair. We've been getting ready together for a couple hours now, meaning we sat and chatted for about an hour and a half and now we're scrambling. I put one final swipe of mascara on, then turn to the screen.

"You're sure my makeup looks okay?" I ask.

She pulls back from the mirror she was leaning into and looks straight at the camera, gaze quickly assessing.

"Yes, it's perfect. Simple but dramatic. I've taught you well, my little fledgling." She pretends to sniff.

"Oh, shut it," I tell her with a grin.

She returns the grin before switching her gaze back to her mirror. I take one last look in mine, seeing a version of me that I'd thought was gone forever. My hair is curled softly, pulled back with bobby pins and clips so that it stays out of my face. The guys bought me some jewelry recently, so a pair of silver hoops hang in my ears, and a silver necklace graces my collarbone, a small circle pendant with our birthstones hanging from it.

My eyes are simple, a black cat eyeliner with some mascara, allowing my eyes to pop on their own. Foundation, a subtle blush, and deep red lip complete my look. I considered doing a brighter or bolder red, but this deep, almost purple color goes with the look instead of overpowering it. Sophie is going full beat, however—contouring, fake lashes, smoldering eyes, the works. I wish I could look as good as she does doing that, but there's something magical about her. She *always* looks good, but she is seamlessly glamorous with the full beat.

"Okay, I think I'm good. I need to head over with the guys," I tell her.

She turns to the camera and sends me an air kiss. "See you soon!"

I send an air kiss back before ending our call. My feet carry me to the the bed where my dress is laid out for the night. The guys haven't seen it yet. It's something I picked up for myself the other day, not knowing if I'd ever actually wear it, but I couldn't leave it either. It's a deep purple, almost black, sleeveless dress. It fits snugly and the side of the dress has a twist in the fabric so it drapes gently over my hips in the front and back. The hemline hits my knees, and the neckline is a cowl neckline. I slide it on, the material smooth and silky as it drapes around me. It feels luxurious, and I shore up my confidence to turn and look in the mirror.

When I catch sight of myself, I freeze. I haven't looked like this in years. My body is visible, I can see the curves of my breasts and hips. The neckline isn't too low, showing cleavage but classy. My legs look long, and the small slit in the fitted skirt lets me move more easily. I turn to the side and raise my eyebrows in appreciation. I have a pretty okay ass in this thing. My feet slide into my dressy flats, and I head downstairs to see if my guys are ready to go. I find them waiting in the foyer, looking like three delicious snacks.

My eyes drink them in, all three of them in black dress slacks and button-down shirts. Colin's shirt sleeves are rolled up to his elbow, Emmett's shirt has one extra button undone, and Jonah is prim and proper with his tie and jacket. They all own their look, and I'm drinking them in like the thirsty bitch I am.

"Fuck me," Jonah says softly as his eyes take me in.

"I did this morning," I tell him with a smirk.

"Come here, you minx," Emmett says, reaching out to pull me close for a hug.

When he goes in for a kiss, I hold him back. "Don't mess up the lipstick. That's for the end of the night."

He chuckles and kisses my cheek instead. I notice Gertie sitting in his front pocket as usual and take a moment to greet her. Then Colin grabs my hand and twirls me in a circle, bringing my knuckles to his lips for a kiss. The action is a perfect mix of cheesy and respectful, and I can't help the pleased flush that runs through my body. I let out a purr of contentment, and the guys all return the purr with their own.

"We sound like a small avalanche," Colin quips.

"The coziest small avalanche," I point out.

Jonah pulls us closer. "Avalanche or not, you guys are all mine and I'm all yours."

A small thundering of steps comes toward us, and I turn to see Princess Biscuits loping our way, bell jingling merrily. I squat down and gather her up in my arms, ignoring the potential for a cat fur lining on my dress.

"Be good while we're gone," I coo at her.

"She's always a good girl," Emmett adds.

I set her down, and before I can take a step, Jonah's there with a fur roller, cleaning up any kitten fuzz that stayed on my dress. *When did he get one of those?* I choose not to question it and go with it for the moment. We all leave the house and climb into the small SUV, Jonah driving us carefully down the road.

"Shit!" I exclaim.

"What's wrong?" Colin asks immediately.

"I never got pre-show cookies from Sophie." My heart breaks from the missing tradition we have.

Emmett rubs my arm from his position in the back seat, and I turn to look at him. "I'm sure she'll bring some cookies with her. She's your emotional-support Sophie, it'll be fine."

Chapter 37

Danika

We walk into the gallery, turning on lights as we go. It's odd being on this end of the exhibit; usually I'm the one just showing up, not turning on lights and unlocking doors. It's nice to see the quiet side of the event, before people can come and create additional noise and take up space. Once we have all the lights on, a small knock sounds on the front door. We're not set to open the doors for an hour yet, but when I look up, I see Sophie waving wildly at me, a grin spread across her face.

"Sophie!" I squeal, doing a small dance. "Jonah, let her in!"

He chuckles and obliges me, opening the door for Sophie and locking it behind her. Sophie's hair and makeup are impeccable as always, and her body con dress is tight around her body. It's long-sleeved, which surprises me since it's early summer now. When she gets closer, I can see that the fabric is sheer on her arms and that explains the sleeves.

"You look fabulous!" I tell her.

"Back at you, babe! Oh! Before I get swept away, I have something for you."

Sophie digs into her purse before triumphantly pulling out a baggie that houses two perfect chocolate chip cookies.

"My cookies!" I shout.

"Told you!" I hear Emmett yell from across the room. I turn and stick my tongue out at him, making him laugh.

"Let me see those bond marks," Sophie demands, and I twist my head so she can see them, almost preening in front of her.

She sighs happily. "They look *perfect* on you. I'm so damn happy, Danika. I really am."

We hug tightly, and I hold her through my reply.

"I know you are. I don't know what I would do without you."

"Oh, you'd be fine," she sniffles and waves me off, trying to keep her make-up from being ruined.

A smirk lines my lips as I open the small bag and scarf down my first cookie. The flavor makes me moan, and three heads snap to look at me.

"I thought we were the only ones who got her to make that noise," Emmett whines.

Sophie and I crack up, tipping our heads back as we laugh. Never a dull moment around here. I finish my cookies and chat with Sophie until it's time to open the doors. Once the doors are open, I move over to my area of the gallery and wait for patrons to pass by and ask questions. The room packs quickly and there's a steady stream of art patrons excited to see what work has been selected to show by each artist. A few pieces have sold, including one of my old pieces, and the conversation never seems to let up.

After two hours of talking, I finally manage to step away for a quick break. I head to the snack table and grab a small bite with a flute of champagne, wishing I had a strawberry to put in it. *Oh, hey, a fruit display!* I sneak a strawberry and plop it right in, taking a quick sip to keep the drink from overflowing. The guys are all mingling with the customers and answering whatever questions come their way. We connect eyes for a few minutes as I look at the art pieces, but if we need to chat, we can always use the link. It's easier than yelling across the room, that's for sure.

I stop by an interesting piece, that I like to call 'blob' art. The artists takes a few colors and swirls them together, in whatever pattern strikes their mood. It can be beautiful, but it can also be just messy. I love seeing what the other artists have created, each one putting their own unique signature down for the world to see.

"*Do you guys see anything you might want to bring home?*" I ask through the bond.

"*I'm lookin' at her right now,*" Emmett quips.

I turn to smile at him, catching the wink he throws my way.

"*Any* art *you'd want to bring home?*" I clarify.

"*Still lookin' at her.*" Emmett smirks.

The guys laugh through our link, and I love that I can hear it even over all the noise. Continuing to roam, I catch a scent I didn't expect to find here. The air purifiers are doing an amazing job keeping scents controlled, but this one manages to sneak by and catch me off guard. A hint of whiskey teases my nose as I look around to find the scent owner. Taking a few steps toward my display, I see a tall man with dark brown hair staring at the painting I revealed during my last showing. The fire painting.

Apprehension grows in me, and I can feel my guys send a questioning feeling down our bond, but I can't put my finger on why I feel like this. My eyes are riveted as this man moves back and forth between the regular light and the black light. Eventually he leaves it on the black light and scrubs one hand down his face before crossing his arms, head hanging low. The gallery noise is muffled now, and my focus is entirely on this man. Another swirl of whiskey hits my senses as I get closer. It's a whiskey I'm familiar with, but it was sharper the last time I smelled it.

When I'm close enough for my own mint smell to waft over him, his shoulders tense, head still down. As much as I want to look away, I can't. My mind won't let me focus on anything else, and I can sense wariness from my bond, but even that's almost undetectable. He sighs, shoulders rising and lowering with the action.

"I'm sorry. For so many things, I don't think I can ever make up for," he rumbles.

My big brother's voice sounds exactly the same, but maybe a little more weary. Disbelief, joy, and anger swirl around in my head. Who the hell does he think he is coming here? He came for me, though, to see me. He waited fifteen mother fuckin' years to do it. Who the fuck does he think he is?

"Why the fuck are you here?" I hiss at him.

He looks up at me, surprised by the venom in my voice, and his light brown eyes connect with mine. The punch in the gut of seeing him again almost takes me out. My big brother who used to try and protect me, even from myself. My big brother who pissed me off daily. My big brother, finally standing in front of me again.

"I wanted to see ya," he replies, voice low.

The world goes blurry as my eyes sting with tears, so I look up and blink rapidly, trying to prevent them from ruining my makeup. I shake my head. The nerve.

"Not here, follow me," I tell him in the same low volume.

All three bonds are now noisy, trying to figure out what is going on, and who the hell I'm walking away with.

"I'm coming with you," Jonah tells me

"No, I can handle this," I insist.

"You can, but I'm coming with you," he insists.

I send him exasperation and love as I lead Tucker around to where the office is. It's noisy enough in the main gallery space that we should have some privacy. I have no desire to shut the door and be stuck in a room with him. He wouldn't hurt me, but I would probably get claustrophobic with just us two. I gesture for him to go in, then I lean against the doorway, my arms crossed.

"So?" I ask.

Tucker rubs a hand on the back of his neck and heaves a deep sigh. "Been thinkin' 'bout you for fifteen years, regrettin' everything I didn't do when we were kids. It's well past time for me to be a man and find ya."

I glance away from him, unwilling to keep eye contact. I have no idea how to respond to that. So naturally I ask him about family.

"How's Ma and Daddy?" I ask, feeling silly for using 'Daddy,' but it's all I ever called him.

"Not good, I'll be honest. Things got real bad for a while, so I found a free care home for packs and mates that aren't balanced. They been there almost ten years now. Don't think they'll ever be fixed."

I scoff and run my tongue along my bottom teeth but stay silent. Serves those two right. I don't think they ever put in any effort toward each other or toward Tucker and me.

"I believe ya," he says in the silence.

My eyes whip up to his. "What?"

"I believe ya. Shoulda done so when we was kids, but I couldn't go another day without tryin' to make it right," he says, eyes full of sincerity and glassy.

How nice for him that he can suddenly find me and gain his absolution. Except he won't be getting that. He was one of the reasons I made the choices I did. I own what happened in the city, I chose that by running, but I couldn't stay in a town like that and live ostracized.

"A little late for that, brother. Do you know what it's like to be a homeless omega in the city? An *underaged,* homeless omega? Because I sure as fuck do."

He shakes his head. "No, I don't know. I believe I never really will since I'm an alpha."

Words are failing me tonight, so I let the silence hang, waiting to see if he'll make any move to have more conversation. Tucker obliges after a moment, clearing his throat first.

"That paintin'. It's from that night, ain't it?"

"What gave it away? The burning forest?" I snark.

He huffs a sardonic laugh, lips twisted into a self-deprecating smile.

266

"I've never seen anything so painful in my life. I've never felt so goddamn worthless in my life than when I looked at that paintin'."

I exhale a sharp breath before looking behind me at my alpha. Jonah shrugs his shoulders and floods me with support. He's behind whatever choice I make. Knowing he's here to back me is like being wrapped in a security blanket. I'm okay and I'm safe with him, he's always got me.

"Go home, Tucker. There's nothing for you here," I say to him.

Turning my back to him I walk toward where Jonah is standing, looking like he's ready to beat the shit out of someone if given the okay to do so. I stop and lean my head down onto his shoulder for a moment before meeting his eyes.

"I'm sure you heard, but can you make sure he actually leaves?" I ask.

Jonah places a gentle kiss on my temple. "Anything for you."

Once I make my way back into the main gallery, Sophie makes a beeline for me. I indicate to her with a nod of my head to go to the receptionist desk. I meet her there, and we step back a few paces so nobody asks us questions.

"Who was that?" she demands.

"My brother," I tell her before taking a swig from the champagne I swiped as I walked over.

Her eyes widen, and for once my best friend is completely speechless. I watch the myriad of feelings flit across her face. Disbelief, sorrow, anger, sorrow again, more anger, then resolution.

"Do we need a shovel?" she whispers.

The question is so unexpected that I toss my head back and laugh. She giggles with me, and it's exactly what I needed. I have no doubt she would actually bring a shovel if we needed to have his body disappear, but offering it at a fancy art gallery event is not what I expected. We link our arms together and lean against a wall, our heads resting against one another.

"Thank you," I tell her.

"Love you, Danika, always and forever," she vows.

Eliza Jonas

"Always and forever," I echo.

Chapter 38

Danika

The next day, my guys are processing purchases and sending invoices for most of the day. The art will stay up for a week before we take it down. I hide in the nest for the day, trying to process the interaction with my brother. Why would he come *now* of all times? How did he even know where to look? When I left town, he wasn't even talking to me, and now I feel confused and frustrated.

Does he think that I'm going to bend over backwards and just decide to be okay with how things were when I left? Honestly, I remember the pain and loneliness, but all the details are fuzzy. It's been a long time, and I didn't try to remember all the details. I tried to just move on. It worked, mostly.

I reach for another chocolate bar as my emotions continue to swirl, and I find that I'm out. I only have a mound of empty wrappers next to me.

Just like me, empty, I think to myself.

Oh god, talk about drama. I need to stop wallowing. I'm clearly getting way too melodramatic. With a bit of effort, I get myself standing and gather up wrappers. I feel fidgety now that I'm moving —nothing is quite right, and I don't want to be still anymore.

Entering the kitchen, I toss the wrappers and look under the sink for cleaning supplies. It's time to scrub. Getting the house clean will make me feel better, I can scrub out all the feelings that are swirling.

Thankfully, I'm not completely in PTSD mode and I remember cleaning gloves. The guys purchased several sets so we won't run out anytime soon. Taking my supplies to the island first, I move all the gathered objects and put them on the counters. That can be sorted later between dishes and decorations. The island gets sprayed down and I get to work, scrubbing harder than necessary as I move the sponge around.

I've managed to clean the sides of the island and the chairs before I'm discovered. Colin walks into the kitchen and stares at me for a few moments. I know it's him based on his scent and bond, but I don't break my cleaning process. He hasn't said anything yet, so maybe he'll just let me do it.

"Sweetheart, you need to stop," he says softly.

"No!" I say, more harshly than I meant to.

Clearing my throat, I try again.

"No, I need to finish this," I insist.

He sighs. "Okay, you can finish the sides of the island, but then you need to be done. I appreciate you have gloves on, but we need to start talking things through instead of trying to clean them away."

His words give me pause, and I turn my head toward him and nod. His position behind me means he can't see my full face, but he can see the movement of my acceptance. Colin moves to lean against the counter, waiting patiently for me to finish. The moment I sit back with a satisfied sigh, he swoops in and puts away all the cleaning supplies. Like the adult I am, I pout and groan before pulling off my cleaning gloves and placing them back under the sink with the rest of the supplies.

Colin pulls me in, and I rest my head on his shoulder, nose positioned toward his neck. That campfire scent gives me strength now—it reminds me of Colin's steadfast love and support, and of my own ability to thrive after pain. No longer does it trigger the bad memories. I let out a deep, shuddering breath and sink further into him.

"Come on, the other two are back from the gallery," he says softly.

He leads me to the living room with our large sofa, and we all pile near each other. I can feel Emmett's joy at our puppy pile, Jonah's satisfied contentment at being surrounded by his pack, and Colin's steady support for everyone.

"I love you guys," I tell them, sinking into the comfort that is our pack.

There are three echos sharing the same sentiment. My heart feels light in my chest, and it brings a buoyant joy I never thought I would have. Of course, that's when Jonah starts speaking.

"Do you want to talk about yesterday?" he asks.

I sigh petulantly. "No."

"Should you?" Emmett asks.

"I thought you were on my team! Team suppress our problems until we can't anymore." I turn and glare at him.

He chuckles. "I admire our current team, but maybe it's time for a change?"

Emmett then tilts his head toward Gertie.

"Gertie agrees," he says smugly.

I turn and give the inanimate hamster a mock glare. "You'll get what's coming to you."

I let myself pout with one more sigh before pulling up my big girl pants to talk about feelings. Princess Biscuits decides she wants in on cuddle time and jumps up to the couch, making her way to my chest where she curls up next to my head. Giving her a smile, I tilt my head to the side and brush my cheek against her purring form.

"So my brother stopped by the gallery yesterday. That was the man who I was talking with."

My three bonds go tense and wary.

"I wasn't expecting it, or I would have warned you guys. He just kept apologizing, and I'm not sure what he wanted from me. Part of me wants to go home and confront him when I'm prepared, but the other part of me wants to just ignore it."

Jonah sighs. "It's a hard choice, baby girl. It's not the same, but when Wonder died, my parents tried to ignore things. Sweep it all under the rug. It backfired spectacularly, and the only way for the rest of my family to move forward was to face our new reality head-on."

I hum in agreement. He does have a point, but nobody died in my situation. Does that mean I still need to face it? Ignoring it might be better.

"Sometimes facing it can be worse, like when I tried to confront some bullies in school. It just got worse," Emmett ponders.

That's not the same situation either. Would I be okay with ignoring it? Always having that empty part of me unresolved? I frown, knowing deep down that I need this closure.

"Will you guys come with me if I go?" I ask.

My bond is filled with reassurance and love.

"Of course we will," Colin answers.

Smiling, I snuggle in close, completely content in this moment with my men.

It feels strange driving down a dirt road to my old town in a nice SUV. The last time I was here, I was speeding away on a stolen motorcycle that I barely knew how to drive. Now I'm back, ready to face my past, healed and making my own life. As we approach the limits to the town, apprehension starts to fill me. My old feelings of inadequacy and fear begin to stir deep within. Before the apprehension or old feelings can take hold, a flood of love and reassurance fills me up.

I turn in my seat to smile at all three of my guys, sending back my own love and appreciation. When Jonah whistles in surprise, I turn to look and see we're at the top of the big hill into town. It looks as sad as I remember, but maybe with a new coat of paint. The woods in the distance are sparse, the front section thinned out and still growing trees stick up from the ground. There's a spot where the ground is still healing from being completely scorched. Almost like a fire pit that's been destroyed.

The street we need to turn onto is coming up quick, so I avoid any conversation about the scorched forest as I direct Jonah on where to turn. We pull up to my old house, and it's a bit run down. I don't remember it looking quite this sad, but I looked at everything with rose-colored glasses in this town as a kid.

"Home traumatizing home," I mutter as I open my door.

Emmett snickers as they follow me out of the car and up to the front door of the house. I'm not sure if I should knock or not, but considering I've been gone for some time now, I choose to knock. Hopefully Tucker still lives here. I hadn't considered he might move. I reach for whoever's hand is next to me and our fingers thread together, squeezing in support.

The door opens to Tucker's shocked face, staring at me first, then evaluating the guys. There's a moment of awkward silence before I clear my throat and decide to make introductions.

"Tucker, this is Jonah, Emmett, and Colin. My pack. Guys, this is my big brother, Tucker."

Tucker clears his own throat, sounding a bit choked up as he talks.

"Pleased to meet ya. I'm glad my baby sister has a good pack."

Emmett smirks. "We could be killers for all you know."

Tucker huffs a laugh. "Nah, she woulda had you kill me by now. Y'all wanna come in?"

I hesitate for a moment before nodding my head. Tucker steps back and holds the door open for us. We file in, and I almost freeze at the difference in here. The outside might not look like much, but the furniture in here is well taken care of, arranged neatly around a large TV, and the kitchen beyond looks spotless.

"Bit of a difference without alcohol and yelling parents, isn't it?" Tucker comments.

"That's for sure," I agree.

He gestures for us to sit wherever but we decline offers of a drink. My brother sits facing us, and I can see him gearing up to talk, but I beat him to it.

"Why?" I ask.

Tucker frowns.

"Why now? Why do you suddenly care? Why do you believe me now after fifteen years? Why did you seek me out?" My voice is unsteady as my throat tightens from an odd mix of anger and sorrow.

"Look, Dani, you don't have to forgive me or anythin'. I'd understand if you don't. I started lookin' for a pack about two years back now, and the one I've been talking with is fantastic. I went out for a drink a while back, just wantin' to not be home, and Benny was there. We lost touch a couple years after you left, I just didn't feel right being his friend anymore.

"Benny drank too much while we were talkin', and he let it slip what happened back then. I don't remember what happened after that, but I do remember Benny on the floor, my fists flyin', then gettin' kicked out. I went into a deep shame spiral, but my potential pack told me any change has to start with me. So, I decided I needed to at least offer you an apology and make sure you're okay."

I don't know how to process all of that, so I surge to my feet and start pacing to help me think. My brother is looking for a pack? He cared before he learned the truth? He doesn't even expect me to accept his apology. Eventually rage wins out. He had to hear it from *Benny* to believe it? I whip around to look at him, glaring with anger and hurt.

"How could you believe Benny but not *me*?" I ask him, my eyes blurry from tears until one finally escapes.

Tucker's face morphs into concern and he stands to face me. He opens his mouth, but I don't want to hear it. I march over and shove him in the chest, but he stands steady.

"Fuck you! You were all I had, Tuck, and you chose to believe that ass-wipe over me. How *could* you?" I'm yelling at this point, furious that he doesn't look as hurt as I feel.

"I'm sorry," he rasps out, his own eyes glassy. "I was a dumbass teenage boy. I got no excuse."

I slap my hands against his chest, letting out all my anger from the years in a wordless cry. I can feel support through my bonds, and I know I'll be okay letting it out. When my anger fades, my sorrow takes over. I missed my fucking big brother but consoled myself that he was an asshole. Now that he can see the truth, he's trying. I just don't know if it's too late.

Tucker wraps his arms around me, and I cling to my big brother, wishing we hadn't lost fifteen years. Wishing things were different. Once my tears subside, I pull away from him, and he lets me go, his own face streaked with tears. I decide not to shut the door on us, and we exchange numbers. Making it clear that I still don't forgive him, we at least agree to keep in touch, even if our relationship doesn't grow into anything deep.

We load back up into the truck, and I decide I want to make one more stop while we're here. Directing Jonah, we get close to Mr. Durst's house, and I can see him out in his yard, tinkering with a cycle. Biting my lip, I ask Jonah to park on the road and I step out, walking over to Mr. Durst, the guys letting me have this one last bit of closure. Mr. Durst looks up, except it's not actually Mr. Durst. He looks extremely similar, but he looks like he's closer to the age he was when I left.

I frown. "Mr. Durst?"

Smiling a little, he replies, "Probably not the one ya want, but yeah, I'm a Durst. The Durst who used to live here was my big brother. Passed away a year ago now."

My face falls. "Oh. Okay, well, thanks."

"You that omega who torched the woods when she left town?" he calls out.

I look at him, surprised. "Um, yeah."

"He wanted you to know he left that cycle out for you, but never got the chance to tell ya. He made sure I knew just in case I was here and saw ya."

Smiling, I shake my head. "Thanks. I always felt bad taking it, but I'm settled now, knowing that he left it out for me."

"He said he always knew you were meant to leave, so he made sure you had a way out any time."

I nod, a smile gracing my face before I head back to the car.

To my men.

To my future.

A Note From Eliza

Did you love it? I sure hope so! The prologue was inspired by the song "Brother" by Madds Buckley. Her song pulls at me and I felt a need to bring it to life within my own imagination, then show the healing.

This book was difficult for me to write, I struggled with motivation and the drive to get it done. However, I felt like Danika's story was embedded in my brain and it needed to be sent out into the world.

Did I expect to write a book with an inanimate featured character? No. Was it fun? Heck yes it was! I always want someone to talk to, and I struggle to talk to inanimate objects, but I love the idea of it. Something that just "listens", and I felt Emmett needed that.

Here's hoping to more fun characters and plenty of steam in whatever I tackle next.

THANK YOU to everyone who read this book, it means so much to me that you're here, reading my words and (hopefully for you) getting off on my imagination.

Awkward statement? Yes. It's my M.O.

Also by Eliza Jonas

<u>Brainstorm Series</u>

Let It Go

Here In Your Arms

Hold On

<u>Stand Alones</u>

Back To December

<u>Matchverse</u>

Knot Gonna Give You Up

Graffiti Heart

About the Author

Eliza Jonas is a Michigan author with red hair, sass, and an amazing family. She feels weird writing in third person, but she's going to give it her best. Eliza grew up with a love of books, and has loved words as far back as she can remember. When she finally felt compelled to self-publish, romance caught her eye from her own experiences. The genre helped her re-connect with that part of herself, and she hopes she can do the same for others. Here are a few fun facts:

Favorite food: chocolate cake

Favorite color: pink

Favorite superhero: Batman

Favorite position: Wouldn't you like to know....